HOSTILE TAKEOVER

An excerpt from *Hostile Takeover*

Seconds later, the woman who starred in all his deepest, darkest fantasies walked into his office. The sight of her made his cock jump to attention again. She wore a polite smile, yet her eyes were devoid of any emotion. He wondered what she'd have to say for herself when he told her what he had in mind. Lydia would probably be suspicious if he deviated in any way from his normal affable self, so Ryder pasted on the jovial smile he gave to all his employees. Too professional and she would sniff a rat; too friendly and she would shoot him down.

"Good news! Prospective clients, high-end, need my best person on the job. And I think you'll do nicely."

Nodding her head, she whipped out a pen and pad. Always ready, Lydia was. It added to her allure. He wanted to knock her off-kilter, just once.

"Give me the particulars, and I'll get on it." She readied her pen to make notes.

Yeah, baby, it's not going to be so simple this time.

"Fantastic! Glad you're on board." Ryder grinned like the Cheshire cat. "Pack your bags. We leave Friday. Seven days at an exclusive resort. The client wants us to experience the place before coming up with a proposal. They were adamant about it, in fact."

Her mouth opened and closed as if she wanted to come up with some excuse as to why it couldn't be her. Like he was going to give her the chance.

"Make sure you pack a bathing suit."

LooseId®

ISBN 13: 978-1-60737-531-9
HOSTILE TAKEOVER

Originally released in e-book format in January 2010

Cover Art by Christine M. Griffin
Cover Layout and Design by April Martinez

Printed in the U.S.A. by
Lightning Source, Inc.
1246 Heil Quaker Blvd
La Vergne TN 37086
www.lightningsource.com

Chapter One

The woman was determined to drive him crazy. Oh she had no idea what she was doing to him; he was damn careful not to show it. Every morning Ryder anticipated Lydia Morris's arrival. His blinds were always wide open to give him a clear view. He had to be the first to see what new confection she had decided to torture every male within a hundred-yard radius with.

On some days, she wore a simple skirt, modestly cut to right above her ankles. In theory, it was conservative to the point of prudishness. Only, with her curves, the skirts hugged her like a second skin. Add in the fact she had a fondness for three-inch 1950s pinup heels and shirts that showcased the most unbelievable set of ta-tas this side of the Rio Grande, and Lydia was a walking wet dream. And she was completely unaware of the fact.

Just once, he longed to rip off those hip-hugging skirts, strip those thin, low-plunging silk shirts, and make her parade around his office wearing nothing more than those damnable pumps and black stockings with the seam up the back. Ryder just knew the lingerie hiding beneath her clothing would be droolworthy in the extreme. Lydia wouldn't deem to wear anything less.

As she walked from his line of vision, he got an excellent view of an ass that would make most grown men weep. Its perfect apple shape was probably what men had in mind when they paid homage to the behind. With each step she took, her perfectly rounded ass cheeks moved like ripe melons waiting to be fondled and squeezed.

His cock jumped to immediate attention at the thought of taking her from behind: slamming his dick between her tight, wet folds and riding her until they were both oblivious to everything around them. The funny thing was, when she'd first started as a temp at his company six months ago, he'd barely spared her a second glance: She was a little taller than he preferred, she didn't wear her hair loose and flowing as he preferred, and she didn't seem one bit impressed by him. Three strikes.

No, she wasn't someone a person took notice of right away. Her beauty was of the unconventional variety, but once noticed, it had the ability to knock a man flat on his ass with her near onyx complexion, large brown eyes that were neither dark nor light and tilted at the corners, and lips so large and plush, he ate his heart out daily when he saw them.

If only Lydia would give him the time of day. Sure, she listened when he spoke; he was the boss, after all. She performed her job flawlessly, coming up with hot ad campaigns for his clients that not only satisfied them but their bottom line as well. But she refused all offers of drinks after work, even in the most professional of settings. Though she came to a few company events, she kept her distance.

She could charm the pants off a prospective customer, schmooze heavy hitters with the best of them, but never allowed anyone to get close, him especially. There wasn't a time when she didn't keep it strictly professional in the office. It didn't help matters that her husky, alto voice stroked his cock, just as surely as if she had slipped it in between those luscious glossy lips. He was getting damned tired of retiring to the men's room to calm his throbbing dick after a meeting with the all-too-tempting seductress.

Ryder didn't consider himself conceited, but he was a good-looking guy with more than his fair share of female attention. He couldn't remember the last time he was interested in a woman where the attraction had not been reciprocated. Most women considered him a catch; he was the owner of his own advertising agency, had a healthy bank account, a nice house on the hill, and a hot ride—two, in fact. Not bad for someone who started out with nothing except a dream, the drive, and a huge set of balls to take the risks required in starting one's own business.

Ryder couldn't for the life of him figure out what the problem was where Lydia was concerned. It crossed his mind that perhaps she wasn't into white guys, but from further observation, she kept all the men, and women for that matter, in the office at arm's length. It was one thing if she didn't believe in dating a colleague, but something told him that wasn't it. She didn't appear to socialize at all. Despite the distance she put between herself and the other employees, she still managed to be friendlier and open with them than she was with him. And he was fucking tired of it.

Before he could change his mind, he informed his personal assistant he wanted to see Lydia in his office—now. Enough was enough. He wasn't going to come right out and ask her why she wouldn't give him the time of day. He wasn't even going to tell her of his interest. What he had in mind was so much better.

New prospective clients wanted an advertising campaign for their “adults only” resort island. In order to get exactly what they were looking for, they had suggested Ryder and an associate spend a week on the island—to get the feel of the place—before coming up with a proposal. They'd offered the same deal to his biggest competitor, and the firm had failed miserably.

Ryder couldn't think of another person he wanted to do “research” with more than Lydia. She was good at her job, and it would give him the perfect opportunity to get to know her one-on-one. It was the perfect excuse to break the ice and finally find out if they'd be as good together as he thought they could be. But he needed to play it smart. If Lydia even suspected what he was up to, she would walk right out of his firm and out his life before he could blink, and that was simply unacceptable.

Licking his lips in anticipation, he rubbed his crotch to ease the ache. His cock was so fucking hard, it threatened to bust the seam of his pants. He wished he had time to rub one out real quick, but that wasn't an option. Lydia would be here in a matter of minutes. Less than that probably. If he'd learned nothing else about her, Ryder had discovered she was punctual to a fault. It took him several deep breaths and thinking nonerotic thoughts for his dick to go down. Just as he got his body under control, his phone rang, displaying his assistant's number on the caller ID. “Yes, Donna?”

“Lydia is outside your office. Should I send her in?”

“Yes.”

Seconds later, the woman who starred in all his deepest, darkest fantasies walked into his office. The sight of her made his cock jump to attention again. She wore a polite smile, yet her eyes were devoid of any emotion. He wondered what she'd have to say for herself when he told her what he had in mind. Lydia would probably be suspicious if he deviated in any way from his normal affable self, so Ryder pasted on the jovial smile he gave to all his employees. Too professional and she would sniff a rat; too friendly and she would shoot him down.

“Good news! Prospective clients, high-end, need my best person on the job. And I think you'll do nicely.”

Nodding her head, she whipped out a pen and pad. Always ready, Lydia was. It added to her allure. He wanted to knock her off-kilter, just once.

“Give me the particulars, and I'll get on it.” She readied her pen to make notes.

Yeah, baby, it's not going to be so simple this time.

“Fantastic! Glad you're on board.” Ryder grinned like the Cheshire cat. “Pack your bags. We leave Friday. Seven days at an exclusive resort. The client wants us to experience the place before coming up with a proposal. They were adamant about it, in fact.”

Her mouth opened and closed as if she wanted to come up with some excuse as to why it couldn't be her. Like he was going to give her the chance.

“Make sure you pack a bathing suit.” He stood up but turned his back before she could see the raging hard-on he was sporting. “The client wants us to participate in some of the outings they have to offer. And bring your laptop. We can start working on the logistics while we're there. Go ahead and knock off for the rest of the day so you can get ready. I have back-to-back meetings, so I will see you when the car comes to pick you up Friday morning. That will be all."

He walked out of his office, leaving Lydia gaping after him. A wry smile graced his lips as he walked down the hall. Yep, sweet Lydia was in for it now.

Ryder was halfway to his destination when the clicking sound of heels drew near. A hand fell on his shoulder. "Mr. Garrison, please wait."

His smile widened to one of sweet satisfaction. Lydia's voice was already sultry, but the breathy whisper of his name was sex personified. It took a great deal of will and concentration to keep his cock from springing to attention. Again. Slowly he pivoted, not bothering to hide his mirth. "Lydia, you know I don't run a formal office. You can Mister and Miss our clients until the cows come home, but my name is Ryder. Say it."

Lowering her long lashes, she dropped her hand and took a step back. "I'd rather not. Um, I needed to talk to you about this trip. I can't go."

He raised a brow. There was no way in hell he'd let her weasel out of this, no matter what her objection. He didn't know when another opportunity like this would present itself, and he damn sure wasn't going to wait when what he wanted was within his grasp. "Oh? I was under the impression you were aware travel was involved when you accepted the position."

“I did, but I didn't think travel involved a weeklong getaway. Anyway, this account sounds like a pretty big deal. Shouldn't one of the senior account managers be handling this? Although I've been here for six months, I've only officially been with Garrison as a permanent employee for two and a half months. I think in all fairness, one of them should handle this assignment.”

Ryder had counted on the little vixen trying to talk her way out of this, but he was prepared for her. “Are you saying you're not capable of handling the workload? Because I can assure you, there are no easy jobs at this company.”

“Of course I can handle the work. I was just saying—”

“Good; since you can handle it, there shouldn't be a problem. As you've pointed out, you've only officially been with the company for a couple months. Keep in mind you're still within your ninety-day probation period. You're not really in a position to turn this down. Understand?”

Her eyes narrowed slightly, and for a second, he thought she'd protest. But instead, she nodded in obvious defeat.

Shit. Was being with him for a week going to be that horrible? Yeah, it was a dick move on his part to mention her probation, but he was a desperate man. There was no turning back now that he'd committed to this course of action. “I didn't hear you. Do you understand, Lydia?”

“Yes, sir.” Turning on her heels with the precision of a seasoned military veteran, she stalked away, her ass cheeks jiggling.

Goddamn.

Lydia was pissed. The last thing she needed was to be alone with Ryder Garrison on a freaking tropical island. She'd worked damned hard to get where she was today, going to school at night and on weekends while holding down a dead-end secretarial position. She had fought, clawed, and climbed her way out of the cesspool she was born in, and she wasn't going back.

The problem was, she just didn't trust herself around Ryder. That man was hot sex on a platter in spades. She kept it strictly professional in the office because she wasn't about to make a fool out of herself. This job was simply too important. In her last position she'd let her crush on a junior executive trip her up.

She had trusted the asshole, and he had used her ideas to get ahead and dropped her like a hot potato as soon as he got what he wanted. She refused to travel down that road again. Sure, this was a little different; Ryder was the boss, but she had learned her lesson all too well. She wouldn't be a rug for anyone ever again.

Her instincts where men were concerned sucked. Maybe it was something she'd inherited from her mother—her ability for picking "winners." Lydia's current stepfather, her mother's fourth husband, was currently serving a twenty-five-year sentence for embezzlement. Wanting something better for herself, she'd left home the minute she graduated from high school. Her dreams had nearly been derailed when she'd fallen in love for the first time with the smooth-talking Kevin, a dark-chocolate dreamboat from Galveston.

Too bad she'd found out too late he was full of shit. Unable to hold down a job, he depended on the meager income she brought in to pay the bills. She'd done her best to stretch her paycheck as far as it would go, but Kevin chose to spend the money on frivolous things like a game system or speakers for his car.

When Lydia complained, he became violent, thus beginning a three-year, hellish nightmare of psychological and physical abuse. It only ended when the police came to their tiny apartment one night asking her to come down to the station. Apparently Kevin had run his mouth off to the wrong person and had been stabbed to death. She wanted to be sad for the lost life of someone she'd once cared about, but she couldn't feel anything but relief. The scars were already too deep for his death to cause her any true grief.

Wanting a fresh start, she'd moved across state and found a job at a prestigious advertising firm, where she'd met Casey. He'd intrigued her because very few men of his ilk had hit on her before. Naturally she was cautious because of the Kevin debacle, but he did and said all the right things and seemed caring and sensitive. When she'd found out he was using her, she had been devastated.

“So I'll just keep it professional.” She reaffirmed to herself with gritty determination.

She could do this. It wasn't like she was going to jump all over Ryder. *Yeah, but you want him.* And who wouldn't? The man could fill out a suit, not that he wore them often, only when meeting prospective clients. He seemed to delight in wearing worn Levi's that showcased the most grabworthy ass ever.

Watching him walk had a woman imagining what those buns would look like thrusting in earnest. That dirty blond wavy hair invited itchy fingers to run through the silky-looking strands. And those eyes! Bright green, always full of laughter and a bit of a dare. The man wreaked havoc on her nerves. To make matters worse, he seemed to enjoy flirting with her. Despite all her resolve not to be a notch on his bedpost, Lydia couldn't help but wonder "what if?" What if he was serious about really wanting her for her? What if he was "the one"? Or worse, what if it was all in her head?

There was a distinct possibility Ryder wasn't trying to get in her pants at all. She was good at what she did; her ideas were fresh and unique. She was so sick of everyone using sex to sell products; Lydia used her wit. Her campaign proposals used humor, a little heartstring tugging, and sometimes sensuality, but not straight-out, blatant sex appeal.

As long as she treated this as just another job, everything would run smoothly. Maybe there was an attraction, but her past was enough to ensure she never acted on it. And she fully intended to make certain she didn't give him the opportunity to either.

Now she had to think of what to wear. Her budget was still tight from the student loans she was paying off, and her mortgage was a little higher than she liked, but her condo was located in a nice safe, neighborhood, something important for a woman on her own. Most of the clothes she bought were from thrift stores.

From an early age, she'd fallen in love with vintage clothing and was able to find outfits with flair for a minimal cost. Come to think of it, one of her favorite consignment stores was having a sale right now.

If she helped land this account, there'd be a big fat bonus in it for her. Ryder paid his employees for hard work, one of the big pluses of working for him. All she had to do was make sure she stayed the course and kept her head in the game. It was perfect.

With a spring in her step, she gathered her belongings to make her way to the shop. She had a few other things to take care of before Friday. Maybe she would even treat herself to a pedicure and have her locs deep conditioned while she was at it. It never hurt to look your best when dealing with new clients. She was *not* doing this to impress Ryder. It was all about the client. Poised, polished, and professional. That was what she would be.

Chapter Two

"Relax, Lydia. If you keep shaking and fidgeting like that, I might start thinking this is your first flight," Ryder teased in an attempt to break the ice. She hadn't spared him anything more than a cursory greeting and single-word responses since he had met her at her condo. Every attempt at conversation had been effectively shut down. Usually she wasn't this distant, even toward him. Something seemed different. It was as if she'd erected an invisible wall between them, and honestly, the more remote she was toward him, the more he wanted to tear that barrier down. He wondered if it bothered her that they'd be in close proximity for the duration of the week.

Lydia gripped her armrest until her knuckles were nearly white. No small feat for a woman with her skin tone, he imagined. Her succulent bottom lip was caught between even white teeth, and at that moment, he wished to God he were those teeth, nibbling and sampling that tender flesh.

"Lydia?"

"It is."

"Excuse me?"

"This is my first time flying." She spoke at such a low decibel, Ryder strained to hear her.

It suddenly dawned on him that she was terrified, but instead of offering her the reassurance she needed, he blurted out the first thing that popped in his head. "Seriously? How old are you?"

She narrowed her eyes and puckered her lips in annoyance, but kept her head forward, refusing to look at him. "I'm thirty-one, Mr. Garrison. Not everyone is privileged enough to afford plane trips."

He felt like a jackass for being so insensitive. "I apologize. There's nothing to be ashamed of. Even seasoned fliers like myself get nervous from time to time." He reached over and took her hand in his.

She looked at him then with a gasp parting her lips. It took a great deal of effort to hold off the smile threatening to turn the corners of his mouth. So she felt it too—that instant spark of electricity flowing between them. Good. This was a start at least. Lydia attempted to pull her hand away, but Ryder tightened his grip, with no intention of letting her go.

"Excuse me. Can we get two glasses of champagne?" he asked the flight attendant who was busily making sure all the members of first class had everything they needed.

"Of course, sir," the gushing flight attendant replied with enthusiasm. "I'll get that for you right away."

"I'm not much of a drinker." Lydia tried to wave the flute away as soon as Ryder took it from the attendant and pushed it toward her.

"It will help relax you. Take it."

With apparent reluctance, she did, much to his relief. She looked about ready to jump out of her skin. Maybe he should have taken the window seat when she offered, but he thought she was just being polite. The flight ahead of them wasn't that long, but it could be nerve-racking, and he wanted her comfortable, at ease. Maybe get her to open up a little. He really wanted to know what made Lydia tick. What did she do when she wasn't at work? What were her favorite foods? How did she like to be touched?

Don't get ahead of yourself, he silently warned himself. She was skittish enough as it was. He couldn't push too hard. Yet. Ryder counted himself very lucky she hadn't asked too many questions about the resort they were headed to. He had told her "adult," but he hadn't told her adult as in erotic. The couple who'd bought the tiny island in the Florida Keys had turned the place into a getaway for those who liked their sex life with a little extra spice. The entertainment ranged from the titillating to the downright raunchy. Ryder had hoped to drop a few hints on the flight, but there was no way he could do that if she was so wound up.

"Feeling better?" he asked after she downed the entire glass. As soon as her glass was empty he motioned to the steward for another. Just another glass or two, then club soda. He waited until she drank the second before attempting any other conversation. Let the champagne take a little effect.

"Much," Lydia fairly purred, sinking deeper into the leather interior of her seat, making his cock come to life.

She was incredibly sexy when she moved like that, kind of like a feline. A half smile graced her glossy lips. What would she do if he leaned over and sucked the bottom one into his mouth?

Slap the crap out of him, more than likely.

"Another glass?"

She smiled, slouching even deeper in her chair. "Don't mind if I do."

Once he took her glass, he held it up in the air, signaling to the flight attendant.

Lydia gulped down her third glass like it was water. "Mmm. That was heavenly. I've never tasted champagne quite like this. I mean, I've had it before, but I don't remember it being so good." It was the most she'd ever said to him that didn't relate to business. The alcohol had definitely loosened her up. "Can I have another?"

With a chuckle, he took away her flute. "I don't think so, darlin'. We don't want you falling all over the place once you get off the plane. But I can think of a better way to relax you."

She raised a finely arched brow. "Oh?"

"Don't look so suspicious." Placing a pillow on the armrest between their seats, he tugged on her shoulder to get her to present her back to him. "Turn your back to me."

"What—"

He placed his index finger over her lips. "Trust me. Turn around."

She pushed his hand away and sighed. "Fine. But no funny stuff, okay?"

Ryder placed his hand over his chest with mock affront. "I'm hurt that you think I'd try something underhanded. I'm a gentleman."

"So was Jack the Ripper," she muttered, turning in her seat.

He liked that she was feisty. There was so much fire in her, and he couldn't wait to see how hot it burned. Once her back was to him, he gently grasped her shoulders and slowly kneaded her soft, supple flesh.

"Ahhh, that feels good." A moan rumbled in her throat.

"That's my goal." He had to concentrate on keeping the massage friendly, not too intimate. It was hard. He'd been dying to touch her for far too long. He wished like hell his hands could caress her bare flesh instead of through the light cotton of her shirt.

"I never knew a massage could feel so good."

Ryder's hands paused as he processed what he was hearing. Never had a massage? Never being on a plane he could see, but a massage? Who the hell had this woman dated? It pissed him off just as much as it relieved him. He had an inkling past boyfriends had, at best, been shitheads. At worst, well, he didn't want to think about it. If her experiences with men were one of the reasons Lydia was so standoffish, he had a battle ahead of him. And he was just the man for the job.

"How is it a beautiful woman like you has never had a massage before?" Ryder dared to ask after her body became more pliant under his fingers. Just a little gentle probing to see how receptive she was.

"Because no one has ever offered." Lydia didn't sound sorry for herself or even as if she was complaining. She just stated it as fact. "There are a lot of things I have never had before or done before, but that doesn't mean I'm not open to new experiences. I just haven't had them yet."

There were plenty of "experiences" he wanted to share with her, like having her beneath him with his cock buried deep inside her sweet pussy. He continued to mold and shape her shoulders, arms, and back. She moaned. Ryder could actually see her visibly relaxing, and when she leaned against him, his dick sprang to life. He didn't want to make any sudden moves, lest she get suspicious, but the intoxicating scent of her flowery perfume was driving him insane.

Unable to help himself, he lowered his head and pressed his lips against her nape. Lydia jumped, but he clutched her arms. "Relax."

Heaven must have been smiling, because she didn't move away. Just a little kiss; nothing more. But his lips slid up her neck to her earlobe. He took a little nip. Not really a full-on bite, just enough to let her know he was there. Her corresponding moan was music to his ears. Moving closer, he pulled her back more firmly against him.

"I'm not sure if you should be doing that. What if someone sees?" Her protest was weak, and Ryder knew he had her.

"Don't worry. No one can see what we're doing. The couple in the seats across from us has been asleep since the plane took off. And the ones behind them are watching the in-flight movie. Relax."

A soft sigh was her only response.

He didn't dare touch her the way he really wanted to. Feeling Lydia up on the ride to the resort would do little to help him break through that wall she had erected around herself. He didn't stop kissing her, though. Her skin was so warm, so damn smooth. She smelled like pure temptation, pulling him in deeper.

“Are you feeling better now, darlin'?” he whispered against her fast-heating flesh. It was gratifying to discover this attraction wasn't one-sided. The champagne might have gotten her to relax, but she was a long way from drunk.

“I'm not your darlin'.” The reply was immediate, but without any real heat.

He was getting to her. He wondered what she'd do when he…

Her head lifted as his descended. The first touch was just a mere brushing of lips. His hands stilled and then tightened, pulling her closer as he deepened the kiss. Lightly biting her bottom lip to get her to open to him, his tongue delved inside, plundering the sweet cavern like a man starved. The need to breathe was the only thing that forced him to let go.

“Did you like that, Lydia?”

“Mmm.”

Ryder ran his tongue along the shell of her ear, grasping her tiny waist and running his fingers along her rib cage, careful not to touch her breasts. “Tell me what you want me to do next. Tell me where you want me to touch you.”

“Mmm,” was her only response.

He gently tugged her earlobe with his teeth to get her attention. “Baby, tell me what you want.”

This time he was greeted with a soft snore.

Fuck!

* * *

Lydia moaned as she was jarred awake. The plane seemed to be bouncing up and down, yet she wasn't bouncing on anything hard. Well, not anything hard and inanimate, like she should have been. Her head was lying on something warm and breathing. The events of what had happened between her and Ryder came crashing back with a vengeance. Oh hell, what had she done?

Jerking her head up, she realized she was no longer on the large 747 that she had boarded in Texas. She was on a very small, very loud transport plane. The warm breathing pillow she had been lying on was none other than Ryder, her lecher of a boss. She took small comfort in the fact that at least this time she wasn't seated next to the window. She had absolutely no desire to see what they were flying over.

"How are you feeling?"

Lydia's eyes snapped up to a visibly irritated Ryder. His normally smiling lips were pulled down into a slight frown, bringing a harshness to his handsome features. How could she have been so stupid as to accept the damn champagne? As much as she would have loved to blame it on the alcohol, she knew that to be a lie. She hadn't done anything she hadn't fantasized about every night since the first time she'd met him.

She straightened up, scooting away from him and pointedly put the armrest down to create a barricade between the two of them. Moistening her suddenly dry lips, she glanced around her. "How did I end up on this plane?"

"The champagne must have done more of a number on you than I thought. I carried you off our plane to the connection flight. You were out of it for most of the transfer, and once we were seated, you were out like a light. Good timing, by the way. We're about to land shortly. Would you like something to drink? I can imagine your head may still be a little fuzzy."

"No. I don't need any more alcohol."

"I was thinking along the lines of some bottled water. It's hot and humid where we're heading, and just going by the amount of champagne you consumed and how you reacted to it, I insist. You're liable to dehydrate the minute you step foot on solid ground. Here. Have some of mine. I've barely taken a sip." He handed her the bottle, which she debated on refusing, but seeing the determined look in his eyes, she knew there was no arguing with him. The bossy bastard.

Lydia snatched the water bottle from him and took a couple of swigs. There was something oddly intimate about sharing the same drinking container, her lips touching where his had been. The very thought of it sent a shiver up her spine. She lowered the bottle and replaced the cap. "Okay. I drank some, satisfied?"

"Not quite, but I intend to be once we finish what we started."

She thanked God for her dark skin, because heat crept to her face and scorched her ears. "I-I do-don't know what you're talking about." Lydia wanted to put it down as an aberration, a temporary loss of control that would never happen again. And her only defense was to pretend it never happened.

He narrowed those incredible green eyes. "You know good and well what I'm talking about."

“I'm telling the truth!”

“So you make a habit of stammering when you tell the truth? Give me a break, Lydia; you know what happened between us, and I doubt your little game playing isn't because you didn't like it. I think you liked it. A lot.”

She turned away from him to stare out the window. “I don't have to take this from you. There is such a thing called sexual harassment.”

“Don't give me that shit. It's only harassment if you don't want it, and you wanted it, baby, just as much as I did. Deny it all you want, but there's something between us. And I'm not going to fight it, and I won't let you either.”

Lydia had no response. He was right. She did want his hands and lips on her. Her skin still burned where he had kissed her. She ached, wanting nothing more than to feel those large, knowledgeable hands on her bare skin. Her body tingled as she thought of how good it could feel. But he was not for her. She had to remember that. She didn't have to admit a damn thing to *him*, though.

And she wouldn't. Lydia would go right on pretending her panties didn't get wet when he had touched her. The simple massage on her shoulders had melted her inhibitions like ice in the hot July sun. Pressing her thighs together tightly, she tried thinking about anything other than the thrill that shot up her spine, recalling hot lips against her nape.

She really needed to get off this damn plane and far away from Ryder Garrison. What did they call it again? Jet lag. She would claim jet lag just as soon as they got to the resort. A cold shower, some quality time with her vibrator, brought in case of emergencies, and she would be right as rain. Too bad she didn't believe a word of it herself. She was going to have to watch herself around him. He was slippery as a snake and twice as deadly. That wasn't good news for her runaway libido.

Chapter Three

"You've got to be kidding me. Please tell me you're pulling my leg and I have a room to myself." Lydia looked around their suite with the look of cornered prey. If she didn't seem so put out by the accommodations he'd arranged for them, Ryder would have been amused. But her obvious displeasure coupled with her pretense that nothing had happened between them on the plane, and the way she'd treated him like a leper ever since, had killed any good humor he'd been holding on to.

He'd specifically requested a double-room suite; that way he could keep an eye on her, and if things progressed as he planned, there'd be no question of whose place they ended up at night. Ryder wasn't exactly sure what he had expected her reaction to be, but this wasn't it. It was pretty clear she wasn't happy. "If you take a look around, you'll realize you do have your own bedroom and private bath. The only thing we'd share is the common area."

"But you led me to believe I'd have my own room. This is unacceptable."

"Why? Because you don't trust me? Or is it yourself you don't trust?"

"Not everything is about you, you conceited ass!" Lydia exploded, looking suspiciously close to tears.

Ryder was taken aback by the vehemence in her voice. She wasn't just unhappy; she was angry. But why? It wasn't like she didn't have her own bed and bath. She still had all the privacy she could possibly need. Who wanted to hang out in a hotel room by themselves?

Lydia did. His conscience took that moment to kick in. *Shit.* He needed to think of something quick before she marched down to reception to demand a private room. It wouldn't be a death knell on his seduction plan, but it would definitely throw in a few kinks. *Think, Ry, man, think.*

"Look, I'm sorry." He conceded that much. "I only wanted to make sure we had a space to work on any ideas concerning the proposal while we're here. I believed you would appreciate that."

He could tell by the fleeting look of confusion that crossed her face he got to her with that one. In a way it was true; they were supposed to be working. Not that Ryder didn't plan on taking full advantage of the situation, but if Lydia was anything, she was dedicated to the job. It was one of the many things he admired about her.

Her nostrils flared as she crossed her arms over her chest. "I'd rather have my own room, please."

"Even if I promise to give you the privacy you require? Look, I thought this arrangement was best because we can keep each other on schedule, bounce ideas between us, and trust me, when an idea pops in my head, I'm ready to work. I believed you'd be up to the challenge of this assignment.

Was I wrong?" It was a low blow, but he was running out of cards to play.

Her beautiful brown eyes flashed pure liquid fire. "But you know full well, setting this up had nothing to do with work. You could have easily booked us in neighboring rooms. If the need arose, we could have met and discussed the project at any time. I'm here to work, nothing more. Whatever game you're playing at, quit it."

He advanced on Lydia until he was inches away from her. "And what game do you think that is?"

Lydia took a step back and turned her head to the side. Ryder could practically feel the heat from her body. He already knew she wasn't as immune to him as she pretended to be. What happened on the plane proved that. If only he could get her to stop fighting it, they'd set the world ablaze.

"I don't know. Maybe you find flirting with me amusing because I don't fall at your feet like the rest of the women in the office."

He grinned. "So you've noticed?"

"That's not what I meant, you cocky son of a bitch."

Ryder moved closer still. "Cocky. Hmmm, I'm definitely that." He looked down pointedly at his now-raging hard-on, drawing her attention to it as well.

Lydia took another step back and then another, effectively trapping herself when her back hit the wall because he pressed his body against hers. She pushed against his chest, but he didn't budge. "Why are you doing this to me? Why can't you just leave me alone?"

"Because I want you. And if you were honest with yourself, you'd admit you want me too."

"No." Her voice trembled.

"Yes," he whispered, lowering his head to do what he'd been dreaming of since the moment he'd laid eyes on her. Lydia turned her head, causing his lips to graze her cheek.

With an impatient growl, Ryder caught her chin and twisted her head to face him. He smashed his lips against hers. She initially whimpered beneath his forceful assault, but there was no mistaking the moan that followed. It was music to his ears. "Open your mouth, baby."

There was no gentleness in his kiss. Had she just accepted the excuse he gave her, as feeble as it was, he could have perhaps held back a little. But instead she had pushed, insisting she wanted to be as far away from him as possible. Well, that just wasn't going to work for him. And he made it his mission to make her as hungry for him as he was for her. His tongue invaded with no mercy, plundering her mouth.

He tangled his hands in the ropes of her shoulder-length locs, forcing her mouth open for his invasion. She didn't fight him. Oh no, quite the contrary. Lydia fought his tongue with her own, nipping at his lips while she buried her hands in his hair and tugged him closer. Her leg made a slow climb up his thigh, causing her skirt to inch up her long, shapely legs. Her heels put her at the perfect height for him to grind his cock against the apex of her thighs.

Hot and wet. He could feel her heat through the light linen of his slacks. Jerking his head back, he glared hotly at her passion-flushed face.

"You don't want me at all, huh?" Grasping her thigh, he pulled her leg higher, then dipped his fingers to stroke the crotch of her panties. A silk thong, of course. "Then why are you so wet?" He pressed his fingers against her clit through the material of her panties.

Lydia moved her head against the wall, her eyes closing as she moaned. "Just do it." She panted, her hips moving against his hand.

Pulling the skimpy underwear to the side, Ryder thrust two fingers deep into her sodden pussy. "Open your eyes, baby," he ordered through clenched teeth. Shit, she was tight. She would milk his shaft dry. "I want to watch you come."

Her eyes snapped open, their brown depths flashing with desire. Hell yes. That was the look he wanted to see. Ryder moved his fingers with brutal precision, curving upward in search of her G-spot. Her pants became whimpers, whimpers turned into little cries of pleasure, each one urging him on. Her pussy clenched around his fingers, practically sucking them deeper.

Ryder couldn't remember ever being with anyone who was this tight or got this wet. And the scent of her arousal was absolutely mouthwatering. He had to get a taste of her. But first things first. As he pistoned his fingers in and out of her juicy cunt, he rubbed her clit with his thumb.

Lydia clutched his shoulders, her nails digging into his flesh through his shirt. Her eyes were closed, and her head rested against the wall. The guttural moans slipping past her lips served to make his already-throbbing dick ache with need for her. It was insane how this woman could drive him to this.

Ryder prided himself on his professionalism and ability to separate work from pleasure. He'd never stooped so low with any woman before, and he'd questioned himself many times about whether he should be doing this. But having Lydia like this with his fingers in her pussy, and her gripping him and moaning so sweetly, he knew without a doubt he'd do it again if given the chance. Something about them together like this felt so right.

"Oh, Ryder." She sighed.

The sound of his name falling off her lips in the heat of passion nearly made him shoot his load right then and there. "Say it again. Say my name."

She licked her lips. "Ryder. Oh yes, Ryder."

"Tell me what you want me to do."

"More."

He grinned. "You're nasty. You want another finger in your pussy, don't you?"

She nodded.

"Beg for it."

She hesitated for a moment, her mouth slightly agape, and for a second, Ryder thought he'd misplayed his hand, until she complied. "Please. Yes. Put another one in me."

A chuckle of pure satisfaction rumbled within his chest. "Whatever you want, sweetheart." He eased another finger in her hot hole, making her scream out her passion.

"Oh God, yes!"

Lydia convulsed against him. Her pussy squeezed his fingers hard. And the heat: the woman could burn him alive and make him like it. Goddamn, she was driving him wild. She orgasmed hard, crying out for his touch and filling Ryder with a deep sense of pride to know he could do this to her.

"Yeah, baby, come on my fingers." Ryder moaned. He stroked her forcefully, enjoying the wonder and arousal on her face. He loved how responsive she was. If this was how she reacted with his fingers inside of her, their coming together would be explosive.

"You like this, don't you?"

"Yes!" she screamed, still riding his fingers as if she couldn't get enough, almost as if it had been a very long time since she'd experienced this level of pleasure. How long had it been for her?

Ryder finger fucked her until the need to taste her sweetness was too much of a temptation to fight. Slowly, he eased his digits out of Lydia, making sure to maintain eye contact before licking her cream off his fingers and hand. He grinned. "I knew you'd taste good, but damn, baby. You should bottle this shit up and market it. Taste how good you are." He slipped his still-dew-drenched fingers over her slightly parted lips and slid them into her mouth. "Suck it."

Lydia knew it was wrong on so many levels, but she didn't want him to stop. Some perverse part of her loved this side of Ryder. She loved the fact he was taking control of her pleasure, of her body, and forcing her to feel what she was too afraid to admit she wanted. Obediently she wrapped her lips around his fingers and sucked them like a cock, bobbing her head back and forth.

"That's it, baby."

Pulling the wet digits out of her mouth, he leaned forward to trace her lips with his tongue. Ryder pulled back just enough so their bodies still touched and their faces were a few inches apart. "Try to deny this ever happened."

The taunt hit her square in the face, forcing her to realize how dangerous this game really was. She had shown him too much by her surrender, small as it was. Now he knew that she wanted him, no matter how she tried to deny it. Lydia widened her eyes and inhaled sharply. How could she have been this weak? He wouldn't stop now. She had given him implicit permission by her words and actions.

She shoved him. "Get off me. Don't ever touch me like that again." Her voice wobbled, and she realized how uncertain she sounded through her anger.

The push she'd given him must have caught him off guard, because he stumbled back slightly. When she attempted to walk away from him, he grabbed her by the arm and swung her around to face him.

"That didn't come out right, but I'm not going to spend the rest of the week pretending like there's nothing between us."

"There is nothing."

"You can say that after screaming my name? After coming all over my hand, riding my fingers like you couldn't get enough?"

She swung her hand before she could call it back. Lydia could feel the burn of it on his reddening cheek. She gasped at what she'd done. “Why are you doing this to me?” A tear slid down her cheek, which she hastily wiped away. Lydia wrenched her arm out of his grip and ran to one of the bedrooms.

She was never going to live this down. She had wanted him and couldn't deny it to herself no matter how she lied to his face, and he knew it too. That part really stung.

Ryder flinched at the sound of her door slamming, followed by the decisive *click* of it locking. *Fuck!* This was not how he'd envisioned the start of their week. He should have kept his damn hands to himself. He just couldn't seem to help himself. Ryder realized he'd behaved badly and needed to apologize, but being so close to Lydia made him lose his fool head. He would be lucky if she let him within ten feet of her.

He was going to have to talk to her. There was no way in hell he would allow himself to screw this up. It had become imperative he become more than just a boss or even a friend. He wanted to be Lydia's man, and damn it, he would do whatever it took to become just that.

* * *

Tell me now how you don't want me, Lydia. Ryder's voice broke through the fog of lust surrounding her. *Look me in the eye and tell me there is nothing between us. Lie to yourself all you want, baby, but don't lie to me.*

He had stripped her bare, leaving her exposed and vulnerable, and she hated him for it. Lydia placed her back against the door, trying to pull herself together. Her knees were still shaky, her nipples like diamonds, pressing against the material of her bra. This was bad. She had to make sure she kept him at arm's length, because she was obviously weak where he was concerned. The vague sensation of feeling cheated would just have to be suppressed. Ryder was not good for her heart; she couldn't afford to let this go any further.

But still, she had never felt so hot and alive. And she wanted more. She'd wanted him to open his pants and give her what she really needed. He had felt so damn thick and long through his clothing. His bulge would have been intimidating if she were thinking clearly. But he was right: she did want him, badly.

The tap on her door made her jump. “Lydia, I'm sorry. I was out of line earlier.”

She didn't bother to answer; there was little point.

Ryder rapped on the door again. “Open the door, and we'll talk about it.”

Was he kidding? There was nothing to talk about. She felt ashamed and humiliated. His apology wouldn't change that. How could she react to him that way after declaring how she didn't want him? How would she manage to look him in the eye? The man was lethal, and not for the first time she wondered if she had the strength to continue working so closely with him when his relentlessness in pursuing her was apparent.

He was the type of man who'd use her. And once he had his fill, he'd discard her. Besides, word around the office was that he liked petite, cuddly women. She was neither. She refused to be his plaything for any length of time simply because he wanted to try something different.

"Go away."

"Lydia, please."

"Leave me alone."

Silence greeted her outburst, and for a moment she thought he had indeed gone away. She was wrong.

"You have an hour to get yourself together. We have a meeting at four with our hosts, and I expect you to be punctual. And if you're not out of your room at the designated time, I will break that damn door down, and you won't like what I'll do if you force me to come get you."

It was on the tip of her tongue to tell him to go to hell, but she bit back her angry retort. This time she listened to make sure he walked away before moving. When she heard footfalls getting farther away from her bedroom door, she released a breath she hadn't realized she'd been holding until that moment.

She wasn't one to give in to tears or histrionics, but she really wanted to break some shit right now.

"I *will* control myself around him," she told herself firmly, thinking that maybe if she said it out loud, she would believe it. Speak it into being or something.

She couldn't blame him for being angry, if she wanted to be honest. She'd let him touch her, put his fingers inside her, drive her to a mind-blowing climax. And she had loved every second. Shaking her head, Lydia decided to shower. She would wash Ryder's touch off her skin. Too bad the steamy water sluicing over her skin only sent tingles of need straight to her core.

Once she had washed off as quickly as she could, she jumped out, dried off, and put on as many clothes as she could stand in the hot Southern climate. A turtleneck would be a bit extreme, so she settled for a prim skirt falling nearly to her ankles and a short-sleeved cowl-necked blouse. Pinning up her locs, she studied her reflection critically in the mirror. Poised, professional, perfect. No one looking at her would ever know less than an hour before she had been pinned to the wall, Ryder's talented fingers pillaging her welcoming pussy. Now to keep it that way.

Head held high, Lydia strode out to the common area, where Ryder waited, drink in hand. He was frowning, looking out the large picture window at the surf.

"I'm ready." Her voice was clear and strong without a hint of her inner turmoil. Ryder Garrison might get under her skin, but he would not break her.

Chapter Four

"So tell us what you have in mind to boost our business, Garrison? I'm prepared to spend whatever it takes." Jasper Rawlings, though an affable host, was if nothing else a shrewd businessman who would accept nothing less than the best. And judging from the magnificent spread they'd spent the afternoon and a chunk of the evening exploring, money was not an issue.

"Please, call me Ryder. And I think the key is not to play up what kind of resort this is, because that will become apparent on its own. I think what will set this place apart from just another adult retreat is exclusivity. The amenities you offer are second-to-none, all-inclusive packages. Yet worth every dime."

"Yes, people would eat that up." Lydia piped in voluntarily for the first time that evening. "Instead of downplaying the price of this place, underline it. I think that strategy would appeal to the snob in a lot of people. They would be paying a pretty penny, but they'd be getting the best. That's what will set you apart."

Jasper leaned forward, his gaze transfixed on Lydia. "I'm listening."

Lydia went into a spiel of how to showcase the amenities such as the free boat and personal watercraft rentals, three different nightclubs, private beaches, fine dining, nightly entertainment, and full-body massages. She even suggested inviting celebrities to vacation here to give their stamp of approval. The economy might be in a downward spiral, but there were still those who craved the best, and that's exactly what Utopia offered. "Everyone is welcome, of course, but the thought of exclusivity will bring people in droves. And might I suggest we launch this campaign on an international basis. I intend to do some more online research later into the demographics of who this club would appeal to and the countries I think we should hit with advertisements. But I can think of a few right now."

"And which countries did you have in mind?" Bev Rawlings asked, joining in on the conversation.

"The Netherlands, England, and Germany would be a good place to start. Each of these countries has a huge sex industry, probably bigger than the US, and the people are a lot more open about their sexuality and about their bodies. At my last job, I had a hand in putting together a catalog for an adult-toy company and learned quite a bit about the industry."

Ryder was impressed. He knew for a fact Lydia hadn't been pleased when she realized just how "adult" this resort actually was, but she was handling it with a professionalism that made him very proud of her. He knew there was more to her than a pretty face, a killer body, and a great ass.

Lydia had a brain and wasn't afraid to use it. It reaffirmed his decision to bring her here. She'd been right to suppose that one of his more-senior team members would have been sent on an assignment like this, but besides his wanting to use this as an opportunity to get her alone, he believed she was capable of handling the job. He wouldn't have chosen her otherwise, no matter how hard she made his dick. And she'd proved him right by the way she asked questions of the client, took notes, and listened to their needs and concerns. He couldn't have made a better choice.

There was only one thing he hadn't counted on. Jasper Rawlings. From the moment he'd introduced Lydia to the resort owner, the older gentleman had seemed fascinated, hanging on her every word when she spoke, his gaze often following the lines of Lydia's body when he didn't think anyone was looking. Never mind that he was married and his wife was sitting at the table with them. Judging from the way the Rawlingses carried on in his interactions with them, their marriage seemed to be an open one.

Ryder didn't give a flying fuck if the two of them invited a million people to their beds; he'd be damned if Lydia became one of them. Lydia was his. Not that Lydia noticed the man's attention. Still, experiencing jealousy for the first time in his life didn't sit well with him.

He shifted in his chair as all these conflicting emotions coursed through his being, the strongest of which was the urge to take her upstairs and fuck her senseless. But after their earlier encounter, he'd have to take things slow. Ryder needed to be more careful with his approach the next time around. And there would be a next time.

Ryder was so deep in thought, he didn't notice Bev scooting her chair closer to him. "Jasper gets so serious when he's talking business. How about the two of us take a stroll outside in the gardens? There's still a lot to see here at Utopia, and I'd love to show it to you." She emphasized those last words as if the resort wasn't the only thing she wanted to show him.

He gulped. Bev was an attractive woman, at least fifteen to twenty years younger than her husband, who looked to be in his late fifties, early sixties. Petite, blonde, and big chested, she was the type of woman Ryder found himself dating on most occasions, but today all he could do was compare Bev Rawlings with Lydia. It wasn't even a close race. Lydia had her beat by a long shot.

Not wanting to be rude, but definitely not wanting to be alone with her, he smiled politely. "I think we should hold off until we finish discussing business."

Bev pouted, poking out a glossy red bottom lip. "They won't mind, I'm sure. Besides"—she leaned over until her lips were only inches from his ear—"Jasper likes black girls."

Ryder's attention snapped back to the pair now engrossed in conversation. Yes, it was about business, but he didn't like the way Jasper leaned in a little too close or touched Lydia's arm as if he had the right to. *Shit.* What the hell was wrong with him? He'd never had problems maintaining his professionalism, so why now?

"Mrs. Rawlings"—Ryder kept his voice reasonably pleasant, but he wanted to leave little doubt that swinging was not on the agenda—"while Lydia and I would be the last people in the world to judge anyone else's relationship, I am very much afraid we have never learned to play well with others."

Bev's brow rose as her gaze slid back to Lydia and her husband. Ah, man, Lydia was going to kill him. There was no way he could take it back now, just like there was no way he was going to let Jasper make moves on her. Nor did he want Bev hanging all over him. It seemed the easiest solution rather than avoiding either of the Rawlingses' come-ons for the entire week.

"You and Lydia are an item?" The woman sounded skeptical, which irritated Ryder. Why wouldn't they be an item? They would make a great couple.

"Yep." Ryder lied through his teeth. "She's my girl. And I don't share."

"Does she know that?"

"You can ask her yourself." He met her gaze dead-on, hoping she wouldn't call him on his bluff.

She pursed her lips and ran a plum-tipped nail on his thigh. "Well, Jasper can be very convincing. I can't tell you how many couples we've met that he's charmed into our bedroom—couples who were just as adamant as you. Guess we'll have to play the 'wait and see' game, then."

Ryder narrowed his eyes. "Is our playing ball part of the deal?"

She waved her hand dismissively. "Of course not. First and foremost Jasper is a businessman. He works hard but plays even harder." She leaned over until he could feel her breath on his neck. "Looks to me like those two are getting awful cozy."

Ryder glanced in Jasper and Lydia's direction. Jasper was getting way too friendly. The older man's hand casually caressed Lydia's thigh. Lydia moved slightly, trying to put her body out of his reach, but the old goat simply moved his chair. Ryder's temperature rose by the second. How dare anyone make his Lydia feel uncomfortable?

"Well, I think we should take a look around for ourselves and hash out some more ideas," Ryder said loudly. A little too loudly, apparently. Jasper looked like a kid who had been caught stealing from the cookie jar. Well, at least he had taken his fucking hand away from Ryder's woman.

"Uh, yeah. That sounds like a good idea." Lydia took the opportunity to slide out of her chair and stand up.

Ryder walked over and took her hand. She made a move to snatch it away from him, but he held it firmly as he looked directly at Jasper to let the man know this woman belonged to him. Other than a raised brow, the other man didn't seem put off by the gesture. "We'll catch up with you tonight at the party."

"Remember it's in the Bay Breeze lounge. Wear something for the occasion. It should be a hoot." Jasper smiled jovially before shooting Lydia a lascivious stare. "And I'm especially looking forward to seeing what you wear."

Ryder could barely bring himself to nod before dragging Lydia out of their hosts' private suite. When they were a good distance away, Lydia snatched her hand out of his. "What the hell was that all about?"

"I was trying to save you from being mauled by the octopus. Yes, this account would be a feather in our caps, but I don't need the business so badly that I'm going to allow that man to touch you. It's why I told Bev we're a couple. That way they'll leave us alone. If you haven't noticed, their lifestyle is a little on the alternative side."

Lydia halted. "What did you say?"

"I said their lifestyle is—"

"No. The other part, about telling Bev we're a couple."

It suddenly occurred to him that this was an opportunity he'd be a fool not to seize. If he could get her to go along with this, there'd probably be some kissing and heavy petting in public just to keep the Rawlingses off their backs. He'd be killing two birds with one stone. They could avoid unwanted advances by other couples, because there were bound to be other people who just wanted to "experiment" on the island as well. And he'd have the added bonus of seducing Lydia. One taste was not enough. He wanted more. Craved it.

"Did you like the old man's hands all over you?" Offense would probably be the best defense here. If Lydia guessed for one second what he was up to, she would probably hand him his balls. "You want to go back there so he can finish chatting you up?"

"That's no excuse to tell them we're a couple." She glared at him. "We are *not* going to go through with this…this—"

"I think *charade* is the word you are looking for. And fine, you want to tell Jasper you're free and available, you go right ahead. Just don't come crying to me when he takes it one step too far."

Ryder would kill the old man without blinking. He had wanted to rip his hands off just for touching her. Lydia didn't need to know that, though. Planting the idea in her head might work in his favor to let her believe he would ever allow someone else to touch her. It might bring her guard down a little. He kept quiet and let her stew a little. Lydia was one heck of a smart woman. She would see the advantages of what he was offering, especially considering what kind of resort this was. And just as he suspected, she did.

"He made me a little uncomfortable—okay, a lot uncomfortable." She shivered and wrapped her arms around her body, making him want to be the one to hold and comfort her.

Ryder had to turn his head to hide his huge grin. He had her right where he wanted her.

"I guess it could work in our favor." She mused half to herself. "That way we don't have to offend a potential client and keep our integrity. But don't go getting any ideas."

"I'm only trying to think on my feet here." Ryder held his hands up in a parody of complete innocence. "What ideas did you have in mind?"

She cut her gaze from his, taking a sudden interest in her shoes. "You know…I don't want you to kiss me or think you can touch me just because you think you can get away with it. I'm willing to pretend, but that's it, okay?"

Not if he had anything to do with it. "Is that a fact?"

Lydia raised her head to glower at him. "You don't have to sound so patronizing about it. And yes, it is a fact."

"Doesn't it stand to reason that some kissing and caressing is necessary to convince the Rawlingses we're genuinely a couple? At the very least there should be some hand-holding."

"Not a chance, buddy."

"So…I should leave you to your own defenses as far as Jasper the Octopus is concerned?" There wasn't a chance in hell of that happening, but he wouldn't tell Lydia that.

A look of pure panic crossed her face, puckering her forehead. "I didn't say that."

"So we'll play it by ear and see what happens. Deal?"

She sighed. "Fine. But I reserve the right to call off this charade at any time. Got it?"

Ryder grinned.

Game on.

* * *

What the hell had she gotten herself into? Lydia played the scene from earlier in her head as she lathered her body with shower gel. Why did it feel like she'd been maneuvered into this? Now more than ever she needed to be on her guard.

He had a point, however. Jasper had gotten way too close for comfort. His touch was unwelcome; it made her feel cheap. Not at all like when Ryder touched her. Her boss had the unfortunate ability to send her body from dormant to blazing inferno within seconds.

The man could kiss like nobody's business. His lips weren't soft or seeking. No, Ryder took with his kiss, invading and conquering, sending her muscles into instant meltdown. He had large, masterful hands too. He molded her curves like a sculptor, caressing her like a real man should. He wasn't hesitant or uncaring at all like her past lovers, but rather had the ability to inspire her body with firm control. What would it feel like to have him pull her hair as he sank that big dick he was packing deep inside her cunt?

A moan echoing in the large bathroom startled her. Lydia blinked, ready to confront Ryder for watching her shower. There was no one. The moan had come from her. Her hands had somehow stopped cleansing and started rubbing. One hand cupped her breast, her fingers pinching her nipples. The other hand…

Damn it. When the hell had she started fingering herself? All it took was thinking about Ryder and she was diddling herself in the shower. But even in her shock, she didn't stop. Ryder's image was stamped on her brain, refusing to go away. That little smirking-smile thing he had going on leered at her inside her head.

Oh, God, she wanted him something bad. Tweaking her clit, she bit back a whimper, imagining it was his blunt fingers inside her right now. Her hips rocked to the remembered sound of his gravelly voice in her ear. *Do you like that, baby? Come for me, Lydia. I want you to soak my fingers with your cum.*

Lydia couldn't hold back the ragged cry as she did just that, riding her hand to glory. With ragged breaths, she rested her head against the shower stall in shame. It wasn't the first time she'd touched herself while thinking of him, but it didn't quell the hunger. She had to get him out of her system and fast. "You can't sleep with your boss, Lydia. Be strong."

She quickly finished bathing herself and stepped out of the steamy shower. Not bothering to grab a towel, because this was her private bathroom, she stepped into her bedroom. The cool breeze of her air conditioner hardened her nipples to tight peaks.

"Gorgeous."

She gasped with a combination of surprise, anger, and lust. Lounging in a chair, casually sipping a drink, probably the scotch he preferred, was Ryder. Smug bastard that he was, he wore a cocky grin, sitting there just as cool as he pleased, as if he hadn't invaded her personal space. Once the initial shock wore off, she crossed her arms over her breasts. "Get out!"

"You're not going to kick me out, are you, darlin'? 'Specially when I brought you a gift." And with an arrogant ease only he could exude, he took another sip of his scotch.

Burning with rage, she turned on her heel and strode back into the bathroom to grab the towel she'd dismissed only moments earlier. She wrapped herself in the fluffy terry cloth, making sure it was secure, then stormed back into her bedroom ready to give him a piece of her mind. What she hadn't counted on was him waiting outside the bathroom door.

Ryder pulled her to him, his mouth swooping down on hers before she could protest. Without waiting for permission, his tongue probed past her lips, demanding and gaining entrance. It wasn't so much a kiss as it was a claiming of sorts. She wanted to beat at his chest, yell at him to let her go, but the balled fists that had been at her sides were now splayed hard against the hard wall of his torso. Her pussy tingled with need.

He pressed his erection against her thigh, hard and heavy. Lifting his head just enough to plant a trail of kisses along her neck, he murmured, “You can't tempt a guy with that body and expect him to walk away.” He cupped her ass and lifted Lydia off her feet to carry her the short distance to the bed.

Before she realized what was happening, Ryder straddled her, then ripped the towel open. His hungry green gaze swept over her nudity with something akin to possessiveness, sending a shiver shimmying through her body. In the back of her mind, she knew she should say something, but her body was on fire.

“Just one taste, baby.” Falling on top of her, he buried his face against her neck, biting and sucking her flesh, sending pulses of pure delight to her pussy. Capturing her wrists in one strong hand, he pushed them above her head as she writhed beneath him. “Keep them there.” He growled.

His lips blazed a trail of erotic torment over her skin. Rough, slightly calloused hands cupped both of her breasts, pinching down on her hard nipples. The slight bite of pain had her already-wet pussy flowing freely. Her body arched off the bed, seeking his solid frame. She wanted him closer, skin on skin. Wanted his clothes gone and his cock so deep inside her, she could feel him in every pore of her body. To hell with maintaining her guard; she needed to be fucked!

“Ryder, I need…”

“I know, baby.” He spoke against her skin, his mouth moving to her breasts. *Yes yes yes!* She wanted his mouth there, and everywhere else. “I'll take care of you.”

She would have loved to come back with a witty reply, but his teeth scraped against her sensitized nipples, sending tiny quakes radiating inside her cunt. Her hands clutched at Ryder's head, unsure whether she wanted to push him away or pull him closer. She just couldn't think.

"Liked that, didn't you?" Forest green eyes burned her every bit as much as his touch had. She couldn't deny it, but she wasn't about to admit it either. "You like it a little rough, don't you?"

Did she? Nothing had ever set her off like this before. Her breath caught in her throat as his finger delved into her sodden core. Her thighs opened automatically, her hips lifting to welcome his invasion.

"Are you going to deny me now?" It turned her on when he was demanding like this. Lydia could have sworn his words caressed her as much as his hands were now doing.

"God, yes. Right there!"

How in the world had he found her G-spot in nanoseconds, when it had taken her a freaking year? There was no way she could ask the question, not when the thrusts of his fingers triggered a microexplosion.

"Fuck, yeah, come for me, baby!" Ryder slammed his fingers into her deeper and harder.

Lydia didn't have time to come down from the spine-tingling orgasm he had given her. Before the last spasm died away, his mouth was between her thighs, his tongue taking the place where his fingers had been. He didn't simply lick her pussy. Oh, no, not Ryder. He consumed her. He used his tongue to bathe her sex, his lips to pull on her clit, his teeth to lightly nibble at her labia. He seemed to sense when he pushed her right to the edge, because he backed up, smiling down at her panting body.

"Do you have any idea how fucking sexy you are?" The way he said it had her believing. A feral light in his eyes sent her pulse rising. She liked him wild like that. Loved how he simply took.

"Damn it, Ryder, let me come!" If she had to beg, so be it. "Please!"

The wicked grin should have been a clue, but it didn't prepare her for the sharp slap against her clit. Fire, lightning, and pure electricity combined and combusted right on her cunt. The scream she had intended to let fly from her lips came out as nothing more than a wheezing whimper. Oh God, she came! He'd spanked her clit and made her come.

"That's for keeping my pussy away from me." Ryder growled, moving from the bed.

Wait. That couldn't have been it. Her pussy still throbbed, aching for more, a true completion.

"What are you doing?" Lydia sat up, staring at him in bewilderment. He couldn't be leaving. He wasn't done.

"Going to get ready for the party, darlin'." He sent her a devilish wink. "That was just something for you to think about tonight when Jasper tries to corner you." He moved to the door, paused with his hand wrapped around the doorknob. "Oh, and I brought you something nice to wear tonight. Be a doll and wear it for me, will you, darlin'?"

He didn't wait for a reply, quickly leaving her shaking in disbelief on the bed.

Chapter Five

After waiting for nearly half an hour for Lydia to come out of her bedroom, Ryder banged on her door. "If you're not out in ten seconds, I'm kicking the door in, and I'm going to spank that luscious ass." No response. He'd be damned if he let her hide out in her room for the rest of the night. "One. Two. Three. Four—"

The door was yanked open, with Lydia in the outfit he'd bought her. The minute he'd seen the gold micromini dress on the mannequin at one of the resort shops, he'd thought of her. A body like hers needed to be covered in glowing silk. He already knew she'd look good in it, with the slinky material wrapping around her body like warm honey, but he didn't imagine she'd look like this.

His cock stiffened, which he didn't bother to conceal. "Hot damn," he muttered more to himself than to her. The only accessory she wore was a pair of large hoop earrings. Her normally pinned-up locs rested in waves around her shoulders, and a light coat of gloss shimmered on her full lips. The halter-style dress dipped so low in the front, it revealed her navel. There was no way she was wearing a bra under that, making him wonder how in the world she managed to keep her tits in place. The skirt rested just below crotch level to reveal thick, shapely thighs. If that weren't enough, she wore a pair of three-inch gold fuck-me heels, the kind with the straps around the ankles.

A grin curled his lips as he remembered being between her legs. He wondered how he'd be able to keep his hands off her tonight. He'd only planned to tease her a little and warm her up—make her more receptive to him when he moved in for the kill. What happened earlier was only supposed to be a prelude of things to come. But seeing her look like hot sex on two legs, all bets were off.

She crossed her arms over her chest. "I'm only wearing this because it seems someone took the liberty of removing what I'd already laid out for the night."

He chuckled. "Didn't want you to chicken out. Besides, you look beautiful. You should wear your hair down more often." He eyed her from head to toe again, unable to get enough of the sight of her.

Lydia touched her hair in an almost-self-conscious gesture. "I'll expect my belongings returned to me in the morning."

"Whatever you say, darlin'."

She tapped her foot impatiently. "Are we going downstairs, or do you plan on staring at me for the rest of the night?"

"As tempting as the latter sounds, our hosts are waiting for us. Shall we go downstairs, my lady?" He offered the crook of his arm to escort her.

Shooting him a hostile glare, she walked past him, ignoring the outstretched arm. It didn't faze him a bit. He'd been counting on her doing that; it gave him a great view of that ass. The way the material of the skirt hugged her bodacious bottom—without pantie lines—it was quite clear she was either wearing a thong or no underwear at all.

Licking his lips in anticipation, he followed her out the door. Oh yeah. He was definitely going to fuck her tonight.

Ryder didn't try to contain the smile pasted on his face once they were inside the party. Lydia stayed glued to his side. It helped that there were more than a dozen or so male gazes leering in her direction. Whenever another man got a little too close, she seemed to get closer and closer, until she was almost a part of him. And he liked that—a lot. It was where she should be anyway, right next to him.

Ever the lady in public, she didn't scowl or complain once, even when his hands wandered to cup the generous cheeks of her ass. She fell into her role as his woman naturally. Especially when they caught the attention of their hosts.

"Are you two lovebirds enjoying yourselves?" Bev Rawlings gushed, beaming at them.

Ryder barely suppressed a snarl when the other woman's gaze roamed lustfully down Lydia's body. He was in no way a prude. Hell, he had enjoyed the heck out of an occasional ménage or two in his wilder days. He just didn't appreciate anyone checking out what was his, man or woman. There would be no other lovers for Lydia if he had anything to do with it.

"It's quite...lively," Lydia answered politely.

That was one way to put it. The party was just short of an orgy. People floated about in various states of undress, kissing and groping openly. Couples and even threesomes on the dance floor were grinding so closely together, it was almost as if they were fucking right there in the open. He could feel tension in Lydia's body, but she didn't show an ounce of discomfort.

"Yes, we know how to party." Jasper's voice boomed amid the revelry, his chest sticking out proudly. "This is a place where people can come and just let it all hang out." The older man wiggled his eyebrows in Lydia's direction, gaze glued to her generous cleavage.

Ryder pulled Lydia to him by the hips, ass flush with his cock, before wrapping his arms around her waist, leaving no doubt in anyone's mind that he didn't plan on sharing. He leaned over and nibbled on her earlobe while boldly sliding one hand up her rib cage to rest just below her breast.

Jasper licked his lips as if he wanted a taste. Too bad for him.

"Let's show everyone how it's done," Ryder whispered in her ear.

"Huh?" She was barely cognizant. Lydia practically melted against him.

"A dance."

As if in a trance, she nodded.

He released her long enough to take her hand and lead her to the dance floor. For once, she didn't fight him. Her body molded to his front as they gently swayed to a beat far faster than the way they were dancing. She smelled so good. Light and sweet with just a touch of spice. Lydia fit perfectly against him, her head resting on his shoulder.

Ryder had held a lot of women in his lifetime, but none fit against him the way Lydia did. He aimed to drive her to the brink and keep her there. He wanted her hot for him and distracted enough to enable him to slip past her guards. He never considered what a double-edged sword that would be. His cock was so hard, he could chisel stone. Everything about her turned him on. He didn't want to wait; he wanted her right now. Ryder snaked his hands through her hair, tugging her head back.

Those sexy brown eyes sparkled up at him, her full, sensuous lips forming a little O. *Fuck!*

"Give me your lips."

He didn't lower his head, didn't move at all. Instead he helped lift her when she stretched up to kiss him. As much as he wanted to let her take control of the kiss, at the first touch of her lips he was a goner. His tongue plunged into her mouth, claiming ownership.

Ryder didn't want to do this here in the midst of the horniest group of people he'd witnessed in a while, but he couldn't stop. He wanted to drown in her taste. Lydia twined her arms around his neck, giving in to his unspoken command. Ryder pulled her hips flush with his. Damn, the dress was too short. He could flip it up and…

"Let's go back to the room." It wasn't a question or a request. He didn't wait for her response. He merely took her by the hand and led her out of the ballroom.

Lydia's head spun. She could have said something to him when he'd gotten all proprietary with her on the dance floor. She could have told him to stop when he had ground his hard cock against her ass. She even could have pushed him away when he took her mouth in a kiss that made her knees wobbly. But she didn't want to. It was official. She was going to be one of Ryder's women—something she'd probably regret after this was all over. The pretense of not wanting him when they both knew the truth was too hard to uphold. No one had ever set her body on fire the way he did. His touch had her feening for more. She was addicted. And that cocky son of a gun knew it too.

She wasn't blind to the fact that he'd orchestrated this week to get into her pants. Out of all the workers at his agency, he could have easily sent someone else. Though she knew she could do the job just as well as any of the other associates, a plum project like this one was generally given to someone with far more seniority than she had.

She'd seen the way he looked at her, how he somehow found a reason to be close to her. And the more she'd rebuffed him, the more aggressive he seemed to get. She should have known she'd succumb. Somewhere deep inside, she must have always known. But there was no turning back now. Tonight they'd fuck. Tomorrow they'd fuck. And the next night…they'd fuck. But when this trip ended, it would be back to business. She couldn't afford to risk her heart. Not to someone like Ryder, who probably collected and discarded them at will.

Ryder yanked her against him; he held her close as they walked the length of the hallway to their suite. Every few steps, he'd stop to kiss her neck or lips. "What's the matter, baby? I lost you for a second."

"I was just thinking."

"Not having second thoughts, are you?"

She shook her head and turned within the circle of his arms until they were facing each other. Looping her arms around his neck, she kissed his chiseled jawline and placed a series of kisses over his mouth and face. She then traced the outline of his mouth with her tongue. "Does this feel like I've changed my mind?"

Something feral flashed in his eyes as he dipped slightly, only to hook his arms under her legs and lift her. Without any words exchanged, he ate the carpet with determined strides to the door. She fumbled with the key card, which he yanked from her hands and slid through the reader. Ryder practically kicked the door open when the green light flashed and he turned the knob.

Without stopping, he carried her to his room, which had a bed bigger than the one in her room. It was obscenely large. But before she could comment on it, he tossed her to the center. "Don't move a muscle." His words were a soft whisper, but it was a command nonetheless. A shiver of anticipation rippled through her. Her pussy was so wet, her juices moistened the insides of her thighs.

Ryder stood by the bed, slowly undressing, his gaze never leaving hers. Lydia couldn't remember the last time she'd been this turned on. No man had ever looked at her with such hunger that promised to give her many hours of pleasure. When she made an attempt to slide off her thong, green eyes narrowed to jade slits. "Don't you fucking dare. The only one undressing you is me."

She licked her lips nervously. Tension rippled his muscular frame, giving proof to the fact he was restraining himself. What would all that suppressed energy be like when he finally took her? Once he stood naked and unashamed, instead of joining her on the bed, he took his cock in hand and slowly began to stroke himself. He was…magnificent. The length and girth of him was well above average, and he had the nerve to just stand there while she lay on the bed in need?

Her mouth fell open with a gasp. No fair. Did he intend to tease all night? "Ryder…please."

He chuckled. "Oh I fully intend to, baby."

Instead of getting down to business, something Lydia so desperately craved, he set out to toy with her. Kneeling on the bed at her feet, he took one leg and placed her foot on his shoulder. Lord, he looked glorious hovering over her like that. Like some kind of ancient warrior prepared to pillage. She just wished he would get to the mayhem. Her body was burning up! Turning his head, he kissed her ankle, his lips moving ever so slowly up her leg. She shifted, then lifted her hips up to offer herself to him, and the damned man ignored her unspoken plea.

"Be good, or I'm going to have to spank you," Ryder chided, his voice thick and smooth.

Lydia decided she just might like that, doing it again. If it were anything like the last spanking he gave her, she was ready for a piece of that action. One smack against her clit would set her off like a Roman candle. Of course, that wasn't all she needed. That weapon he called a dick looked like it would be satisfying, and she wasn't leaving this room until she was good and satisfied.

But he didn't spank her. Instead he hooked his fingers in both sides of her thong and pulled the material against her weeping cunt.

"You're so wet, baby." He moved so he was face to pussy. "Is all that for me?"

"Nope, it's for the guy I'm planning on meeting tomorrow." It was a smart-ass thing to say, but she couldn't help but wonder what he would do about it. A little evil voice inside her head whispered to her to push him, to see what he'd do next. If that made her freaky, well, it was Ryder's fault for bringing it out in her.

Ryder cocked a brow, scowling down the length of her body. "Is that so?" He didn't growl, didn't threaten, didn't betray a thing by the way he watched her. Yet Lydia could see implicit danger flashing in his eyes. Not the kind where he would hit her or anything like that. No, Ryder looked like a man determined to make her eat her words. How delicious.

"Yep." She grinned. "Wouldn't want to get bored while I'm stuck here with the boss."

That did garner her a pussy smack. Unfortunately it was muted by the cloth covering her opening and clit. Instead of giving her an orgasm, it only made her itch for harder contact—skin to skin. Before she could open her mouth to protest, his teeth scraped over her covered nub, followed by the most incredible suction right through her panties. He repeated the action once more, then ripped the side of her underwear, exposing her to his hungry gaze.

"There will be no other man for you tomorrow"—Ryder ran his finger leisurely across her labia—"or the next day either." He kissed her—not on the mouth, but French-kissed her pussy, dipping his tongue deep inside her, then curling it up to swipe her clit as he rose. "I won't allow it."

Something she should have voiced much sooner came to mind. "Uh, Ryder…shouldn't we use protection?"

"You've got to be kidding me. When I'm finally inside of you, I want nothing between us. But if it makes you feel better, I have a clean bill of health. I'm regularly tested, and you'd be the first woman I've had unprotected sex with."

"So why now?"

"It just feels right."

"How do you know I don't have anything?"

"Do you?"

"No."

Ryder ran his finger along her slit, making Lydia shiver. "Well, we have no worries, then, right?"

She shook her head.

"Good, because tonight you belong to me."

His possessiveness would have given her pause in any other circumstances, but right now it was a fucking turn-on. She wasn't sure how she'd feel about it afterward, but she'd play along for now. Her pussy ached, and her body needed him. She went willingly as he pulled her up into a sitting position, his finger deftly unhooking the back of her dress.

The look he gave her as he lifted her dress over her head made her toes tingle. There was a touch of roughness when his hands tangled in her locs, pulling her into his kiss. He tasted wild with a hint of Lydia love juice on his tongue. His lips were hard and demanding. She quickly found herself swept up in a fog of pure carnal cravings.

She wasn't aware of when he settled her on his lap as he knelt, couldn't really say when her legs wrapped around him in a lotus position, bringing her pussy against his rigid cock. Lydia became hyperaware of every part of him.

“Put me inside you, Lydia.”

With greedy fingers, she grasped his hard length as she raised her hips just enough to position the helmet-shaped head of his erection against her slit.

Ryder reached down and parted her nether lips with his fingers as she got the tip of him inside her, eliciting a collective gasp from both of them. “That's it, baby. Take it. Take every single inch.” She slowly lowered her body, impaling herself on his cock. It wasn't easy; he was so thick, he stretched her almost to the point of pain. But she was far too gone to give up, though. Rolling her hips, she worked it until she was fully seated, every bit of his cock stuffing her to the brink. She wiggled her hips to adjust herself to his immense size.

“Don't move.”

He had to be joking. *Don't move?* How the hell was she supposed to not move? The sensations set off by having him inside her were amazing. She had to have more. When she ignored his instructions and moved anyway, a heavy hand fell squarely on the cheek of her ass.

“I said don't move, Lydia. I meant it.” He gritted his teeth. Her disobedience earned her another slap on the ass.

“I can't keep still.” The need to move was almost overwhelming. She needed the friction so bad, she could taste it.

"You move when I say so. And not before." Ryder gripped her hips to ensure she didn't disobey again.

Lydia was dying. She could feel every delicious inch of him throbbing inside her cunt as she nearly cried tears of frustration. She needed it, damn it! Her eyes shut as she strained to tighten her muscles, suck him inside a little more, anything to add friction.

"Look at me, baby."

Ryder's voice turned tender, swirled in with white-hot desire. She was almost afraid to open her eyes, but she did so anyway. His gaze spit green fire as he raised her off his dick nearly to the point where he was almost out of her, before bringing her back down. Hard. She reveled in the sheer strength of him and the way the muscles in his arms flexed as he repeated the motion over and over again. He didn't speak, but his eyes said plenty. The sensation of being taken so forcefully as he stuffed her so deliciously with his cock sent her closer to the edge with each thrust. She hovered between the brink of pleasure and pain and loved every second.

When she attempted to turn her head away, he growled. He actually growled. "Don't you fucking look away from me." Eyes narrowed slightly. "No. One." He thrust, hard. "Is. Ever." Another thrust. "Going to be." Two quick, deep ones. "In this pussy." One thrust. "But me." Three thrusts. "Ever again."

She was lost in his gaze, her body automatically moving in time with his. The rigid flex of his thighs as he pistoned deeper and deeper inside felt oddly soothing against her legs. She anchored her feet on the bed and slammed her body down as he surged upward. It was so good, so fucking good.

"Do you understand, Lydia?" Ryder grasped her chin. "No one. Ever."

He took such control over her pleasure, she could believe in this moment, she would never have another lover. At least for now. Right now there were only the two of them, the sounds of their bodies coming together, and the exquisite tension building deep in her belly.

She gripped his arms, loving the feel of his taut muscles between her fingertips. She was sure to maintain the eye contact he demanded. "Oh God, Ryder! Feels so good."

"This is my pussy. Say it, Lydia."

She panted, barely able to get the words out. "Yours."

"Say the words. I want to hear them. Tell me this is my pussy."

"Your pussy. All yours!" She squeezed her muscles around his dick.

"Damn right it is. All mine. And don't you forget it." He dug his fingers through her hair and took a clump in his fist before giving it a healthy tug. It brought her head back to expose the column of her neck. Ryder kissed the side of her neck before catching the highly sensitized flesh between his teeth and biting down. Combined with the hurting he was putting on her pussy, it sent a burst of lightning through her body. "Oh God! I'm going to come!"

"Don't hold back. Come for me, baby."

Digging her nails into his arms, breaking skin, she let go, coming hard and fast. Her orgasm must have spurred him on, because he stiffened and shot his hot seed inside of her hungry pussy.

As she slowly came down from her high, Ryder pulled away and gently laid Lydia on her back. Sliding next to her, he dropped tender kisses along her cheeks and neck. “So beautiful,” he murmured.

Lydia balled her fists against her sides, unable to return the affection he so easily gave in the aftermath of mind-blowing sex. Sex, rough-hot-heavy, she could take. But the tenderness would be her downfall if she weren't careful.

Chapter Six

"We're quite pleased with the ideas you've come up with for the resort. This is certainly an angle we hadn't thought of." Jasper rubbed his chin as he looked at the PowerPoint presentation Lydia went over with him. Bev had decided to opt out of this meeting in favor of overseeing some last-minute arrangements for the Fantasy Ball they were having that night.

Jasper was every bit the hard businessman now, giving suggestions and letting them know exactly what he wanted. Ryder watched for the most part, allowing Lydia to take the reins. He was impressed. She was confident in her work and presented the client a package that not only suited their needs but exceeded expectations. The ideas she'd come up with and her professionalism in what could have been a leery situation validated why he believed she was one of the best associates in his agency.

From time to time, however, he found himself staring at her lips and counting the seconds to when he'd get to taste them again. His cock stirred as he thought about getting her alone. Last night had been amazing. It wasn't simply fucking. It was a meeting of the souls. No woman had ever made him feel so many emotions he once believed to be beneath him:

jealousy, possessiveness, and uncontrollable lust. Lydia had the ability to make his dick hard 24-7 without blinking an eye.

She'd bewitched him, and he didn't care. Ryder wanted more than sex. He wanted to know what made her smile, made her laugh and cry. What was her favorite color? Season? Food? He simply wanted her. For keeps. The revelation thrilled and scared him at the same time. He'd always believed love was a trap he was too clever to fall into.

Was he in love now? He wasn't sure, but if it was being completely obsessed with someone to the point every waking thought was about them, or feeling bereft when they weren't near, then maybe he was. Sure, he'd had crushes when he was younger, but none compared to what he felt for Lydia.

Ryder had had his life planned out. Obtain his MBA. Check. Work for one of the largest advertising agencies in the country to gain the much-needed experience while building up a list of contacts. Check. Start his own business and make his first million by the age of thirty. Check and check. Once he'd accomplished his goals, he'd rewarded himself by enjoying the lifestyle he'd earned: women, parties, and high living. He figured one day he would eventually settle down, get married, and have a couple of kids, but there'd been no rush.

Now here he was on the verge of thirty-eight and feeling like something was missing in his life. Ryder now realized what that something was—the right woman. He was almost certain Lydia was she. His parents would more than likely object to his relationship with a black woman, but he'd stopped caring what they thought a long time ago. There were only a few people he was close enough with to care about their opinions—his sister and a couple of friends he'd known since he was a kid. They wouldn't give a damn either way, as long as he was happy.

With the newness of this discovery surrounding his feelings for Lydia, a sense of dread descended on him. He hadn't been too caught up last night to notice she'd held a piece of herself back. She'd given him that delectable body of hers, but that's all he'd gotten. What was worse, he'd woken this morning to find she'd returned to her bed. If she thought this was just a fling, she had another think coming. And Ryder didn't plan to rest until he had her heart, body, and soul.

Impatiently he shifted in his chair, waiting for their meeting to be over, adding his comments when necessary, but for the most part letting Lydia do her thing. So it came as a huge relief when Jasper stood up with a satisfied grin on his face. "I do believe I like what I see, little lady. Beauty and brains. Have some figures to me by tomorrow, and we'll talk contract." The older man took Lydia's hand and held it a little longer than Ryder liked.

Ryder stood as well, clearing his throat. "I think we could come up with some figures that will be satisfactory to both parties."

"Good to hear." Jasper barely spared him a glance as he smiled at Lydia. "Bev and I are really looking forward to seeing you two tonight at the Fantasy Ball. It's going to be a hoot. Can't wait to see your costume. You will be coming, won't you?"

Lydia looked at Ryder as if seeking direction for how to answer. Ryder liked that. She was so his, and she didn't even know it yet.

"Yes. We'll be there. As a matter of fact, we're going to take advantage of one of your shops and go costume shopping. So if that concludes our business, and if you don't have any other questions, I think Lydia and I should get going."

Jasper looked a little disappointed. "Oh, shoot. I was hoping you would have drinks with us. Tomorrow Bev and I are taking you out on our yacht for the entire day. Bring your laptops so we can discuss finances on board. And your bathing suits for the water. We're not taking no for an answer."

"Sounds like a plan." Ryder casually walked over to Lydia and slipped his arm around her waist, essentially guiding her away from Jasper without making it too obvious. "We'll see you tonight at the ball, then."

"Of course. You'll save a couple dances for me tonight, won't you, Lydia?" Jasper's gaze roamed her body before settling on her face.

"Uh, sure."

Later, after they packed up their equipment and headed back to their room, Ryder took Lydia by the elbow, halting her.

"What?" She spoke for the first time since they'd left the conference room. She seemed a bit distracted about something.

"You will not dance with that man tonight."

Brown eyes narrowed. "Excuse me?"

"I said you won't dance with him tonight or any other night." Ryder was angry. No, he was way past anger to full-on rage. He knew there was something between them. Why was she so set on holding back?

"One night does not give you any kind of say over what I do with my life." Lydia poked her finger in his chest. She was so sexy when she was indignant like this. Not that it curbed his ire one drop.

"No, one night doesn't." He gave her that point, but that was all she was getting. "And if that was all there was, I wouldn't give a shit about Jasper. But we both know there is a hell of a lot more going on between us than sex, and you know it."

That got her. She looked like an adorable fish plucked out of the water with her mouth opening and closing, but not a sound emerged from those luscious lips. Something flickered in her eyes. He caught just a glimpse of it before she pointedly looked away. Damn it, he wished he could get into her head. He wanted to understand why she was so dead set on holding herself back from him. It made no sense. They had the kind of chemistry that just didn't happen every day. He didn't understand how she could just walk away from it.

Lydia not only walked away from him, she ran. Ryder allowed her that for now. Following much more slowly, he wasn't surprised she wasn't in their suite by the time he made it there. Truth be known, he was a little relieved. He needed to work on a new strategy.

When they had left Texas, his only goal had been to sleep with her. He couldn't have predicted how she would affect him. It was cliché, perhaps, but sleeping with her only made his attraction worse. Ryder wanted more than her body. He wanted her to come to him with all her problems. He wanted to be the first person she shared good or bad news with. He wanted to shower her with flowers and candy. Man, how corny was that?

Ryder Garrison, Mr. Romance. No one who knew him would believe it, but it was true. He wanted Lydia something fierce. The thought of anyone else touching her made him near-homicidal. But how was he supposed to get her to trust in him when she refused to acknowledge their connection was stronger than sex?

Perhaps it was just too soon. Maybe he just had to keep working to get behind her barriers. Not by concentrating on a purely nonphysical relationship, however. That may work in the movies, but he was a flesh-and-blood man. Hell, all he had to do was think about her and he was hard and ready. There was no way he could stop himself from fucking her. He didn't even think that was possible. Lydia was like a drug—completely addicting. But what he could do was put chinks in her armor, bit by bit.

By the time they returned to Texas, he would know what it was that made Lydia Morris tick. He would seduce it out of her if he had to—and he was probably going to have to. At least then he would know how to combat the ghosts that kept her from letting it all go. A week wouldn't be nearly enough time for any real relationship to develop, but it wouldn't stop him from trying.

"Whatever you're plotting, forget about it."

Ryder smiled as Lydia stormed into the suite, holding her laptop in front of her chest like a shield. There wasn't a hint of the intimacy they had so recently shared in her body language. She was just as standoffish as she'd been before they arrived.

"Why don't we go hang out on the beach for a little while?" Ryder suggested, completely ignoring her little comment. She was looking for a fight, and he wasn't about to give her one.

She looked at him suspiciously, hugging her computer. Ryder was careful to keep his relaxed sprawl, not looking away from her face. He was a somewhat-patient man when the situation called for it; he could wait. Time to show Lydia there was more to what they had than hot sex.

"Why?"

He wanted to laugh out loud at the bewildered look on her face. Why indeed?

"We've done a fantastic job in such a short time. We deserve a little break." He leaned back into the cushions of the overstuffed couch.

Ryder watched her mull over his suggestion. Perhaps she was trying to find a way to say no politely. A little prodding and she would give in. Despite her tough talk, Lydia was sweet at the core. It was one of the intoxicating things about her: the dichotomy between the tough, cool professional woman and the vulnerably sweet sex kitten underneath. It was probably why all her clothes were understated yet incredibly seductive at the same time.

Any one item taken on its own seemed conservative, almost prudish, but she always managed to look like a siren in them. It was an unconscious challenge for a real man to step up and take it. When she looked as though she wanted to protest, he went in for the kill. “Look, Lydia, I'm not going to hide the fact that I find you extremely desirable. Nor will I pretend that I didn't enjoy what we did last night. And I sure as hell won't stop wanting to do it again. But all things aside, we're going to be here for another five days and nights, and I don't see why we can't just get along and go with the flow.

“Arguing back and forth is not conducive to this paradise island. Let's bury the hatchet right here and now. What do you say? Truce?” He hoped to appeal to her more-sensible nature. Ryder waited with bated breath for her response as he observed several emotions flutter over her lovely face.

“All right.” She finally acquiesced with a sigh. “I'll go change.”

“Meet you out here in ten.” Ryder smiled, climbing slowly to his feet. “I'm glad we can be friendly, aren't you?”

He walked away, not bothering to wait for a reply. Let her think what she wanted about the vague statement. The less cautious she was, the better for him.

* * *

Lydia lay on her stomach, half dozing on the blanket Ryder had laid out for them. When they'd come outside, he immediately procured a beach umbrella in a prime spot on the sand, close enough to hear the crashing sounds of waves, but far enough away from them not to get wet, which was just fine with her. She was tired and didn't feel like going into the water for a swim. She'd barely gotten any sleep the night before. After Ryder fucked her to an earth-shattering orgasm, he allowed her to rest only long enough for his dick to get hard again, not that she'd complained, much to her chagrin.

Every time she resolved to not give in to him, he somehow found a way to shatter her defenses with just a look. And when he touched her, forget about it. She was putty in his strong, masculine hands. She wished she weren't so weak when it came to him, but somehow he managed to see right through her. Yes, she wanted him. Wanted him, with the likes of nothing she'd experienced before. And even though she tried to convince herself in the light of day that it had been nothing more than plain old hot sex, a nagging voice within told her otherwise.

After Ryder had finally drifted off to sleep, she lay awake in the circle of his corded arms, trying not to memorize the feel of his caresses or the way his lips had tasted. The man was too lethal for his own good. Whenever she tried to ease out of his embrace, however, he'd murmur something in his sleep and tighten his hold. So she'd waited until he fell into a deeper slumber, and finally escaped.

Unable to sleep, Lydia decided to work more on the proposal for Jasper and Bev. Careful not to wake Ryder when she eased out of his grasp, she'd returned to her room. It was dawn by the time she was exhausted enough to sleep, but even then, she'd only gotten a couple of hours of fitful rest. Her dreams were dominated by a man who had the power to take her heart and smash it to bits.

As cool as she tried to act with him, Ryder somehow made her feel foolish for even putting up a fight. *Damn him.*

It's how she'd ended up with him on the beach. To her surprise however, Ryder pretty much left her alone while he went out for a swim. She'd slept longer than she'd thought, because the backs of her legs stung a bit. She must have repositioned herself while she slept, because her legs now hung outside the protection of the umbrella.

"You're going to need some lotion for that. Let me."

Lydia raised her head just enough to see Ryder taking a seat next to her. His hair was wet and curled around his face, and water glistened off his body in rivulets. He had an incredible physique from the toned chest sprinkled liberally with dark, honey-colored hair to washboard abs that tapered to lean hips. The way his trunks hung low on his hips to reveal his pelvic bone made her mouth water. It was obvious he took good care of his body. She quickly glanced away, uncomfortable with the effect he had on her.

"It's okay; I'll just move into the shade." She scooted back under the umbrella until the shade fully covered her once more.

"With the heat alone, you'll need something. It won't hurt."

Before she could protest, he whipped out a bottle of sunblock and squirted a generous amount in his palm. His hands felt incredible as they slowly kneaded into her legs. She tried desperately to hold back the shiver working through her body. Try as she might to feign indifference to what he was doing, her pussy clenched and her clit throbbed.

"Very sexy," he whispered. "You have beautiful skin, so rich, dark, and smooth."

Lydia bit the inside of her lip to keep herself from moaning.

Ryder poured more lotion directly onto her back and shoulders where the bathing suit exposed her skin. “I love this suit you're wearing. It's far sexier than any of the skimpy string bikinis and thongs women tend to wear these days.”

“I kind of like retro clothing,” she said for lack of anything else to say that wouldn't make her look like a complete idiot.

“I've noticed. This bathing suit, though, it kind of reminds me something Bettie Page would have worn, the halter style that silhouettes your body perfectly and the saucy little skirt.” He wasn't so much as rubbing the lotion into her skin as he was caressing it in.

“I, umm, I'm a fan of hers.”

“Oh yeah?”

“Mmm hmmm.” Lydia balled her fists so that she wouldn't reach between her legs and relieve the ache building within.

“You're very tense. Would you like me to massage you?”

That was it. She couldn't take any more. Rolling away from his touch, she quickly rose to a sitting position. “Uh, that's okay. I'm fine. Guess I'm just worried about making this deal. It's my first big account, so it's important to me that I do well.”

Ryder raised a brow but didn't say anything for a moment. Maybe she'd imagined that brief twist of his lips signaling displeasure. He leaned back, planting his hands on the ground at either side of him. “You have nothing to worry about. You're doing a fine job, and I'll be very surprised if Jasper doesn't agree to sign with us tomorrow."

She moistened her lips with the tip of her tongue, wondering what he'd think if she told him she wanted to go back to the room. She'd probably look like a coward, but what choice did he give her? "Uh, maybe I should head back upstairs?"

He grinned. "What's the rush? The ball doesn't start until nine, and we have plenty of time to kill before then."

"But I have nothing to wear."

"I have that covered."

"But you told Jasper—"

"I told him that so we could have some time to ourselves. I didn't think you'd take pleasure in having to fend off his advances for the remainder of the afternoon."

He had a point there. As much as getting this account meant to her, sleeping with her client was not something she was willing to do to secure it. It was bad enough she'd already screwed her boss. "Yeah, but I should probably check to see if we've gotten a response from our finance team with those numbers. I've been waiting for a callback."

"Our BlackBerrys are right here. If someone from the office needs us, we'll talk to them then. Relax. And tell me a little bit about Lydia."

She stiffened. "What do you need to know that you already don't?"

"Where you're from. Likes and dislikes. That kind of thing."

"There's really not much to tell. Since you seem to be in such a sharing mood, why don't you share something about you?"

"What would you like to know, darlin'? I'm an open book."

"Dunno. You tell me."

"Well, I was born and raised in Texas in a little town not far from Dallas. I have one sister, who I'm pretty close with. Mom and Dad, not so much. Played football in high school and was good at it, but found I didn't really have the heart for it, much to my father's disappointment. That was just one in the string of many letdowns for the folks, so that didn't matter. I got an academic scholarship to Texas A&M, where I received my bachelor's in business, with a concentration in marketing. Went to grad school at Duke University. Worked with a firm in New York for a few years but realized I missed my home state and used that opportunity to start my own company in Austin. That's me in a nutshell."

"Why don't you and you parents get along?" She wanted to kick herself the moment she'd asked him that. Lydia didn't want to care, but he'd piqued her interest. As someone who'd had a tumultuous relationship with the only parent she had, she could sympathize with anyone who didn't see eye to eye with their parents. "Sorry."

He shrugged. "Don't apologize. It is what it is. My parents are basically failures in life who've tried living vicariously through their children. But I wasn't willing to play ball. So now we only see each other on holidays, and we have that one obligatory phone call a week."

"That sounds sad."

"I'm used to it. I guess it's not as big a deal when you realize you'll never please them so you might as well please yourself. Admittedly I did have a hard time with it before I came to that realization. And what about you? What is your family like?"

She was completely disarmed. Before she could check herself, words flowed out of her mouth.

"It was just me and my mom for a while, before she remarried." Lydia shrugged, suppressing bad memories. "I left as soon as I was legal."

"I take it you and your stepfather didn't get along?"

"Depends on which one you mean. I just felt like I was kind of a ghost, you know? Like I didn't really matter. So I left."

"That's it?" Ryder prodded, playing with one of her locs.

Had it been anyone else, she would have yanked her head away. Not so with Ryder. It felt comforting just lying here with him, just talking.

"Yeah, that's pretty much it. I went to night school while working crappy jobs during the day, and here I am."

"Why are you single?"

Why indeed? Because men were shits in general? Because she attracted the worst kind of guys? Oh the places she could go with that loaded question. She wouldn't, though. Lydia doubted he was really interested. It probably just seemed like the right thing to say. How many of his past women had fell for that mock concern?

"Why are *you*?"

"Guess I was just waiting for the right woman."

Something in his gaze caused her to squirm. He seemed so earnest, like he was trying to tell her something. That was foolish. She was probably just projecting what she wanted to see. One night did not constitute a relationship. “Yeah, well, I'm sure she's out there somewhere.” Cool with just a touch of flippancy. That was exactly what she wanted to project.

“I know she is.” His intense gaze never wavered from her face.

What the hell does that mean?

Chapter Seven

Lydia blinked at her reflection, not believing what she saw. The gossamer fabric floated around her as she moved first to the right, then the left to check out how she looked from every angle. The waist was lined with tiny golden coins, standing out against the stark white of the material. There was no way she could walk out of this suite looking like this.

Her legs were bare on the sides to her waist. The billowing white material cascaded down the front and back of her legs, stopping right after covering anything important. One stiff breeze and the gold thong she had on underneath would be revealed. It was beautiful, there was no doubt about that, but it was scandalous to the extreme. The skirt rode low on her hips, leaving her midriff bare. The bandeau top stretched tightly across her ample chest was also edged with tiny golden coins. The costume made a stark contrast against her dark skin.

This wasn't a costume as much as it was an open invitation. The golden armbands and circlet, along with four-inch-heeled sandals that laced up her calves completed the outfit. She looked exotic—sexy even. If she swung the other way, maybe she would have been tempted to ask herself out.

She looked good, she could admit that, but she didn't think she could go out in public like this.

"Hey, Lydia, are you ready?"

She should be annoyed he bought this for her to wear, but she was more flattered than anything else. At least he thought she could pull it off.

"Hot damn!"

Lydia jumped at the sound of Ryder so close. She hadn't heard him come in.

"Did you forget to knock? How do you know I wasn't…"

Oh God, he was one tall drink of water. A leather kiltlike thing hung on narrow hips and his chest was completely bare; his brawny arms had leather armbands. He looked every inch the warrior god or whatever the hell he was supposed to be.

Throw me over your shoulder and take me away, Mr. Bad Man.

"Wasn't what?"

Damn his cocky hide. That smile of his could melt an iceberg.

"I can't go out like this." Lydia changed the subject. No talking about nudity tonight.

"You look stunning." Ryder moved far too close for comfort, his voice dropping an octave. "I knew you would."

Her breath caught as he trailed a single finger over her collarbone. His touch sent chills down her spine. "You don't look too bad yourself."

His smile widened. "Yeah?"

"Bev will be pleased, I'm sure."

The grin fell, and she wished she could take the words back. Though she hadn't meant to be catty, she couldn't let him know just how much he affected her. Still, she owed him an apology.

"I'm sorry."

"Forget it. We should probably head downstairs. The ball is getting under way."

Lydia placed her hand on his arm. "Ryder, that was uncalled-for." She didn't want to lose the peace they'd forged earlier that day.

Ryder looked to where her hand rested, a slow smile returning to his lips. "Do you realize this is the first time you've voluntarily touched me?"

"So it is. Don't let it go to your head, buddy." She found herself grinning with him.

The atmosphere changed all of a sudden, and an unreadable emotion flickered within his eyes. "I wish you'd do more of that when I'm around."

"More of what?"

"Smile. It seems like you have a ready smile for everyone, but me. Why, Lydia?"

She lowered her lashes, hoping he didn't catch the longing she'd felt. How was it possible to want someone so much even though you knew he was no good for you? "Ryder, let's not go there. Please."

He sighed. "Fine, but remember you're my date tonight, and I have no intention of sharing you. Just promise me this. Let go. And have fun. Can you do that for me?"

When put like that, the request didn't sound that unreasonable. Tonight she could let her inhibitions go. Just one night. “Okay.”

Ryder captured her chin between his thumb and forefinger, holding her head immobile as he brushed his lips lightly against hers. “Just enjoy yourself tonight. And don't worry about your costume; I'm sure there will be women wearing far less than you.”

And he wasn't kidding. Lydia was practically overdressed compared to some of the costumes she saw. A handful of the women were dressed as bare-chested vestal virgins. One woman was wearing a vine that was carefully draped around her body, barely concealing her private parts. She'd even seen a completely naked woman in high heels being led around by her leather-clad partner with a dog collar and leash.

“Pretty wild, isn't it?” Ryder leaned close to talk because the music was so loud.

“That's an understatement. Before I thought I wouldn't fit in because I'm not wearing enough clothes. But now I don't think I fit in because I'm wearing too much.”

“Don't worry about it; you look fantastic.” Something must have caught the corner of his eye, because he let out a groan. “Oh Lord.”

Jasper and Bev made their way over to them, both in pirate costumes, although Bev's outfit had less material than the bathing suit Lydia had worn earlier. The blonde moved away from Jasper and pressed her body against Ryder's. “You owe me a dance from last night, you naughty boy, and I've come to collect.” She pressed her large, probably surgically enhanced boobs against his chest. Lydia didn't know why it bothered her so much, but it did. And she didn't like feeling this way. She had no claim over him.

Jasper used that opportunity to take Lydia's hand. "And you, goddess, definitely owe me one." Without waiting for an answer, he pulled her out to the middle of the dance floor. She looked over her shoulder to see Bev with her arms wrapped around Ryder. His gaze was on her, and he didn't look happy.

Lydia didn't know whether he was angry because Bev's advances were unwelcome or because she was with Jasper. Either way, she didn't have a chance to analyze it, because Jasper pulled her against his body. His big hands roamed her naked back, and she tried not to flinch from revulsion. It wasn't that Jasper was an ugly man. In fact he was quite good-looking and well preserved for a man his age. The salt-and-pepper hair, broad shoulders, and lean physique probably attracted a fair share of women. But Lydia simply wasn't interested in playing games with a married man, no matter how open his relationship was.

"Relax, honey. I won't bite. Unless you want me to." He wiggled his eyebrows to emphasize his words.

This could cost her the contract, but she needed to say what was on her mind. "Look, Jasper, Garrison Advertising would really love your business, but I'm not part of the deal. If that's a condition to your doing business with us, then we're not the company for you."

A silver-tinted brow shot up. "Is that a fact, honey?"

"Yes, it is. And I'd really appreciate it if you'd call me Lydia."

She braced herself for his wrath. Ryder would probably be pissed to lose what had looked to be at least a million in revenue for the company. Instead Jasper threw his head back and let out a huge belly laugh. What the hell did she say that was so damn funny?

"Umm, Mr. Rawlings?"

"Now, don't you go getting formal with me again, Miss Lydia. I'm laughing because you obviously thought I'd be mad at you for being straight with me, when in fact, I appreciate your candor. Of course I find you attractive, but first and foremost I'm a gentleman, and if you say no, I respect that. Quite honestly, you're the first woman I've been interested in for a long time."

"Really? Aren't you and Bev free to be with other people when you want to?"

"We are, but old fool that I am, I went and fell in love with my wife. Our relationship started out as an open one, and at this late stage of the game it wouldn't be fair to change the rules."

Poor Jasper. All in one moment he'd gone from a man she would have crossed an ocean to avoid to a man she felt sorry for. "Maybe you should tell her how you feel."

"Don't pity me. I don't. It's the life I chose. Maybe one day she'll get tired of it all too and settle down. Maybe even give me some kids."

"She'd be a fool not to realize what she has."

"Why, thank you. He's a lucky man, you know."

"Who?"

"Ryder. Your lover. I can see why he's so possessive over you. At this very second my wife is over there trying to get into his pants, but he only has eyes for you. That boy has it bad."

Lydia seriously doubted it, but she didn't argue. She and Ryder were after all pretending to be a real couple. She and Jasper talked about island life, the resort, and just life in general as they swayed to the music with no real intimacy. She realized she liked this man very much with his witty retorts and comical anecdotes. He made her laugh out loud, which was rare for her. She was having such a good time, she didn't notice the song changing. It wasn't until a pair of strong hands fell on her shoulders to pull her against a hard body and out of Jasper's arms that she noticed anyone else's presence.

"I believe you've had your dances." Ryder uttered the words tight-lipped. When she turned her head to look up into his face, she gasped at what she saw. Fury.

"I will leave you two to it, then." Jasper bowed out graciously and then hurried off toward a pouting Bev on the other side of the room.

Lydia gulped, equal parts thrilled and horrified that Ryder was so obviously upset. While it secretly pleased her to see Ryder so aggressive, there was really no reason for it. They weren't a real item, so what was up with the jealous-boyfriend routine?

"Were you having fun?" Any thought of playing him off vanished at the ice behind his words. He was really, really pissed off.

"Actually, I'm kind of glad I got the chance to talk to Jasper alone." She wasn't going to lie; she had earned a new respect for the older man.

"Is that so?" He sneered down at her, whirling her around before yanking her firmly against his hard frame. "Maybe you've forgotten what we discussed last night?"

What the hell had they discussed last night? She honestly couldn't remember any kind of conversation. All she could recall was the way his skin felt hard yet smooth at the same time and the way his mouth possessed hers. The way his tongue felt stuffed deep in her cunt. If there had been any kind of meaningful conversation, she'd missed it.

"I meant every fucking word I said, Lydia. I will not share you."

"Um, okay, but—"

"What did he say to you? I look over and see you two laughing it up, and I have to wonder. Maybe you would like to join our clients in their room?"

Lydia stopped all pretense of dancing. Heat infused her face as her blood began to boil. No, he didn't just say that to her.

"You know what, jackass? You can go fuck yourself!"

She attempted to storm off, but Ryder was too quick. Her body was brought back against his in a heartbeat.

"Oh, but baby, haven't you figured out I would rather fuck you instead?"

It was so many different kinds of wrong to be turned on right now, but she was. She had gone from mad to horny in seconds. Add in the fact that he was honest to goodness jealous of a man who couldn't hold a candle to him on his best day and Lydia was in serious danger of losing her heart. That was the one thing she couldn't afford to do.

"If this is how you act when I even look at another man, it won't be happening again."

The need to take her right there was almost overwhelming. Seeing Lydia in Jasper's arms had pushed him further than he'd expected. When the two had started laughing, looking for all the world like they were sharing some delicious secret, Ryder couldn't take another second of it. He had left Bev with the briefest of excuses and stormed over to take his woman. Whether she wanted to admit it or not, she *was* his woman.

"You wanna bet?" he challenged, his dick growing harder the more she fought him. "It's going to happen again and again, until we both drop from exhaustion. And that will only be the beginning."

"Let me go, Ryder." Lydia snarled, making a halfhearted attempt to pull away.

Her hard nipples and rasping breathing gave her away. Ryder would bet anything that if he dipped his fingers between her thighs, he would find her wet and ready.

"That isn't going to happen, sweetheart." Not now, not ever. Cupping her ass, he brought his hips next to hers. He ground his cock against her, loving the way her eyes glazed. "Let's go."

Surprisingly she didn't try to stop him from half dragging her out of the ball back to their room. As soon as the door was closed, he pinned her against it, taking her lips. She tasted so damn sweet; he couldn't get enough. His hand tangled in her hair, jerking her head back, drinking her moan.

The costume had perhaps been a mistake. As good as she looked in it, he didn't appreciate the speculative looks in her direction. He'd originally picked it because he couldn't wait to see her in it. But he hadn't taken into consideration how other men would ogle her.

The second they'd stepped into the ballroom, Ryder noticed the lustful glances sent in Lydia's direction from men and women. And then there was Jasper. Barely tamed rage ran through his veins as he saw how the man caressed his woman's naked back. Coupled with Bev's unwanted advances, Lydia laughing with Jasper like he'd told the funniest joke in the world had been the final straw. Even in his anger, he knew he was edging his way over the line of insanity where Lydia was concerned, but he couldn't help it.

Even now with his body pressed so tightly against hers, and the taste of her sweet mouth on his lips, he couldn't get enough of her. He needed to consume every last bit of her. He trailed his lips along the side of her face, leaving her panting—just how he liked her. Releasing the grip he had in her hair, he grasped the bandeau top between his hands and ripped it apart. Her breasts bounced as they were set free. Ryder cupped her breasts and ran his thumbs over her nipples. The dark-chocolate tips came to life beneath his caresses. "So damn beautiful. Your body is responsive to my touch, isn't it, Lydia?"

She groaned in response, her head lolling back and forth against the door.

"Tell me what you want, sweetheart. Do you want my mouth where my hands are?"

Lydia opened her eyes; the dark depths were glazed with passion. "Mmm."

Ryder pinched her nipples none too gently, making her gasp. "You have to say it."

Her tongue shot out to run along her top lip. "Please. Put your mouth on them."

He grinned. "Well, since you asked so nicely." Lowering his head, he took one turgid tip between his teeth. He nibbled, licked, and teased it until her entire body shook. Satisfied by her reaction, he sucked the nipple into his mouth, tugging on her breast as he continued to roll her other nipple between his fingers.

Lydia dug her fingers through his hair. "Ryder, that feels so good."

Spurred on, he added his teeth, dragging them with just a little pressure down to the pointed tips of her nipples. A hiss *whooshed* from her lips. Ryder nudged her legs farther apart to better position himself. He pressed his erection against her core, grinding it and leaving her as hot for him as he was for her. The moist heat radiating from her pussy scorched him, making Ryder wish he had two mouths instead of one.

He hungered to taste her sweet honey coating his tongue, but he didn't want to leave where he was currently feasting. Pushing her round, plentiful breasts together, he sucked both nipples into his insistent mouth, sucking down hard as he pressed his thigh against her core. The musky scent of her arousal had his senses reeling. It beckoned him to taste all she had to offer.

Fuck! She writhed against him, just like when he was buried deep inside her. He wanted her to come. He needed to drink her nectar.

“That's it, baby.” Ryder groaned, coming up for air. She looked so sexy with her head thrown back, her eyes laden with passion. “Show me how much you want this.”

Small quakes of pleasure raced though his body as she did just that. Her pussy seemed to vibrate against his skin, soaking through her scant underwear. He dropped to his knees, positioned one thigh over his shoulder, then pushed aside the material of her panties with his teeth and dived in. Her unique flavor burst on his taste buds, making him crave more. The tugs on his hair gave proof to how much she enjoyed his attention. She made him feel like the master of the universe with the way she fell apart so sweetly in his arms. He wanted to drive her higher and higher, until she couldn't deny him or this ever again.

“Oh God, Ryder, yes!” she cried out as his attention turned to the hard nub of her clit. “Please, give me more!”

He planned on it. He slid two fingers deep into her cunt, lapping at the juices surrounding his digits as they entered. Lydia groaned her pleasure, trying to spread her legs wider to let him in. He crossed the two fingers inside her, then curved them upward to stroke against her G-spot. Her response was immediate. With a keening wail, she literally jumped, her other leg coming hard around his other shoulder. She bucked her pelvis against his open mouth, giving him everything, but it still wasn't enough.

Ryder needed Lydia's complete and total surrender. He needed her whimpering and begging for his touch, because damn it, he was whimpering and begging for her. Maybe not out loud, but he needed this woman like he needed air to breathe. A common-enough phrase he had heard a lot, but never before understood until this woman.

"Don't you fucking hold back on me." He growled against her savory, fragrant pussy. He could feel the tension radiating through her body. He knew she was close. "Come for me, Lydia. Give it all to me."

His mouth went to work double time, alternately sucking, licking, drawing deep on her pearl, then lapping up her juices. So sweet, so damn good!

"Ryder! Yes! More!"

Her pelvis thrust hard against him, her cream coating his fingers. He loved the way she came—her hands grabbing his hair in a death grip, her body convulsing beautifully. And he had driven her to this. Only him. He would be the only one to do so for the rest of their lives.

Without letting her go, he rose to his feet, allowing her body to slide down just enough to wrap her legs around his waist. As much as he wanted to take her right there against the door, his need to dominate her overrode the need to fuck her. He wanted so much more than sex. Somehow he managed to stalk to his bedroom, tearing what was left of the costumes from both of their bodies with one hand as he went along. By the time he made it to the bed, they were both gloriously naked, hot, and oh so ready.

"On your hands and knees," he ordered, his voice gruff with yearning so deep, it was damn near a physical thing. "Now."

God, but she could never make it easy for him could she? Instead she stretched out her succulent body, then turned slowly before climbing to her knees in languid movements. It was a move meant to tempt and tease; he knew that. But knowing and not allowing her antics to affect him were completely different things. A moan escaped his lips as his hand encased his throbbing cock, stroking himself from root to tip as he watched. He could see her glistening pussy clearly as she spread her legs and looked behind her shoulder at him with a siren's smile.

"Like this?" Lydia used her forearms to support her upper body while presenting her ass. Her knees were spread far enough apart to reveal her cunt. Damn, she had a pretty pussy. Its yummy cherry center was encased in dark chocolate. It was better than any drug or aphrodisiac, and it was all his.

Aw, hell.

There was absolutely no way he was going to last once he was inside of her. Fisting his cock, he pressed the head against her entrance. "Beg for it."

Lydia wiggled her ass, pushing it back. "Please don't tease me, Ryder. I need it."

He cracked his palm against her ass. He loved the way it jiggled beneath the force of his hand.

Lydia cried out, but he suspected it was more from shock than pain.

"If you want it so bad, tell me how much."

"Give me your cock. All of it. I need it. Want it."

He swatted her rear again. "Beg me to fuck my pussy."

She whimpered, still pushing back. Her pussy wept. Juices slid down her inner thighs. "Please fuck your pussy, Ryder. Don't keep torturing me. I need it so bad."

Ryder chuckled. "That's my girl." She moaned when he slid the tip of his dick inside of her. He grasped her hips then, and with one swift thrust, he was completely encased inside her wet heat. Her walls clamped over him in a choke hold. Wrapping her locs around one hand, he yanked hard as he slammed inside. He leaned over, then bit down on the tender flesh of her ear, neck, and shoulders, never losing his rhythm. He was going to fuck the shit out of her and take away any doubt she had about whom she belonged to.

"Can anyone else make you feel like this?" Ryder smacked her ass in rapid succession as he dug deeper still.

"No! No one!"

That was what he wanted to hear, but he was a long way from being done.

"Will you let another man touch you like this?" He was perhaps treading dangerous ground, but she needed to understand he was serious. She was his. No ifs, ands, or buts about it. "Will you ever let someone else touch what is mine?" The question was accompanied by a twist of her nipple. Damned if her pussy didn't contract around him as he did it.

"Yours"—Lydia panted—"only yours."

"Damn right!"

Lydia's head spun. Each thrust brought her closer and closer to the edge of something she was half-afraid to experience. He filled her to the point of overflowing, his cock stroking her so good, it hurt. And she wanted more. She shoved her ass up higher, desperate for more, even though she wasn't sure she could handle it. There was just something about Ryder that made her wild, made her crave to give everything she had to him. She'd be sore in the morning, and there would probably be marks all over her body where he bit and pinched her, but she didn't care. All she could think about was the here and now.

"You fit me so damn good, baby." She heard him groan in her ear. His words alone could make her cream shamelessly. "Tell me you feel it too. Tell me you love it."

"I do," she admitted on a broken sob. "Oh God, I feel it."

"Do you love it?"

She squeezed her eyes tight and concentrated on how deep his dick was inside of her. "Yes!"

"Is that all you love, Lydia?"

What the hell did he mean by that? She didn't answer, and thankfully he didn't press her as his breathing grew shallower. Lydia could tell he was close to his peak. Whatever he'd meant by that question, she refused to think about it. It wasn't something she could even wrap her head around at the moment. She loved his dick. That was it.

Pushing away thoughts that threatened to ruin the moment, she welcomed his now-frenzied lunges. She could never tell him, though. To admit it out loud would only mean certain doom. So she held it inside and swallowed the words. She opened herself in every other way.

The sting of her hair being pulled back until her head rested on his shoulder fueled the untamed hunger slamming through her. Her back arched as she bucked back against him, giving as good as she got. She loved it. She loved the way he hissed his approval, his free hand cupping her swinging breast in a near-brutal grip. She was going to explode.

"Yeah, baby, fuck me back!" Ryder roared, his hand moving slowly down her front to rest on top of her clit. He didn't move his hand, just pressed his palm against her nubbin. She needed more than that. She craved the delicious friction she knew he could provide.

"Please, Ryder," she begged, tears gathering in her eyes. She was so close.

"Please what? Tell me what you want, Lydia. Say it."

"Let me come!" Damn it. Why was he torturing her? She was right there. So very close.

"I want to hear you say it again."

She could barely get the word out. "What?"

"Tell me you belong to me." He scraped her neck with his teeth. She shivered at the primitive move. She knew he was marking her, but she was too caught up to protest. She wanted him to take it. "Tell me this is mine, that you are mine."

"I'm yours!" she cried, taking small solace in the fact he would never know how true the statement was.

“What is mine, Lydia? Your body, your pussy, your heart? Which part? Say it, baby, and I'll let you come.”

She knew he was just as close as she was, but he was holding back. How he could, she didn't know.

“Your body, your pussy.” She wouldn't say heart. She couldn't. “Please, Ryder, I need to come so bad.”

It was enough. It must have been, because he smacked her clit, sending sparks shooting from her pussy to set her entire body ablaze. Then he pinched it, twisting just enough to send her over.

“Ryder!” Lydia screamed from the sheer force of it. Her body shook from the inside out, detonating completely. She couldn't seem to suck in enough air, couldn't see. All she could do was feel, feel his cock expanding, feel his seed shooting deep inside her. Her world spun on its axis, sucking her down into a vortex of pure bliss.

“I love you, Lydia.” She could have sworn she heard him say from somewhere far away as she slipped into the blessed quiet of sleep.

A trick of the brain. It had to be. Ryder Garrison was a fling. For the remainder of their stay here, he could have her body. She'd give that freely, but that was it. Her heart and her pride couldn't take anything more.

Chapter Eight

There was no way Lydia could stay around her lonely condo after Ryder dropped her off. Her body hummed with need; the thought of going to bed alone made her feel cold. It took her about five minutes pacing her living-room floor before she was in her car and heading to the only place she found solace.

Sammy Jo White was the one person Lydia could always rely on. Through thick and thin, they had been best friends since grade school. Both women came from less-than-supportive homes. There were often times when they only had each other against the world. Sammy Jo had been there for her throughout the Kevin debacle; she'd been her shoulder when Casey had used her and thrown her away. Lydia had practically lived at Sammy Jo's after Marvin White, Sammy's husband, had been killed on the oil rig where he'd worked.

Lydia couldn't understand why three years after Marvin's untimely death, Sammy Jo still hadn't been able to let go. A pair of the man's work boots still stood by the front door of the small but cozy home in which she lived. His coat hung on the coat rack by the door; his clothes still hung in the closet; his chair still held a prominent place in the living room. No one was allowed to sit on it. Lydia couldn't understand that kind of obsessive love. It scared her how faithful Sammy Jo was to a memory—unable to move on, unwilling to let go.

"Aunt Lydia!" Melody, Sammy Jo's precious six-year-old daughter, flew into her arms as soon as she opened the door. Melody was a miniature version of her mother, not that her mother was much taller. Her dark-chocolate skin seemed to gleam with health and vitality, her dark eyes sparkling with laughter. Lydia could never resist a playful tug on her ponytail and a tweak of her chubby baby cheek.

Lydia never knocked; she had a key. It wasn't like she was going to catch Sammy Jo doing anything more than cleaning or taking care of Melody. As always, she had to suppress a shiver as she walked past Marvin's boots and coat with Melody still firmly in her arms. His pictures were all over the tiny living room. Sammy Jo said it was in order to remind Melody of her father, but Lydia suspected it was more to give Sammy Jo comfort. Melody didn't even seem to remember her father and never noticed she might be lacking in something.

"Hey there, sunshine. Where's your mama?"

"Right here." Sammy Jo frowned in her direction. "Melody, honey, go finish your homework. Aunt Lydia will still be here when you're done."

The little girl pouted but went to do as she was told. Sammy Jo waited until her daughter was out of the room before swinging a critical eye in Lydia's direction.

"Come sit down and tell me about it." Sammy Jo had to reach up to wrap her arm around Lydia's shoulder, a move that usually made her smile. Her best friend in the world was a short little thing, all feminine and curvy. Usually Lydia felt like a giant just standing next to her. Not today, though.

Today, Lydia basked in the motherly comfort. There wasn't another person she could trust with her confusion about Ryder. Before long, the entire sordid story of the weeklong sexfest came pouring out, along with her confusion about her boss. Tears Lydia wouldn't dream of shedding in front of anyone else flowed freely as she sniffed out almost all of it: The hot sex along with her unaccountable desire to let down her guard. How she wanted nothing more than to snuggle in his arms afterward and give in to the girlie urge to "talk."

"Well," Sammy Jo said with a sigh after listening quietly to Lydia's confessions and fears, "do you want this to go anywhere?"

"No. Not really." That was so not true it wasn't even funny. She knew the only person she was fooling was herself, and she didn't even believe herself. "Okay, don't say it. Yes, I do, but it won't happen. Men like Ryder don't get serious about women like me."

"Lydia, please don't make me smack you. You're a hell of a woman. Don't let a couple of bad experiences color your opinion of all men."

"So you think I should continue to fuck my boss, then?"

Sammy Jo shook her head while rubbing her back. "No, hon, that isn't what I said. I can't really give you advice about that 'cause I don't know him. I do know you tend to be overly cautious since Casey. I keep hoping you'll let it go and give love a chance, but I don't really think your boss might be the best move."

Hello pot, meet kettle, Lydia thought to herself but didn't dare say out loud. Sammy Jo's inability to let her husband go was a sore subject. No matter how she tried, Lydia could never get her friend to see how she was doing herself more harm than good by holding on to a ghost. There was nothing wrong with Sammy Jo loving her husband even though he was gone, but the man was dead. There was no coming back from that.

"I can't do it, Sammy. I can't have an affair with him. There is no way I could without losing my heart." It was as honest as she could be. Lydia seemed to excel in self-delusion, but she had made herself a promise she wouldn't ever delude herself into another heartbreak.

"Well, we will just have to make sure you don't, won't we?" Sammy Jo engulfed her in a bear hug, making Lydia almost believe everything would turn out okay.

Somehow Lydia doubted it would.

* * *

Ryder picked up his phone after the third ring. "Yeah, Donna. What can I do for you?"

"I have a call for you on line three. I know you said you wouldn't be taking any calls today, but it's your sister, and she won't take no for an answer."

Damn, he'd meant to call Mickey when he got back from his trip, but when he and Lydia had flown back to Austin, he'd been exhausted. He'd asked Lydia if she wanted to stay at his house for the rest of the weekend, but she'd mentioned something about having things to do. He didn't press, even though he wanted to, realizing she'd need her sleep for the upcoming workweek considering they'd been dog tired. He spent the rest of the weekend sleeping and working through all the work e-mails he'd gotten that week.

"Okay. Put her through."

"Sure thing." A *click* indicated that the phone had switched over to his sister.

"Hey, Mickey. Sorry I didn't get back to you sooner. I've been playing catch-up since I've been back."

"Cut the crap. Didn't you fly back on Saturday? It's Monday now. You mean to tell me you couldn't spare ten minutes of your time between then and now to pick up the phone?"

Ryder groaned inwardly. Mickey could put a guilt trip on people that would have made a Catholic nun proud. "I was tired. It's been a long week. To what do I owe the honor of this phone call?"

"I wanted to know how it went. You seemed a little edgy about it before you left. Were you worried because this would be one of your company's biggest clients to date?"

"Among other things. But I was fairly confident my colleague and I could present them with a package they would find satisfactory."

"And did they?"

"Yep. They signed the contract on Friday. And with this kind of revenue coming in, we'll be able to expand again maybe next year sometime. I was looking to open another office in either Dallas or Houston. But we'll see once the logistics have been worked out."

"So if you weren't jittery about the deal itself, then what were you so nervous about?"

Ryder sighed. He might as well tell her. She'd find out soon enough anyway. "Well, actually the purpose of the trip was twofold. One, to secure a contract with the client, and two, to finally get some alone time with Lydia."

"Lydia? Who's that? Don't tell me you're sleeping with one of your employees. That could easily blow up in your face in this litigious society."

"Fine. I won't tell you."

"No way."

"Yes way. I know it's not a good idea to get involved with the people I work with, and I've never had that issue before, but with Lydia…it's different, you know? I wouldn't even have mentioned this to you if it weren't something more. I'll admit, when I first engineered for her to join me on this business trip, the idea was strictly to assuage this obsession I had with her."

"You jeopardized your company to get a little booty?"

"I'd never do something that reckless. I already knew Lydia was more than capable of handling the job, which by the way turned out better than I anticipated. You should have seen her in action."

"Good to know, but you're going off on a tangent now."

"Sorry. As I was saying, what I didn't plan on was falling head over heels in love with her. So I guess you're right. It did blow up in my face."

There was a long pause on the other end of the line, and for a second Ryder thought his sister had hung up on him. But finally she responded. "I don't know what to say other than I'm shocked. I never thought I'd see the day when you'd be bitten by the love bug. You used to tease me every time I announced a new love."

"Well, you have to admit, you did do it with some frequency."

"I was young. But we're not talking about me. Tell me about the woman who's finally brought the great Ryder Garrison to his knees."

"You don't have to sound so happy about it."

"What can I say? I didn't know there was a woman alive who'd make you want to reform your he-whore ways. Now stop stalling and tell me everything there is to know about her. I'm assuming this is someone you see a long future with."

"Try forever."

"Wow. It's that serious?"

"Yes, it is. Lydia started out as a temp some months back when I was expanding. I needed a few new associates, but I wanted to try them out first before deciding to keep them on. She was the only temp who actually worked out, so I hired her on a permanent basis. Since then she's proved to be a valuable asset to the company. Even though I didn't realize it at the time, I think from the moment I first saw her, I was smitten. I'd never met a woman who was so sexy and didn't seem aware of it. I'd find myself walking by her desk just to see her smile. When we talked, I'd get as close to her as good manners would allow just so I could smell her perfume."

"Sheesh. You really do have it bad."

"Hey, I'm still talking here. You wanted to hear this."

"Sorry. Go on."

"Lydia is so amazing. She's beautiful, smart, and witty. She's the kind of woman whose company I'd never get tired of."

"So why did you feel the need to engineer the situation in order for her to take this trip with you?"

Ryder pushed his fingers through his hair. "By rights a more-senior account associate should have had dibs on an account like this, but I wanted to spend the week with her. It was a little unethical, but like I said, I was more than confident she was capable of doing the job."

"And you couldn't ask her out on a date like normal people do?"

"She didn't want anything to do with me outside of work." It was embarrassing to admit, but there it was. If Ryder hadn't forced Lydia to go on the trip with him, he'd still be pining for her while she ignored him. A smile curved his lips. There was no way she could ignore him now. He couldn't wait until she came into the office just so he could see her face again. If love was for fools, then he didn't mind being the biggest one of all.

"And now?"

"I think we've reached an understanding. The trip started out rocky, but toward the middle something really good happened. She relaxed and opened up to me. We laughed and got to know each other better. It only reaffirmed what I felt about her."

"Well, if Lydia makes you happy, then I'm happy for you. I'd love to meet her. You know once Mom and Dad get wind of this, they will too."

He groaned. Ryder had forgotten about them completely. "I'm sure they won't be too happy for me when they meet her."

"What? She's a Democrat?"

"Uh, we never talked political affiliations. No, it's something that would be way more obvious."

"Okay, now you're starting to scare me. What's wrong with her?"

"Nothing's wrong with her. She's perfect in every way, although I doubt the parental unit will think so. She's black."

"Uh. Yeah. They'll have plenty to say about that. But hey, it's your life, and my only concern is your happiness. Why don't you bring her over next weekend? Graham can barbecue some steaks. The kids would love to see their uncle Ryder."

"I'll see what she has to say about it. Let's not make any plans just yet."

"Okay, then. I need to check on the demon seeds. The twins are way too quiet right now. That means they're probably up to something. Gotta run. Love you."

"Love you too." Ryder hung up with a smile on his face. Glancing at his watch, he saw that it was just past ten. Lydia should be here and settled by now. Maybe it was time to take a little stroll.

His step was light as he made his way through the office smiling a greeting to each person he passed along the way.

There were plenty of kudos from sales reps and support staff alike. A big contract lifted all boats, and he and Lydia had landed a pretty big one. Junior staff would be jumping through hoops to be on the team; the bonuses were bound to be substantial. He had decided to head this one himself, along with Lydia. It would mean long hours working together. He couldn't think of another person he wanted to work long hours with. It would probably entail working outside the office, in his house, perhaps even in his bedroom.

He smiled from ear to ear by the time he stopped outside her cubicle, all kinds of nefarious plans bouncing around inside his head. He needed to pull it together for just a little while longer. Lydia had been reserved on the flight home. But that was only to be expected. Perhaps she was letting everything that happened sink in a bit. He also put it down to exhaustion.

When they weren't working, they were making love. If she hadn't reacted so sweetly and given herself to him with such wanton abandon, he might think she was putting some distance between them. But that wasn't possible. Not after what they'd shared and especially not when he'd been explicit that theirs was no casual fling. Just thinking of the time they had spent together their last two days on the island had him hard and wanting. Two nights had been far too long to sleep without her. He'd called her last night on the pretext of making sure she was okay, but the truth was, he'd just wanted to hear her voice. She didn't answer or return the message he'd left. Again, he put it down to her being tired.

Finally, after what seemed like an eternity, he'd see his Lydia again. Damn, he'd missed her. His heart flipped within his chest when she came into view. The sight of her took his breath away. He couldn't move even if he'd wanted to. Every fiber of his being cried out for her. Her hair was pinned on top of her head, accentuating high cheekbones and a graceful neck. His palms grew sweaty as he remembered kissing that neck. Her dress was simple, dipping just enough to show a hint of her pert globes. It hugged her curves yet managed to be understated at the same time. She was like a ray of sunshine, shining just for him.

"Hey there." Ryder smiled at her, leaning against the partition. "Get some rest?"

Instead of a smile, small or otherwise, he got a slight frown. "Good morning, Mr. Garrison. What can I do for you?"

That was definitely unexpected. Gone was the soft, willing woman who had lain beneath him so recently. In her place was a cold stranger who looked at him as if she wished there were anyone other than him standing in her cubicle. "Lydia, are you okay?"

"Couldn't be better."

Maybe she was just having an off morning. "I tried to call you last night, but you didn't answer, so I assumed you went to bed early."

"Yep." She turned back to her computer screen, effectively shutting him out.

"So it's like that?"

She began typing, her fingers flying across the keys. "I don't know what you're talking about. But if you'll excuse me, I have a lot of work to go through since I was out of the office for an entire week."

Thinking fast on his feet to get some alone time with her, he blurted the first thing that popped in his head. "Oh? Well, I need to see you in my office regarding the Rawlings account." He needed to tread lightly or he would lose any ground he might have gained. Confronting her in public would kill all his best efforts. "Now, if you have the time." He put a little steel in his words to let her know it was not a request but an order.

It was cold comfort to see her nipples tighten at his command, proof that she was all his. Ryder stepped back to let her pass, his gaze roving over every inch of her, not bothering to hide his desire. Despite his irritation at Lydia's lack of recognition that they had shared something special, that they had shared anything at all, he couldn't help but appreciate the way she looked. There was no doubt in his mind Lydia belonged by his side.

All he had to do was figure out how to keep her there. Having little experience with long-term, serious relationships, he knew how to seduce her into his bed. He just didn't have a clue how to keep her outside the bedroom. The woman was prickly. He had no idea what was up with her hot and cold act right now.

Well, that wasn't exactly true. They were back at work, after all. Maybe she really thought it had been a mere fling, but as soon as he got her into his office he would quickly disabuse her of that notion. He could have picked a better venue perhaps, but her cool posture toward him rankled too much. Ryder couldn't go through the day like this. His earlier high had hurtled to earth, and he didn't appreciate it one little bit. He kept his fists balled at his sides to stop himself from reaching out and grabbing her to him. He wanted to touch her so bad, he ached for it.

"Lydia! I thought my eyes were playing tricks on me when I saw you earlier. What are you doing here?"

Ryder had been so caught up in his thoughts and the sway of Lydia's hips, he wouldn't have noticed a herd of elephants prancing down the hallway. The voice belonged to the new account manager he had hired right before leaving for the island. In some of his earlier business dealings, Ryder had come into contact with the young man and had been impressed.

Casey Werth had been on the fast track to a junior partnership before he had suffered some kind of family emergency. Long absences had knocked him out of the running from moving up the ladder. Now that his family situation had been resolved, he was looking to get back into the game somewhere fresh. Ryder was a firm believer in second chances, especially if the thing that had knocked the person out was beyond his or her control.

So how in the hell did Werth know Lydia? And why the hell was he standing so close? A tic formed in his clenched jaw as he forced himself to hang back a step. He had a feeling if he demanded answers from Lydia, she would close up tighter than a clam. He wanted to form his own opinion first and then ask her about it.

Lydia halted, her body stiffening, and if it was possible, the icy mask she'd worn for him earlier had grown chillier. "Yes. I'm a junior account manager." Her lips barely moved as she spoke, as if she couldn't be bothered to address the other man properly. Well, that was something.

"That's fantastic!" Werth beamed as if he had some kind of vested interest in her success. Not good. "I knew you would make it."

"I just bet you did." The sarcasm was thick on that little statement. "You work here? At Garrison Advertising?"

One overly eager male and a recalcitrant female did not add up to a story Ryder wanted to hear. He wasn't sure he could keep his cool where Lydia was concerned. There was history between these two. The tension crackling between them was palpable. It was time to break up this little reunion.

"Werth, I see you've met Garrison's rising star." Ryder stepped up to stand almost flush with her backside. For once Lydia didn't flinch or pull away. In fact, she seemed to edge a little closer.

Werth noticed. His eyes narrowed as his gaze fixed on where Ryder's hand rested on her arm. Just to send a little proprietary signal, Ryder squeezed it.

"Lydia and I worked closely together at PRL." Though Werth spoke to him, his gaze remained firmly riveted on Lydia's face. There was a wealth of meaning in his words, and Ryder didn't like it one bit.

Did they now? Yeah, they knew each other, all right. A little too well.

"We were colleagues once. Nothing more." Lydia's glare could stop a charging bull from fifty feet away.

He'd noted on Casey's résumé that he'd come from the same company as Lydia, but didn't give it much thought until now because PRL had a couple of different branches, and it would have been likely that their interaction was minimal if at all. Judging from the tension oozing from Lydia's body, he could surmise what happened.

Casey Werth was at least part of the reason Lydia had left Prichard, Reynolds & Lee abruptly. When he had called her former employer, the supervisor wasn't happy over her departure. Lydia had left with little notice, though the woman had no idea why she had done so. Lydia herself had been evasive, murmuring something about PRL's not being a good fit. Now he knew why. Lord help Werth if he had hurt Lydia in some way.

The fact that Werth had known Lydia first rubbed Ryder raw. He didn't like to think of her with any man other than himself, irrational as the thought may be. Working with someone who had possibly known her in the biblical sense would be hell. Especially when she was giving him the cold shoulder again. Was Werth the reason for that? Had an office romance turned into something ugly? That would make her reluctance to give him a running chance understandable.

"Yes, well, Lydia and I were just about to meet to discuss a new client." Ryder gently nudged Lydia in the general direction of his office. "I'm sure you two will have plenty of time to catch up later. Welcome aboard."

"Yeah. Lydia, I'll see you later, okay?" Werth reached out to pat her free arm. Ryder didn't bother containing his frown, and he let Werth see it clearly. "I think we really need to talk."

That was more than enough for Ryder. He quickly brushed past the other man, Lydia's arm firmly in hand. No way was he letting her out of his sight until he got some answers.

“Donna, hold my calls.” Ryder threw the words at his assistant as he strode by without pausing.

He knew by the stormy look on his face and the shell-shocked look on Lydia's, rumors would be flying around the office of possible disciplinary action in minutes. They wouldn't be that far off base. Discipline was definitely in order here, but the kind he had in mind would shock the shit out of the people who worked for him.

“Sit.” He gestured to the seat in front of his desk as soon as the door was closed.

“I'm not a damn dog.” She raised her chin in defiance.

“Lydia, you really don't want to push me right now.” Ryder chose to sit in front of her on the edge of his desk rather than behind it. He didn't want anything between them.

She sat with a heavy sigh. Ryder was surprised by the brief flickering of disappointment that flashed through him. He had half wanted her to defy him, fight him, something other than give in with a mere sigh. That just wasn't like her.

“I take it this isn't about the Rawlings account.” Resentment dripped from her tongue.

Lydia sat with her arms wrapped protectively around herself, her gaze fixed on the floor. She looked upset, but he wasn't sure whom it was directed toward. Her composure slipped just enough for him to catch a glimpse of the scared, or perhaps vulnerable, woman inside. Rarely had Ryder ever felt so moved to violence as he did at that moment. That any man could have made this gorgeous, intelligent woman doubt herself for even a second made him want to punch Werth's face in.

"Tell me." Ryder knelt in front of her and lifted her chin with his finger. "Am I wrong to assume you were more than just colleagues with Casey Werth?"

Her gaze darted away from his. "I don't want to talk about this."

"You're going to have to, because I'm not letting you out of here until you do."

There was a sheen of unshed tears in her eyes. It tore at his soul to see that.

"I could always fire him." It was unethical without a good reason. And he risked a lawsuit if he did. But for Lydia he would—as crazy as that was.

He moved to stand, but she stopped him.

"No!" Lydia flew out of the chair, both hands on his chest to make him stay put.

If she only knew how her touch burned through the suit he wore. What this woman did to him should be illegal.

"He didn't do anything. I did it to myself."

Damn her for caring about a man who didn't deserve her consideration.

"I knew what I was doing, and I…I had a relationship with him anyway. It's my fault for ever getting involved, knowing the risks."

He had figured that one out all by himself. Hearing it was far, far worse than suspecting. And yet he pushed. “What kind of relationship?” He didn't want to hear this, but he needed to.

“We were lovers.”

Even though that's precisely what he'd been expecting, it hurt to hear her say it. How the hell was he going to work with the other man knowing he'd touched Lydia intimately? That he'd kissed and caressed her. Had fucked her. And then broke her heart. Though Lydia hadn't admitted to the last part, she didn't have to. The way she'd looked at the other man said it all. The image of Lydia beautifully bare for Werth made his stomach churn.

As much as he wanted to storm out of his office and beat the shit out of Werth, he kept his cool—just barely. Ryder stroked the side of Lydia's face. A ray of hope shone through when she leaned into his touch momentarily before jerking back. He'd definitely have to tread lightly. “If he approaches you, promise me you will come to me.” Jealousy swamped him.

“Of course he'll approach me, Ryder. We will no doubt be working together sometime in the near future.” She looked at him like he had grown a second head. “There's an office manager and HR to take care of this kind of thing.”

He didn't trust the man; he couldn't imagine Werth not wanting Lydia back. What red-blooded man wouldn't?

“Look, Lydia, I care about you. If this guy makes you uncomfortable in any way, please come to me.”

She sidestepped him, dropping her hands that had until that moment still been resting on his chest. “I think it's better if we keep things professional, don't you, Mr. Garrison?" That tone could freeze a lesser man. Ryder was inordinately proud of the fact that nothing on earth could cool the fire inside of him that burned for her.

"Oh?"

"Yes. I think the less time we spend around each other, the better."

The perfect pivot on the heel of her "fuck me" pumps was a thing of beauty. Truly a masterful parting stroke, had he allowed it.

"Given how closely we will be working together on the Rawlings account, I don't think that's going to be possible, darlin'." He purred silkily to her back. "Congratulations, you got the co-lead. With me. Be prepared for very long nights…working."

Her spine stiffened, but she didn't turn back around. And to her credit, she didn't slam the door as she left.

Chapter Nine

Work on the Rawlings account would begin next week. Lydia wasn't anxious about the actual work. She loved her job, loved coming up with something new and fresh. She loved everything about the advertising business. She even watched television mainly for the commercials. It was always good to know what the competition was up to. No, her stomach wasn't doing somersaults because she was nervous about the ad campaign. It was Ryder who had her tied up in knots.

They had been back from the island for one week, and not a day went by that he didn't remind her of their sordid affair in some way. Oh he never came right out and said anything overt. He was way too smooth for that. Instead he would give her a look, touch her arm, or just deliver a knowing smile that made her pulse race.

It shouldn't have bothered her so much. She should have been able to shrug it off. The problem was, whenever he aimed one of his steamy come-hither glances in her direction, she got wetter than rain. Every night since their return her body had craved his next to her. Her pussy felt so empty, so cold. She'd had to change the batteries in her vibrator twice.

How was she supposed to work the long hours on a campaign thinking up ways to sell a freaking sex resort to consumers with him so close? Despite her best efforts, Ryder invaded her dreams at night. She caught herself fantasizing about the way he moved inside her. Lydia would squeeze her legs tightly together to try to relieve the ache those memories brought on. He was a fantastic lover. Too good to be true.

But it seemed that lately, Ryder was the least of her problems. Casey Werth brought on issues of a far-different kind. Memories of her time with him didn't cause anything to ache, except her pride. How silly and easy she must have seemed to him. She had fallen for his slick words and nice smile like a freshman dating a senior. She had been so awed that he had even asked her out in the first place. She didn't think of herself as any less than any other woman, but before Casey, well-educated, upper-middle-class men had never looked in her direction.

Lydia realized now it didn't matter where a man came from or what color he was. Any man could be a shithead. Casey certainly fit the description. He had lied to her, used her, and left her behind without so much as a thank-you. His cutting-edge ideas for the Real Women Clothing account that had propelled him to up-and-coming-superstar status at PRL had come from her. Every bit of it. He had asked her for her thoughts and ideas. She had even worked on the storyboards and overall presentation for him. Then he'd passed her ideas off as his own without a hint of shame.

Now he was here, somewhere she had hoped to carve out a place for herself, constantly begging for her to talk to him. Every time she turned around he was trying to get her to go to lunch or for drinks after work. So far she had managed to ward him off with small excuses, but it was only making him more insistent. He claimed he could explain, that if she would just give him a chance, he could perhaps make amends.

She really didn't want to hear his explanation. One day they were hot and heavy, the next he was done with her. After her experience with Kevin, Casey's betrayal had been a devastating blow. It made her realize that love was just too painful to deal with. Maybe she was a coward, but at least this coward would keep her heart intact.

The last thing she wanted or needed was to follow her mother's example. The woman always seemed to fall for the sorriest excuses for men—black, white, Hispanic, it didn't matter. Every one of them had been a loser; none of them had lasted very long. Who needed to live a life like that? It seemed to Lydia there were far more bad times than there had ever been good ones. What was the point of that?

She pinched the bridge of her nose trying to stave off the tension headache building behind her eyes. She'd been staring at the same page of her document for the last half hour without making any progress. With a resigned sigh, she logged off her computer and pushed away from her desk. A walk outside would clear her head, she decided. There was a path behind the building a lot of her coworkers utilized during breaks and lunch. Being outside didn't make things any better, however. Five minutes into her walk, she realized all her thoughts were still centered on Ryder and Casey, and she had no idea how to handle either. She didn't notice someone was behind her until a hand fell on her shoulder. "Mind if I join you?"

Lydia nearly jumped a foot off the ground. She whirled around to see Casey. "Jesus Christ! Don't you know not to sneak up on people like that?" She pulled away from his touch.

"I'm sorry. I didn't mean to frighten you, but I did call your name a few times. Guess you were in your own little world. I asked if I could join you."

"I heard you the first time, and your question was would I mind? Yes, I'd mind. I'd mind the hell out of it, so if you'd please excuse me, I'd like to continue my walk. Alone."

He shoveled his hand through curly auburn locks, his frustration evident. Casey was the type of guy who had things easy all his life and couldn't deal with it when he couldn't get his way. It was probably how he was able to stab her in the back without batting an eye and smile while doing it. Someone with his looks and charm always found a way to get by. "Please. I just need a few minutes of your time. We'll be working together in the future, I'm sure—"

"And I intend on documenting every conversation we have and saving and dating it on a hard drive so that I can keep a running record of *my* ideas. One can never be too careful, you know. There are a lot of snakes in this industry."

He winced. "Ouch. I guess I deserved that and a whole lot more. I have no right to assume you'd welcome me in your life after what I did."

"How observant of you." She glared at him, not bothering to hide the sarcasm.

"Look, Lydia, this isn't easy for me."

"And you think it was easy for me to sit in front of the partners while you presented my idea as your own? I felt like such a fool, but at least I can thank you for opening my eyes. Now I'll be on the lookout for jerks like you. We may work for the same company, and we may even have to collaborate on some projects, but I'd thank you to keep your distance from me if what you have to say is not work related." With every intention of walking away, she halted when he called to her.

"I'm sorry."

She wasn't expecting that. Men like Casey didn't apologize. They simply took as if it was their due. Lydia crossed her arms over her chest. "Sorry about what? Or are you saying you're a sorry individual in general?"

"Both." His quietly spoken word was full of contrition, and she saw something in him that she really didn't expect. Sincerity. Was he genuinely sorry for what he'd done, or was this a ploy to get close to her and use her again?

"And what exactly are you sorry for? That you didn't have the originality to come up with your own idea or that you're a jackass?"

"Lydia, you can call me whatever name you like, but won't you please hear me out? Not a day has gone by when I didn't regret what I did."

She snorted. "Funny, because I'm pretty sure I was on the receiving end of you telling me that you were moving on to bigger and better things and a woman like me didn't fit into your plans. What exactly did you mean by that comment anyway, Casey? A woman like me? Did you mean a woman who comes from the wrong side of the tracks or a black woman?"

"It wasn't that at all. And you know I'm not a racist. If I were, do you think I could have held you the way I did? Loved you?"

"Excuse me if I cry bullshit. You never loved me. You loved what you could get out of me."

"What I did was inexcusable, and there's probably no way I can make up for it. But I would like to try. Look, I have a two-o'clock meeting, but can we meet for dinner one night to talk?"

"You've lost your mind if you think I'd go anywhere with you."

"One dinner. That's all. Just to talk. If after this dinner you don't want to even spit in my direction, I'll respect your wishes and leave you alone. You won't even see me unless it's work related."

She flared her nostrils and placed her hands on her hips. This man had a huge set of balls. He had the nerve to basically blackmail her into seeing him. "I could easily go to HR and say you're harassing me."

"You could. Or you could give me the opportunity to explain myself. I think you at least have the right to know the hows and whys. I owe that to you. Don't tell me you never wondered why."

He had her there. Countless times she'd wondered, and now she had the opportunity to find out and finally lay this ghost to rest. She'd probably regret it, but curiosity had ahold of her and wouldn't let go. "Fine. We can meet at a coffeehouse. No dinner. And you only have a half hour to state your case."

"Seriously?" He seemed surprised by her agreement.

"Yes. When?"

"Tonight?"

"Can't tonight. I'll be working late and won't feel like going out afterward. I'll be free Saturday evening, say six o'clock?"

"Saturday evening it is. Okay, I'm going to head back in. My meeting will be starting soon."

She nodded. "I should head back as well."

As Lydia started to walk back to the office, Casey fell in step with her. Neither said a word, which was just fine with her. She didn't have a clue what to say to him anyway. When they made it to the door, Lydia's foot caught on a lump in the carpet, and the next thing she knew she went hurtling face-first toward the floor. Before she crashed, however, Casey caught her. "I've got you."

Lydia clutched his forearms to gain her balance. She was breathless by the time she righted herself. "Thanks. I was almost a splat on the carpet." Realizing the comedy of the situation, she laughed.

Casey grinned, which turned into a full chuckle.

"Am I interrupting something here?"

Lydia jumped away from Casey as if she'd been scorched. She turned to see Ryder looking—no, glaring—at them both. If looks could kill, she and Casey would both be dead on the spot.

Conflicting emotions assaulted her. On one hand, something primal within her was turned on by his jealousy. He knew she had history with Casey, and he didn't like it. On the other hand, it was a bit like a dog with a bone. They weren't involved in a relationship, so where the hell did he get off acting as if they were? What really got her was the guilt that swamped her under Ryder's accusatory gaze. She had nothing to feel guilty about. She didn't like the fact she couldn't seem to shake the irritating emotion even more than she resented that look of his.

"Are you okay, Lydia?" Ryder literally moved his body between her and Casey.

This was not good. She needed to defuse the situation quickly, before things got out of hand.

"I'm fine." Lydia made sure her voice was firm and clear. "Casey saved me from an embarrassing spill; that's all."

"Right. So I'll see you tomorrow, Lydia?"

"Yeah, right, tomorrow."

Ryder waited until Casey was out of sight until he said anything.

"Tomorrow?" Ryder had to choke down the anger threatening to erupt.

"What I do on my off time has nothing to do with my job." Lydia smoothed the wrinkles from her skirt, essentially dismissing him.

Ryder didn't answer her right away. He simply stared at her, biting his tongue as he attempted to rein in his temper. When he had driven up after his lunch meeting, the first thing he had seen was his woman talking to her ex. Already frustrated by her refusal to even acknowledge his overtures, seeing her with someone who knew her intimately chafed like hell.

He had almost allowed himself to believe whatever had happened between Lydia and Casey was in the past. He noticed the way she seemed to suddenly become busy whenever Casey approached her, or the way she hurried off when she saw Casey coming in the opposite direction. Ryder figured that whatever Casey had done, he had blown his chances with her. Which made things free and clear for him, or so he had believed. Now he wasn't so sure.

It had only been a week since the last time he held her, and he was finding it hard to sleep without her. He walked around with a constant hard-on because of her. Not that she had done anything deliberately to tease him. Lydia made sure to stay as far away from him as she could. Whenever he came around, her guard went up. She didn't avoid him quite like she did Casey, but she was a long way from welcoming.

As much as he'd tried to be subtle, to give her space, he was fast coming to the end of his rope. He knew that she desired him. The signs were still there. Her breathing grew shallow when he was near. More than once she let out a tiny gasp when his body casually brushed against hers. Occasionally he'd caught her gaze wandering to his crotch and lingering, her tongue peeking out to swipe at her lips. And damn, did he ever miss those lips.

So what was up with her going out with Casey? Did she think to replace him with some other man? Did she think he would simply stand back and watch this happen?

"See, darlin', that's where you're wrong." Ryder didn't growl; he didn't snap. She wouldn't react well to that. He kept his voice low and even, though it was one hell of a battle. "It's very much my business what you do outside of work. If I haven't made it clear before, you belong to me."

Her brows flew up. "You're joking, right?"

"I've never been more serious about anything in my life. Maybe you *think* what we shared at the resort didn't mean anything, but it sure as hell did to me. In fact, I know there's something special happening between us. Why else can't I keep my thoughts focused on anything or anyone other than you? You haunt my fucking dreams every night. Since you've been with this company, I've lived and breathed you. And when we touch, I know I can never be with another woman without comparing her to you."

"Sounds personal. Now if you'll excuse me, I have a ton of work to do." She sidestepped him in an attempt to walk away, but he caught her wrist.

"You can't tell me you're unaffected. Even now those tight little nipples are pressing against your blouse, practically begging me to take a little bite. I told you once, you can lie to yourself all you want, just don't waste your breath lying to me."

Ryder waited, wondering if she would cut him to the quick with a sharp retort, or would she yield? He never knew what to expect. She had been like this in the beginning on the island, but eventually he had broken through. What was it going to take back here in the real world? Hell, if he had to, he wasn't above demanding they work on the Rawlings account on the island if she kept running from him. He was beginning to think he was going to have to do something drastic. Like get her pregnant.

The thought rocked him back on his heels. Get her pregnant? He must have it bad or be insane, because resorting to something along those lines had never entered his thought process before. He had been very careful since he became sexually active to always protect himself at all costs.

Not once had he used a condom when they were together at the resort, however. Did Lydia realize that? After that initial time she'd asked, probably not, considering how hard she was trying to push him away. His gaze flickered to her stomach in wonderment. Could she be pregnant? The thought of having a child had always been in the back of his mind, stored away for the future.

He had planned on it one day. As soon as a woman he was dating brought it up, however, he was usually out of the door so fast, he left a smoke trail. Not so now. The idea of Lydia round with his child made his cock throb painfully in his pants. When it came to her, he was damn near primal with the urge to push her down in the grass and make it happen.

Taking a deep breath, he took a half step back, trying to get control on his unruly emotions. He was taking things way too fast. For all he knew she was on the pill. Actually, someone as meticulous as Lydia probably was. But if she weren't and it had already happened, that was fine by him. More than fine actually. She wouldn't be able to push him away anymore. But he wasn't going to jump the gun. It wasn't fair to her. Ryder was just going to have to win her the old-fashioned way—work for it.

Lydia sighed, her shoulders slumping somewhat. He had broken through somewhere but wasn't sure he liked her posture. He hadn't wanted to break her; he just wanted her to give him half a chance.

"I'm not lying to anyone. I never said I wasn't attracted to you. I said this—you and I—isn't a good idea. You're my employer, Ryder, and relationships in the workplace are never a good idea. Believe me."

Ryder had the distinct impression there was more to it. The way she'd stressed that last part almost seemed as if she was trying to tell him something. "Why? There are no fraternization rules at this company. Why are you fighting this thing so hard when we both know your body goes up into flames the second you're in my arms?"

"It's just lust. Nothing more."

"The hell it is!"

"Look, can't you just respect the fact that I'm not interested in dating someone I work with, or anyone for that matter? My main priority in life at the moment is my career."

"Yet you're willing to go out with Casey? What is that about, Lydia? Tell me how that works, particularly when you act like you can't stand being near the guy."

She winced as his words came out a little more forcefully than he had intended. It was gratifying to know he'd scored a direct hit with her.

"It isn't a date; not that it's any of your business."

"You are going out to dinner with the guy, darlin'. That sure as shit sounds like a date to me. Yet here I am begging for an opportunity to show you how good it can be between us, and I get what? A cold shoulder every damn time."

Lydia looked around, her cheeks turning an interesting shade of burgundy. At this point Ryder couldn't be bothered to care if someone overheard them. He was about ready to pull his hair out with the roller-coaster ride she had him on.

"Why don't we just chalk last week up to the atmosphere and forget about it, okay?"

Forget about it? There was no way in hell! Tightening his hold on her wrist, he moved her a little ways from the glass door that led to the Garrison offices. He doubted very much she wanted others to hear what he had to say next.

"Can you forget about it, Lydia?" Ryder growled low, moving into her personal space so that her back was up against a wide oak facing away from the building. "Because I can't." Moving in closer, he dipped his head until they were nose to nose. "I can't forget about the sweet taste of your pussy on my tongue. I can't forget the way that tight little cunt milked me, squeezing so damn tight, I didn't know whether to come or die. I can't forget the way you screamed my name or the way you dug your nails into my skin. I don't think you can forget either. That's why your nipples are so hard they could probably cut that lacy little nothing of a bra I know you're wearing right now to shreds. I think your pussy is so wet, I could slide right in, right here, right now." The little needy whimper as a response made his dick jump. He could have her right now, he knew it, but she would hate him for it afterward. That would only make the situation worse.

Stepping back, he ran his hand through his hair, trying to gather his wits about him.

"We need to go over our attack plan before we announce our team next week. Be prepared to work late tonight."

He knew he had already told her that, but he wanted to reinforce the edict should she decide to bolt. The one thing he could always depend on was Lydia's professionalism. Too bad his seemed to have flown right out of the window.

Chapter Ten

Something told her she could possibly be making the biggest mistake in her life by showing up for this meeting with Casey. Common sense alone should have had her telling him hell no. But part of her wanted that explanation he'd talked about. He seemed sincere, but then again, he'd charmed her once before.

The only reason she'd agreed to see him in the first place was the realization she no longer felt anything for him. Not even contempt. Slight annoyance was about all the emotion she could conjure up where he was concerned. This meeting was simply her closure. Besides, Casey wasn't her biggest problem. Ryder had him beat hands down.

After their confrontation yesterday, Lydia was literally shaking by the time she'd made it back to her desk. The need he had awakened earlier hadn't gone away; it had grown throughout the day until her clit thrummed, painfully seeking stimulation. She was terrified if he pushed her, she wouldn't be able to say no. Lydia was barely able to concentrate, but somehow she'd managed to make it through the rest of the day without having a complete meltdown.

Thankfully Ryder hadn't wandered by her cubicle, as it seemed to be a habit of his lately. Their late work sessions had been professional, only going over the elements of the account, though the looks he threw her way could start a forest fire. At home, things weren't much better. He had ignited a need only he could put out.

Even when she poured herself a glass of wine and pulled out the suspense-thriller novel she'd been reading, Lydia couldn't get past a few pages without images of Ryder invading her thoughts. Her body throbbed in need of his. Before long, she found her fingers inside her panties, rubbing away at her clit. She pretended her hand belonged to Ryder, and he was fucking her with his forceful digits. After bringing herself to an orgasm, she was left feeling disappointed. Masturbation had at one point been something to ease her sexual desires, but having been with Ryder, it was no longer enough. She'd just have to find a way to get him out of her system for good.

Transferring to another company wasn't an option in the current state of the economy. And truth be told, she enjoyed her job at Garrison's. The work was challenging, and for the most part, she got along with her colleagues. In addition, there were several opportunities for growth. She'd be hard-pressed to find something better and for around the same pay. She had to admit, Ryder was generous with his employees when it came to the benefits package. No. She wouldn't let him run her off from a good thing. Maybe he'd eventually get tired with the chase and leave her alone. Yet every time that thought occurred to her, she had a sinking feeling in the pit of her stomach.

A tap on her car window brought her out of her musings. A quick glance at the clock on her dashboard told

Lydia she'd been sitting in her car for ten minutes. She rolled her window down. "You have a habit of sneaking up on a lady."

Casey's sheepish grin gave him a boyish quality. It was no wonder some of the women in the office thought the "new guy" was hot. Too bad none of them knew what a weasel he was capable of being. "Sorry. Didn't mean to scare you. Thought I saw you pull up into the parking lot, but when you didn't come in right away, I feared you might have changed your mind, and I was hoping to convince you to come inside."

She shut off her engine and slid out of the vehicle. "I didn't drive all the way to turn back around. I'm here now. I was just thinking. I do that from time to time."

"Oh okay. Thanks for coming."

She shrugged. "I said I would."

"I know you did."

They didn't speak again until they were seated. "What would you like? Do you still like caramel lattes with a double shot of espresso?"

"Haven't had one in a while. Trying to watch my caffeine intake. That stuff will kill you. Chai tea with skim milk will be just fine."

He stood up. "No problem. I'll go get it for you."

Lydia dug into her purse for her wallet. "Wait, let me give you money for my tea."

"Don't worry about it. It's on me. I invited you out, remember?"

"But I insist. It's not like it's a date or anything."

He pursed his lips. "I'm quite capable of paying for a four-dollar cup of tea without reading anything into it."

When put like that, it didn't seem like that big a deal. "Fine. Thank you." She crossed her arms over her chest and sat back. She remembered a time when she couldn't wait to spend time with Casey, and how excited she'd get when he even deigned to look her way. And now she couldn't wait to get this thing, whatever it was, over with. It was one of the many reasons she knew Ryder was no good for her. He brought on the same kind of excitement Casey once had, only with Ryder it was way more potent. Yes, he turned her on like no man had before, but when the novelty wore off for him, she'd be the one left in the dust. She didn't want to go through that again.

What the hell had she been thinking to have sex with him on that island? And without a condom, to boot. There was no telling what his sexual history was, despite his assurances. At least she didn't have to worry about pregnancy, as that wasn't likely to happen with her erratic cycles. He made her throw all caution to the wind, and it scared the hell out of her that any man was capable of bringing her to such a pass.

"A penny for your thoughts?" Casey placed a cup of tea in front of her.

"Thank you."

"My pleasure." He smiled. "So what were you so deep in thought about?"

She picked up a stirrer and whirled it inside her cup. "Nothing you'd be interested in, I'm sure."

"Try me."

"I'd rather not. Besides, I'm here for one reason only."

He lowered his lids, hiding his expression from her. "Right. It just seems so surreal sitting here with you after all this time. I really missed you, Lydia." He reached across the table to grab her hand.

She snatched it away as soon as their fingers made contact. "Don't. I told you I didn't come here for that, and if you don't start talking, I'm out of here."

"I can't begin without prefacing what I have to say with this—what I did was wrong. Not a day goes by when I don't replay that look on your face. I will admit that at first, I did get close to you because you were always so full of ideas, but something happened along the way: I fell for you. By the time I realized my feelings, I was already on a course I couldn't stray from. And not only did I hurt you, I ended up losing in the end anyway."

Lydia found that hard to believe considering what he'd done had elevated him to a promotion at PRL. "Pardon me while I interrupt, but I say bullshit. The only person you cared about was yourself. You thought it was fun to play around with the black girl's affections and then discard her all willy-nilly."

"That's really not what I thought at all. And if I could do it again, knowing what I know now, I wouldn't have done it. As you know, I was sort of the 'golden boy' at PRL; the bosses loved me because I was the ideas guy and I knew how to schmooze with the best of them. But something personal happened in my life. I was stressed, and basically the well ran dry. I couldn't come up with a thing, and I knew I needed to in order to get that big bonus, salary increase, and possibly some initials behind my name."

"Of course. You needed to make the money to enjoy the good life." She didn't bother hiding the bitterness she felt.

"No. That wasn't it at all. I won't lie and say my motivation hasn't been making lots of money in the past, but at that point it wasn't. I'm a twin. My sister, Karen, and I were extremely close. Neither of us wanted for anything growing up, except for our parents' attention. They were of the 'children should be seen and not heard' ilk. I think that was probably one of the reasons my sister and I were so close. I'm not saying my parents were bad people. They simply didn't know how to deal with young kids, and they compensated by giving us stuff. We grew accustomed to the good life, so when our parents died our junior year of college, it was a pretty devastating blow to learn they were so far in debt there would be no money left after the burial and all their creditors were paid off. I was determined to finish school; however, Karen... Well, she just wasn't cut out to struggle."

Lydia raised a brow. "You mean she was too lazy to work?"

Casey turned bright red, and it was obvious he wanted to respond. "That wasn't the case at all."

Shame washed through her. Lydia didn't know his sister to make such a snap judgment. "I'm sorry. That comment was uncalled-for."

Without acknowledging her apology, he continued. "I won't say that Karen was lazy, just that she was used to having everything handed to her. She ended up leaving school and marrying her high school sweetheart. Things seemed to be going well. I graduated college, and Karen seemed happy. I was lucky to land a job at PRL, which afforded me the money to attend grad school. Then Karen got sick. Her husband couldn't take it and left her."

As much as Lydia didn't want to care, she felt bad for his poor sister. "What was wrong with her?"

"An extremely rare form of cancer. She moved in with me because she couldn't afford to keep her home with no means of support."

Lydia remembered Casey never inviting her to his place. It made sense why he didn't now. "Her husband should be horsewhipped for leaving her in her time of need."

Casey shrugged. "Some people just aren't cut out for dealing with sickness. Anyway, I was unfortunately unable to add her to my insurance, and it was basically a struggle to get her on Medicare and signed up for disability benefits. It was an absolute nightmare. So I bought Karen her own policy, which cost the earth because of her preexisting condition. That's when we learned that she'd need an autologous stem cell transplant. It wasn't a common treatment for the type of cancer she had, so the insurance company deemed it medically unnecessary. I was looking at six figures that I needed to come up with. That's where you came in. I believed what I did was for the greater good. I needed that money so badly, I didn't consider how you'd feel. If it's any consolation to you, all the while I was presenting your idea as mine, I felt like a piece of shit." He lowered his head, his shame evident.

"And your sister? Did you at least use the money to help her?"

"By the time I got the money through a bonus commission and a personal loan, it was too late. Karen died the day before her surgery was scheduled." Tears glistened in his eyes.

"That's awful. I'm…I'm sorry."

"There's no need for apologies. You didn't know. And even though I thought I had a good reason to treat you the way I did, there was no excuse. I should have found another way to raise the money."

This time it was Lydia reaching over the table to take his hand. She'd demonized this man in her mind for so long, she didn't stop to think that things weren't always as they seemed. As he'd said, there was no excuse for what he'd done, but Casey had paid the ultimate price with the loss of his sister. She could forgive him, but she would never forget. "It's in the past now. And we'll let bygones be bygones. We'll probably be working together on a project or two, so we may as well bury the hatchet."

He nodded. "I see. Is there any way we could be friends?"

"I don't know, Casey. What you did will always be in the back of my mind. But I don't see why we can't be friendly."

"So there's no chance for something more?"

She shook her head slowly. At one time this man had meant something to her, but now all she could feel was pity and sadness for his loss. Acknowledging this was like a big weight off her shoulders she hadn't realized she'd been carrying around all this time. "That ship has sailed. I'm not the same woman I was then."

"I kind of like this new you. You're more confident. It's sexy."

"Thank you. But I'm also more cautious."

He frowned. "I did this to you."

"You're not completely to blame. But the fact still remains, there's too much water under the bridge."

His lips twisted in displeasure. "I have to confess that when I saw you again, I thought maybe I would get a second chance."

Lydia shook her head. "Sorry. But no."

"Doesn't mean I won't try to change your mind."

He had a pair the size of grapefruits, but she found herself giggling. "Yeah, like that's going to happen."

"I'm dead serious." Casey squeezed her hand.

"So am I. Look, I really appreciate you telling me about your sister. At least now I don't think you're as big an asshole."

An auburn brow flew up. "Oh? But I'm still an asshole?"

Lydia smiled. "A little. But you have to be a bit of an asshole in order to get ahead these days. So tell me. What did you do after…"

The mood turned somber once more. "After Karen passed? I left PRL. I didn't feel right staying there knowing what I'd done and that I hadn't earn my place in the company fairly." That he'd resigned from such a prestigious agency raised his credit in her eyes. Most people wouldn't have cared one way or the other. "Then I sold my condo. I couldn't live there anymore, because I'd see her face in every room. I finished grad school and worked at a small start-up for a while. I made my way through the ranks, but I realized I needed a bit more of a challenge. That's how I ended up at Garrison's."

"So how do you like it so far?"

"I love it. Plenty of room for growth. Garrison is a bit intense, though."

She tried to maintain an air of casualness at the mention of Ryder. Lydia took a sip of her tea before responding. "What do you mean?"

Casey took a sip of his coffee. "Dunno. When he hired me, he seemed like a cool guy, but since he came back from that business trip you two were on, he seems annoyed with me about something. Sometimes it seems he's looking right through me and doesn't like what he sees."

"Well, he can be intense. But I'm sure you're just imagining things." The last thing she needed was for him to find out about her affair with the boss.

"I'm not so sure about that. But at the very least I'm glad to see you're doing well for yourself. You deserve all the success that comes your way."

"Thank you. It means a lot to hear you say that."

"Speak of the devil," Casey muttered, glancing toward the entrance.

"What?"

"The boss is here. And he doesn't look happy."

It couldn't be. Lydia whirled around in her seat to see Ryder march toward them with purposeful strides, determination etching his face. He stopped at their table. Barely avoiding rudeness, he nodded in Casey's direction as acknowledgment. "Get your purse, Lydia, and let's go."

Her eyes widened. So much for keeping their affair a secret. "Excuse me?"

"I said let's go. You can either walk out of here on your own steam, or I'll carry you. Either way, you're not going to sit there with him for another minute." Her mouth gaped open.

Chapter Eleven

Casey stood up. “Hey. Is there a problem?”

Ryder refocused his attention on his adversary. “There will be, if you don't stay out of this.” He turned back to Lydia. “I'm not going to repeat myself; let's go.” He almost wished she'd defy him just so he'd have the pleasure of tossing her over his shoulder and paddling her luscious ass as he walked out the door.

“I'm sorry, Casey. I have to go.”

The other man looked uncertain. “Are you sure, Lydia?”

Ryder was two seconds away from knocking Casey's teeth down his throat.

She nodded. “I'll be fine. See you at work.”

Ryder allowed her enough space to gather her purse and walk past him. When they were outside, he took her by the forearm and guided her to his vehicle.

“Hey. Let me go. I'm not going anywhere with you.” Without saying a word, he opened the passenger-side door and waited for her to get in. “You are nuts if you think I'm getting in your car.” He waited, not trusting himself to speak, lest he say something he couldn't take back. She must have read something in his expression, because she huffed. “Fine.

Wherever it is you plan on taking me, I'll need you to bring me back here so I can get my car and go home."

He waited until she got inside and closed the door behind her. Little did Lydia know, she wouldn't be needing her car for the rest of the weekend. Sliding into the driver's seat, he flexed his hands over the steering wheel, trying to get his temper under control. The jealous rage burning inside was eating away at him until he could barely breathe.

How did he end up like this? Going from just about every coffeehouse in a twenty-mile radius from where Lydia lived just to bust up this date. He knew it was crazy, was downright stalkerish even, but he couldn't stop himself. Her being with another man was literally driving him up a wall, and he couldn't take it. Whatever it took, he vowed to spend the remainder of the weekend staking his claim.

"This is ridiculous!" Lydia broke the silence after they'd been in the car for a few minutes.

"What's ridiculous is your not realizing we were meant for each other. Seems like my words aren't getting through to you, so it's time I showed you."

"If you think I'm sleeping with you again—"

"Sleeping is the last thing we'll be doing."

That cut off any other comments she might have made. Glancing at her profile, Ryder could clearly see confusion warring with what he hoped was desire in her expression. She wasn't looking at him but rather staring out of her window biting her bottom lip. As much as he wanted to reassure her, he couldn't. Jealousy was riding him too hard to utter any kind of comforting words. He would only wind up snapping.

He had walked away from her Friday convinced he had gotten through to her in some small way. But had she come to him? Had she even tried to talk it out? No, instead she had gone out with the asshole who'd hurt her. Ryder had gone to her condo to talk things through. Since she had avoided him Friday afternoon, he figured she'd had more than enough time to think things over. Instead of her thinking about him, she hadn't been home at all. Remembering the little incident between her and Casey outside the building, he had driven himself crazy in his attempt to locate them.

Visions of Lydia entwined in Casey's arms had tormented him with every passing second. The drive to find her before Casey could talk his way back into her bed and heart was overwhelming. Lydia was his, damn it; he needed her to know that.

The drive to his house on the outskirts of town took less than ten minutes, when it should have taken at least twenty. Lucky for him there were no policemen lying in wait to write him a ticket. Ryder hadn't trusted himself to say anything until the garage door slowly descended behind his parked vehicle. He couldn't chance her bolting.

"This isn't a good idea, Ryder." Her voice was soft, almost gentle. There wasn't any fear, at least none he could detect. Good. Though he didn't want her to be scared of him, he was done playing. She needed to understand that.

Looking at her now, Ryder was blown away by the beauty of her quiet strength. She was the kind of woman who made a man step up his game, the forever kind of woman. He wasn't going to give up; he was going to fight harder to get through that tough shell. He would tell her tonight. Just not in his garage. "Let's take this inside."

He was grateful she didn't argue with him for once. As resolute as he was that Lydia would be staying the night, he didn't lead her to the master bedroom quite yet. Instead he settled into the large suede couch in the den, taking a seat beside her. She scooted away from him, but he simply followed her until she had nowhere else to go except the floor. She scowled something fierce but still didn't complain.

Blowing out a heavy breath, he clasped her hands in his, surprised she was shaking. Maybe she was scared, after all. "I would never hurt you, Lydia." He meant it to the depths of his soul. He only hoped she would believe him.

"Maybe not intentionally."

Is that what she really thought? That he would walk away and leave her heartbroken? Didn't she realize he'd rather rip out his own heart than hurt her?

"Look, Ryder, I love my job. We work well together—in the office. When this thing between us ends, and it will, I'd find it difficult to be the same around you."

"Is that what happened between you and Casey?" She had told him bits and pieces; now he wanted to know the whole story. "Because I'm not him. I don't want to walk away. I don't want this to end. I want us to be together in every way. Hell, I'll give you anything you want—money, jewelry, even a stake in my company." That came out wrong. He knew it as soon as he said it. And just as he suspected she would, Lydia picked right up on it.

"That's mighty expensive for a piece of ass." The open scorn in her voice cut him deep.

"That's not what I meant, and you know it. I want you to feel protected. I'd like for you to be comfortable enough around me to let go and be Lydia. Most of all, honey, I just want you. This isn't about a piece of ass. I can get sex anywhere."

"So why don't you?"

"Because no one exists for me except you. I want you in my bed and by my side. At work, at home, at play—just you."

Ryder had been a lot of things in his life, but scared had never been one of them. He was scared now. Shaking in his boots that Lydia would once again rebuff him. He was running out of ideas and getting tired of figuring out his next strategy to get closer to her. He wanted his woman.

Dragging her to his lap, he wrapped her locs around his hand to tilt her head back. He gave the thick tresses a gentle tug, making her mouth open for his kiss. He poured all his pent-up frustrations and desires in the act, taking as well as giving.

Lydia didn't pull away. With a deep sigh, she seemed to melt into his kiss, her body pliant against his. He hugged her tighter against him, his free hand moving down her back until it came to rest on her ass. Lydia had a great behind.

He squeezed until she opened her legs and straddled him. Ryder rocked his hips upward, rubbing his jean-clad bulge against her core until she moved on her own. He needed to make her so hot, she would forget about fighting it, at least for a little while. The kiss became a battle of wills—tongues dueling, lips smashing against each other. He was determined to win this round. He couldn't let her walk away again.

She twisted her head away, panting heavily. "Ryder, I can't." No matter what she moaned, her body told him an entirely different story. His grip tightened because he was half-afraid she would get up and leave.

"Yes, you can, and you will."

Lydia was lost in a sea of sensations clashing around her. She hungered for him, but she couldn't say the words. She should stop him—should demand he take her back to her car, but no sound would leave her lips except throaty moans. His lips demanded, his hands were everywhere, and God help her, she didn't want him to stop. Lydia arched her neck for his biting caress as she swayed her pelvis against his rock-hard erection. She was so wet, she knew he could probably feel it through the denim of his jeans. She swiveled against him, trying to get just a taste of the sweet ecstasy she knew he could give her.

"Let me show you, darlin', and remind you how good it can be." It was good. So damn good, it was addictive. *Yes* was on the tip of her tongue, but she couldn't force it past her lips. Instead she spoke with her body, offering him the only thing she could. When he rose to his feet, she wrapped her legs around him, giving him implicit permission to make love to her.

She had no chance to see the house as he carried her toward what she assumed was the bedroom. She was too caught up in the fire he'd set within her. She burned even more than she had on the island. The longing was so acute, it bordered on pain. It suddenly dawned on her what she'd been missing, what she had denied herself for too long—Ryder. The dark desire whirling within made the wait much worse than if she had no clue what would happen next.

Lydia opened her eyes when he dropped her on the bed. A gasp escaped her lips at what she saw. The look in his eyes reminded her of some wild animal with prey in its sights. She got wetter just watching him watch her. This was the Ryder she remembered, the one she dreamed about each night. She hadn't realized her hand strayed down between her legs until he stopped her with a barking command.

"Don't you dare touch my pussy! I will give you what you need. Only me." She shivered as his gravelly tone caressed her. Her skin was tight. It suddenly seemed as if the lightweight skirt and blouse she wore were too heavy, too constricting. "Take it all off. Every stitch." Lydia wanted to weep with relief. Her fingers flew to obey as she pushed thoughts of the power he had over her from her head. He made her weak with wanting, thereby making her vulnerable. And deep down, she loved it.

She loved the way he made her feel feminine and soft. The way Ryder dominated her without taking anything away from her was so fucking hot. She had projected toughness to the world for so long, it was starting to wear on her, but Ryder stripped it away. She would be strong again, but for right now she'd give herself to him completely and freely.

With her clothes quickly discarded, she was eager to have him where she needed him. She watched with desire as he slowly undressed, her gaze sweeping over every exposed inch. The proof of what she did to him sprang from his jeans as soon as he unbuttoned his fly. His shaft stood straight out, its head glistening with drops of precum. Licking her lips, Lydia watched it bob slightly like it was greeting her. It was a heady sight, sending her already-overexcited libido spiraling out of control. Without really understanding why or what possessed her to be so bold, Lydia decided that for once in her life, she was going to push it. She was going to take this to the limit.

She lay on the bed panting with anticipation for him to kiss, caress, or hold her—anything, as long as it involved him touching her. She'd never needed anything as badly as she did right now. Ryder watched her with a predatory gleam in his eyes as he discarded the remainder of his clothing. She whimpered when he continued to stand by the bed, watching her as he palmed his magnificent cock. Damn him for getting her this excited and teasing her. Lydia decided to take matters into her own hands.

"Did you miss this, Ryder?" Cupping her breasts together, she pushed them up like an offering. "Did you dream about it? Did you touch yourself when you did? Did the memories of what we did back on the island keep you hard for me all week long?" The low growl that answered her was thrilling. Throwing a siren's smile in his direction, she turned to lie on her stomach, curving her back so that her ass was on full display. "I'm thinking maybe you forgot what to—"

Before she could finish the sentence, Ryder was on her. He dived on the bed, covering her body completely but using his arms to catch the brunt of his weight. His skin on hers burned so right. She wiggled her ass beneath him, nudging his full cock. Catching her wrists in one large hand, he pushed them above her head and pinned them to the bed.

Ryder used his other hand to get a firm grip on her nipple, twisting the hard nubbin just right. He ground his cock on her rear, forcing her hips against the mattress. The slight friction wasn't nearly enough to ease her ache. She needed more. She thrust back harder, forcing his cock to lay flush against the seam of her ass. Lydia had to smile at the heavy groan in her ear. She had him now.

"So you wanna play, do you, darlin'?" She did, but she wouldn't give him the satisfaction of saying so. "Cat got your tongue, baby? Let's see if we can find it."

Releasing his grip on her wrists, Ryder flipped Lydia on her back, not missing a beat. Capturing her wrists again, he forced them over her head. She liked it a lot. She found she liked a lot of things she had never dreamed of before Ryder. *For now; you can't have him for keeps.* She forced the thought away as quickly as it came. Tonight she could have it. She could have it all, and she was going to take it. Tomorrow she would pick up the pieces and worry about the consequences later. If only he would stop playing around and get down to business. He seemed to delight in tormenting her. Despite the fire in his eyes, he took his sweet time moving his hands lightly over her body, avoiding her breasts and pussy. Why was he doing this? It was damn near killing her.

Arching her back, she let a little moan tumble from her kiss-swollen lips and brushed against him again like a cat. She needed tonight to last a lifetime; she wanted it all. Ryder first took one nipple then the other in between his teeth, giving each a sharp bite before sucking away the pain. He used his tongue to lave each point until she purred with pleasure. He hadn't gone anywhere near her pussy, and she was already close to coming. “Damn it, Ryder, just do it!”

That only made him smile. It was a feral twist of his sensual lips, bringing to mind so many naughty thoughts, she trembled. Oh the things those lips could do. “Do what, baby? Tell me.” His deep Texas drawl made her pussy spasm. He raked his teeth over her neck, then bit down on the sensitive spot at the crook. “Say it.”

He didn't have to tell her what he wanted her to say, she knew. “Fuck me, Ryder.”

“No.”

He couldn't be serious. Not when his lips traveled across her chest with such deliberate ease. Not when his hands molded her body, kneading her shape like he wanted to commit it to memory. Did he know she had no intention of letting this get further than the here and now? Did he suspect she was planning on this being the very last time she ever allowed him to touch her like this? He wouldn't leave her wanting, not when she could feel his hot, hard length against her thigh. She bent her leg to increase the pressure against his dick.

“Are you sure about that?” Where had that sultry voice come from? Lydia barely recognized herself around Ryder. It scared her as much as it excited her. “Because your body is telling me a different story.”

Lydia didn't have to see his face to know he was smiling. She could feel it against her stomach, where he seemed to be fascinated with her belly button. "There will be no fucking tonight, baby doll." The cooling breath against her flesh after the heat of his mouth caused goose bumps to break out all over her skin.

"Then what are we going to do? Talk?" That was the last thing she wanted to do. It was hard to keep up the pretense of being a seductress. She wasn't that. She was just Lydia, a woman so afraid of being played once again, she tried to keep her heart firmly behind a wall of stone. This man was determined to break through it; she just couldn't allow that. She was playing with fire as it was, just being with him. This was madness, but she couldn't stop. She needed this. She needed to feel like a woman.

"What we are doing is making love."

Chapter Twelve

A sudden spark of insight blindsided Ryder. All she expected from him was sex—hot, sweaty, nasty sex. He wondered if anyone had ever bothered to really take the time to make love to Lydia before. Sex wasn't the best way to prove he was in this for the long haul, but it was too late to back off. Not when he could feel her heat.

But he could make love to her, slow and easy, even if it killed him—and it just might. His dick already leaked copious amounts of precum, throbbing fiercely. He was impatient to be cocooned deep inside her. It took herculean effort to work his way back up her body once he reached her pelvis. Ryder pressed kisses on Lydia's taut belly and over her breasts. Her body shuddered underneath his touch, welcoming him to take what he wanted.

"I don't want that." Panic radiated underneath the panted words, but he wouldn't be deterred. "Damn you, Ryder, just fuck me!"

She undulated relentlessly and had somehow managed to coil herself around him. Lydia rolled her hips, almost managing to capture his rod between her labia. Ryder had to still her movements in an almost-brutal grip while trying to distract her in a devastating kiss. The problem was, whenever he kissed Lydia, he was the one more likely to lose control. Her supple lips against his inflamed him. They made him greedy for more.

"Shhh, baby, relax." He crooned against her mouth. "Let me take care of you." *For now, forever.* "Will you let me?"

She looked like a doe caught in headlights. Lydia stared back at him wide-eyed and guile free. In that skittish gaze, he saw he had been right; no one had ever bothered to make love to her before. How could the men in her past have been so clueless? She was female perfection. He would go to bed with praise on his lips every night, recognizing what a priceless treasure she was.

A slight nod was the only confirmation he had that she had even heard him. It was all he needed. With infinite care and precision, he began the process of leisurely working his way back down her curves, making sure to worship every inch. He whispered sweet nothings as he went along, murmuring tributes to every part he touched. "Your skin is silky smooth, darlin'. So sweet, you melt on my tongue. I love the contrast of your skin against mine. So fucking sexy."

Ryder ran his hand along the flat expanse of her belly, reveling in how soft she felt beneath his fingertips. There were nights when he'd lie in bed and just fantasize about doing exactly this. He loved the way she quivered with each caress. His head pounded as his carnal cravings made him ache.

"Oh God, Ryder, you're killing me." He knew the feeling. Still, he refused to be rushed. Slowly making his way down the length of her body, he planted kisses on her heated flesh, circling her navel with his tongue.

Lydia pushed against his shoulders in an obvious attempt to make him go lower. He chuckled at her impatience. "Easy, baby. We have all night." Shrugging out of her grasp, he continued to nibble and lick the little indentation in her stomach, knowing she wanted more. He wanted her to be crazy for it, just as he was for her. "Tell me how bad you want it, darlin'."

"I need it. Ryder, please eat my pussy." She lifted her lower body, bucking beneath him like a cat in heat.

The scent of her arousal was too tempting to ignore any longer. "I love it when you beg. It would be my pleasure." As he settled between her silky thighs, he kissed the insides, nipping at her tender flesh. Gently, he parted her nether lips to display her clit to his gaze. Lydia had the prettiest pussy he'd ever seen. Nudging his nose against the taut button, Ryder inhaled deeply, nearly dying from her musky fragrance. It was far headier than any aphrodisiac.

A man could get hooked if he weren't careful, but Ryder didn't want to be. This was his cunt and his woman, and it was his intention to savor every inch of her. He curled his tongue around the pink pearl before suckling it gently between his lips. Then, getting high from the taste of her, Ryder increased the pressure with fervent tugs. Lydia cried out sharply, practically mashing herself against his face, smearing her juices on his mouth and chin. Placing a hand on her belly to hold her still, he raised his head. "Not so fast, baby. This is a marathon, not a sprint."

"I need it so bad. Stop fucking teasing me!" Digging her fingers through his hair, she yanked his head forward. Ryder latched on to her clit again, this time with his teeth, taking little bites as he eased his middle finger inside her damp heat. Her breathy moans and gasps were such a turn-on, he was tempted to give in to her demands and take her right then and there. Instead he reminded himself to go slow, although it was killing him as much as it probably was her.

"More!" Lydia tugged on his hair again.

Slipping another digit inside of her, he fingered her hard and fast, showing no mercy. His tongue delved, licking, lapping.

"Yes! Ryder! Yes, just like that."

Something within him snapped. Ryder pulled his fingers out of her wet hole and latched his hands under her thighs and attacked her pussy with French kisses, licks, and bites. He swiped his tongue from her clit to her tight rosette, leaving no inch of her unexplored. Ryder could eat her pussy for days if he thought she'd let him. Lydia had the sweetest, juiciest cunt he'd ever tasted, and it was all his.

Lydia's body tensed. "Oh shit, Ryder. I'm going to come!"

But he didn't stop, couldn't stop, even as she wiggled and writhed like a wild woman beneath his hungry mouth. Warm honey flowed from her pussy. Ryder lapped at her cunt, not wanting to miss a single drop. Only then did he begin his trek back up, stopping to worship her generous breasts, then moving his mouth along the column of her throat.

"Open your eyes and look at me, Lydia." He waited until her sole focus was on him before he slowly eased his cock inside her. She was damn wet, so tight he had to grit his teeth to keep from surging. "Feel that, baby? Do you feel how good we are together? Let me in, baby. Let me love you." He wondered if she really understood what he was asking. Never taking his eyes from her, he moved with deliberate control, rocking his hips in a slow, steady rhythm. His arms curled around her, holding her close as he poured everything she refused to hear into his movements. "How can you walk away from this?" He damn sure couldn't.

"Please, Ryder, harder." Her pretty little pleas wouldn't work. He needed this, and so did she. Without changing his leisurely pace, he dug deeper, however, determined to fill her up. Her channel vibrated around his cock, threatening to shatter his control, but Ryder fought through it. Tightening his arms around her, he stopped her pleas with his kiss, moving his tongue in and out of her mouth in time with the movement of his hips.

"I love the way you fit around me, baby." He had to distract himself. Maybe by sharing what he was feeling, he could take his mind off the burn in his balls as they screamed for release. Lydia wrapped her legs tightly around him, the heels of her feet digging into his ass, urging him to go faster. She was killing him.

"You're so damn tight, baby. So hot. Give it to me. Give me everything." Her nails dug into his shoulders as her eyes took on a suspicious shine. Oh God, if one tear fell, he would be a goner.

"It's too much." Lydia moaned, shaking her head, trying to look away from him. "I can't—oh God, Ryder, I can't!"

"Don't turn away from me, Lydia. Look at me! Don't you dare hold back. Give it to me, baby. Come for me." Even though he'd demanded it, he was unprepared for the quake that followed. Her pussy clasped down on him so tightly, Ryder lost it. "Fuck! Ah, baby." He bucked like a bronco, rearing up and plunging down wildly. There was no way to take it slow now. Not when Lydia was gyrating right along with him, her pussy milking him so thoroughly. He could feel his release boiling up, but God help him, he couldn't stop. Not even when he roared toward his own release. He didn't pause while taking her legs and placing them over his shoulders, pushing deeper inside.

She tore at his back, breaking skin. "Ryder! Oh God, I can't take it!"

Like hell she couldn't. "Yes, you can. Take me. Take it all." He didn't recognize his own voice. This woman drove him to a place so primitive, until all he could think of was branding her as his. He had a burning need to drive all thoughts of any other man out of her mind for all time. She cried openly now, her hands clutching the cheeks of his ass, her pussy spasming like crazy.

His head was swimming, and he still couldn't stop. Not even with his second orgasm fast approaching. Ryder wanted more. He wanted her out of her mind. Reaching down, he flicked at her clit with his fingers, relentlessly until she howled. It wasn't any coherent word he could distinguish. It was, however, the most perfect sound he had ever heard. With more of a whimper than a roar this time, he followed her right over the cliff.

Slowly coming down from his cloud, he rolled to his side, pulling Lydia with him. He held her clasped to his body. Even in a sweaty, disheveled state, she was the most gorgeous creature he'd ever laid eyes on. No matter how much she fought, he'd be damned if he let her go. Ryder placed a kiss on the tip of her nose. "At the risk of sounding corny, was that good for you?"

Lydia rolled her eyes with a laugh. "That was way corny, but yes, it was very good for me." A soft sigh of contentment fell from her lips, and she snuggled closer, causing his chest to swell. At least that was something. He could tell she was warming to him more and more. The last time they'd had sex, she resisted his holding her and only gave in at his insistence. This time she was peaceful as a kitten.

Ryder stroked her back while he stared at her face, committing every curve and line to memory.

She shivered.

He tightened his hold on her. "Cold?"

"No. It's just..."

"What?"

"The way you're looking at me. It's so intense."

"I can't help it. Have you any idea how lovely you are, darlin'?"

Her lips twisted to a half smile. "I'm sure you've been with lovelier women."

"They weren't you."

"There really isn't anything special about me. I'm just a woman trying to get by in the cruel, hard world on her own. I'm no different from a lot of people."

"So you think. Can I tell you what I see when I look at you?"

She shrugged, not answering either way.

Ryder unraveled his arms from around her and caught her face between his hands. "I see a woman who doesn't know her own worth. Someone with a loving heart, but afraid to show it. A determined woman. Smart, funny, witty, but sometimes a bit uncertain when she has no reason to be. I see the woman I'm falling for."

"Ryder, don't—"

"Don't tell you how I feel? My heart skips a beat when you're near, and I can't get enough of you."

"It's way too soon. I can't deal with this."

"But I've been dealing with it for months, Lydia; seeing you in the office and not being able to hold you has driven me mad. I can no more control what I feel for you than the need to breathe. I know you've been hurt before, and I'm willing to wait until you're ready to open up to me. But I want you to know I will be here. I'm not going anywhere." Ryder leaned over and brushed her lips with his. The darkness of her eyes gleamed with what looked like tears.

He bit the inside of his lip to keep the smile off his face. The wall she'd erected around her heart was starting to crumble, and he would be there when it finally came tumbling down.

Chapter Thirteen

Lydia rolled over on her stomach with a groan, her eyelids still heavy. But the aroma of freshly brewed coffee made her want to open her eyes. As the smell drew closer, she popped one lid open to see Ryder walking into the bedroom with a tray in hand. He lowered it on the nightstand and slid in the bed next to her. “Your breakfast awaits, m'lady.”

She groaned again, reluctantly opening both eyes. “I don't usually eat breakfast, but a cup of coffee would be nice.”

He placed his hand over his chest in an overly dramatic gesture of mock hurt. “Are you telling me I slaved over a hot stove for nothing?”

She playfully smacked him on the chest. “Somehow I seriously doubt that. What did you make? Toast and cereal?”

“I'll have you know I made bacon, sausage links, scrambled eggs, and French toast lightly sprinkled with powdered sugar.”

“That sounds like an awful lot of food. Did you stop at the IHOP before I woke up?”

“Bite your tongue, woman. I'm not as useless in the kitchen as you obviously think I am.” He took the tray and placed it on his lap. “Sit up.”

With a sigh, she did as she was told, eyeing the array of food arranged on the plate. “You seriously did all this yourself?”

He held up his right hand. “As God is my witness. Don't look so surprised; I've been a bachelor for a long time. When I didn't have two dimes to rub together, I had to learn to cook, because I simply couldn't afford to eat out all the time. Some of the stuff I concocted in my younger years wasn't fit for zoo animals.” He picked up a slice of bacon and held it to her mouth. “Open up.”

Lydia took a bite. The bacon was crispy, just how she liked it. She chewed and swallowed before speaking. “Mmm, not bad. It's funny, because you never struck me as someone who's had to struggle.”

He raised a brow, feeding her the remainder of the bacon strip. “Why is that?”

“Dunno”—she munched—“you just seem to wear your wealth well, kind of like you've had it all your life.”

“I admit I didn't want for anything growing up, but that was mainly because my parents suffered from 'keeping up with the Joneses' syndrome. But we were far from rich. My dad had a middle-management job and was never really able to get beyond that, and Mom spent money faster than he could make it. I didn't realize until much later in life how much in debt they were. When my business took off, I was able to get them out of the hole they'd dug themselves.”

“That was a really nice thing for you to do. I thought you said you weren't close to them.”

“I'm not really. I mean, not like a son should be with his parents, ya know. But when it comes right down to it, they are still my parents, and I had the means to help them out, so I did. It wasn't a big deal.”

“How much debt were they in…if you don't mind my asking?”

“It was over six figures.”

“Oh my God. I maxed out my credit card once to pay for school expenses, but the card only had a five-thousand-dollar limit. I was panicking then, so I can imagine how they must have felt.”

“I'm sure it was no walk in the park for them, but you never would have guessed by the way they acted. Some people just spend money as if it's their right, without thinking over the consequences.” He cut a piece of the French toast and fed it to her.

Lydia didn't say so, but she was impressed. Not having a close relationship with her mother, she wondered if she'd help if her mother needed it. It spoke highly of Ryder's character that he'd do something like that. “That's kind of harsh.”

He fed her a sausage link. “It's the truth. If I hadn't paid off their debt, they would probably have filed for bankruptcy and lost their house. I couldn't allow that to happen, even if we don't always see eye to eye. Don't get me wrong; they're not the worst people on earth, but my relationship with them is kind of complicated. Know what I mean?”

She nodded, her mouth still full.

"What about you? I know you mentioned that you left home early because of some problems with your mother. Were things really bad? You never talked about your father."

Lydia took another strip of bacon off the plate and nibbled on it to buy some time before answering. Unsure of whether to share with him some of her more-painful memories of the past, she chose her words carefully. "I've actually never met my father. Honestly, I'm not sure if my mom even knows who he is. She claims she does, but who can say, with her past."

"Sorry."

"Don't be. There are millions of kids who grow up without one parent or another. It's something I'm used to."

"But surely you're curious about him?"

"When I was younger, I used to dream he'd come for me, and in these dreams, I knew exactly what he looked like, smelled, talked, and walked like. I imagined him with a pipe and a cardigan sweater. He'd be an adventurer who searched for precious artifacts in far-off lands, kind of like Indiana Jones. And he'd have a big, bushy mustache. I don't really know why, but in my mind, all daddies were supposed to have mustaches, because it made them look distinguished. I know it sounds silly, but there you have it. I had this imaginary character built up in my head, and every birthday and holiday I prayed he'd come, but he never did. By the time I hit puberty, I let go of that dream."

"So you never tried to find him?"

"I didn't really see the point, nor did I have a lot of information to go on. My mother mentioned a few things here and there. But I barely think about it anymore." She thought about it all the time. But Ryder didn't need to know that. She didn't want his pity.

"Maybe if you talked to your mother, she could point you in the direction of possible—"

"No, thanks. I don't need my life turned into an episode of the Maury show. Like I said, it was just a silly childhood fantasy. I'm over it."

"Are you sure?"

"Yes!" It came out a little more forcefully than she'd meant. "I mean, I'm used to taking care of myself anyway. I don't need a father, and I barely had a mother."

"Were things really that bad with your mom? I'm sorry if I'm being nosy, but you have me curious."

She laughed with unease. "What is this, twenty questions?"

"I've already told you I want to know everything there is to know about you. Besides, I told you about my parents."

He had her there. She sighed, knowing this subject would eventually come up again if she didn't tell him something. "Like you said of your parents, my mom wasn't terrible. Actually there were times when she could be a lot of fun. But my mom is the type of woman who needs a man in her life to feel validated. And sometimes she didn't make the best choices. I learned early on that I would always come second to her love life."

Ryder frowned. “Did any of these men try anything with you?”

“Tried, but I was pretty adept at staying out of the way.”

“And your mother didn't do anything about it?”

Lydia pursed her lips as she pushed away old feelings of resentment. “She only saw what she wanted to. But when I was old enough, I left. I talk to her on occasion. She remarried a few years back. Husband number four. I attended the wedding, which was the last time I actually saw her. She seemed happy, but it apparently didn't last, because he's currently in prison for embezzling money from a pension fund.”

“That's terrible.”

Lydia shrugged. “I'm sure she's bounced back. She made no mention of it when we spoke last month, but she seems happy. Maybe she's found a new man.”

“Oh, baby…” Ryder cupped the side of her face. She could feel his sympathy and hated it.

Lydia turned her head away from his touch. “Don't feel sorry for me.” Having already said enough, she plucked another sausage link from the plate and stuffed the entire thing in her mouth.

Ryder tactfully remained silent as she ate most of the contents from the plate. Lydia finished off the sausage, bacon, and half the French toast and washed it down with a glass of freshly squeezed orange juice. When she was done, she wiped her mouth with the cloth napkin he provided. “That was really good. Thank you for breakfast, Ryder, but I think I really should get dressed so you can take me to my car."

"I'll take you later. Hop into the shower while I put these dishes in the dishwasher. I'm taking you out today."

"Ryder—"

"No arguing. I'll take you to your car afterward."

Somehow she knew arguing would do no good. "But my clothes. I can't wear what I wore yesterday."

Ryder wiggled his eyebrows at her. "I won't tell if you won't."

"I'm serious."

"Stop fretting, darlin'; it's taken care of. I threw your clothes, underwear included, in the washer. They're drying now, so by the time you get out of the shower, I'll have them all nice and laundered for you."

"How long have you been up?"

"A few hours. I'm usually up by five to run, but I thought I'd take care of a few chores while you slept."

"Wow, you are pretty handy around the house. You're a rare man. Good-looking, can cook and do laundry. Most women would love that."

He grinned. "So you think I'm good-looking, huh?"

Lydia snorted. "Fishing for compliments? You know you are."

"Why, thank you, ma'am. And for the record, I don't care what most women want. I'm only interested in one in particular." He leaned over and gave her a slow, lingering kiss, taking his time as though savoring the taste of her.

Unlike the many other times when he'd initiated intimacy, she didn't fight. She didn't want to. Lydia returned the kiss enthusiastically. "Mmm." He pulled away with a smile. "Any more of that and we'll never get out of here. Go get in the shower, babe."

When he was gone, Lydia sat in the bed, the covers still wrapped around her, wondering how this man continued to get through her defenses. But for once she didn't mind.

* * *

He was getting through to her. What's more, she was getting more comfortable with him. One step at time and soon he'd find a way into her heart. He couldn't keep the smile off his face as he attempted to keep his attention on the road, although he stole glances at Lydia's regal profile whenever he could manage. Damn, she was beautiful.

She'd shared more of herself with him this morning than she ever had, and hearing about how she'd longed for her father as a child explained so much. It was probably where her mistrust in men had begun. Her unconscious reactions to the male sex reflected something deeper than what had happened in her past relationships, perhaps to the point where Lydia didn't even realize it. He still had a long way to go to completely melt the ice around her heart, but he was halfway there.

Ryder took one hand off the steering wheel and reached over to take hers in his. He brought her hand to his lips to give it a light kiss. She didn't pull away. Another good sign. "You're awful quiet."

"I was wondering where you're taking me and how much longer will we be? We've been in the car for at least a half hour. You're not taking me out to the desert to dump my body in an unmarked grave, are you?"

He chuckled. "Not before I have my wicked way with you."

"I'm serious. Where are you taking me?"

"I'm serious too. I plan on having my wicked way with you."

She snatched her hand out of his and folded her arms across her chest and pouted. She was so darn cute.

"Relax, Lydia. We'll be there in a few minutes. As a matter of fact, we're turning into the development now." He maneuvered his car past several large houses and turned down three side streets before pulling up in front of a big white house. "Here we are."

Lydia peered out of the window. "Where's here?"

"This is where my sister and her family live."

"Your sister? You didn't tell me I'd be meeting your sister! I can't. I look a mess."

"Relax. You look beautiful. And Mickey won't care what you look like. She's really laid-back, as is her husband. You'll like them both, as well as the kids, even though they can be a handful at times."

"I can't believe you're ambushing me like this, Ryder."

"How am I ambushing you? I've already made it quite clear to you how important you are to me, so wouldn't it make sense that I would want to introduce you to someone else I care about?"

Her mouth opened, but no words came out.

He had her. "Come on, sweetheart. Let's get out." Ryder had to practically drag her out of the car and up the walkway. When Mickey came to the door, she catapulted herself into his arms like a tiny blonde ball of energy. "Ryder!" He caught her in a bear hug. He'd always been close to his little sister, and their bond had only grown stronger when they grew up.

"Easy, kiddo. We're past the age where I can swing you around like a monkey."

She laughed, releasing her hold on him. "Glad you could make it, after standing me up last week."

"Couldn't be helped, Sis. But we're here now. Mickey, I want you to meet Lydia. Lydia, this is my sister, Mickey."

Mickey turned her attention to Lydia with a wide smile. "Ryder, she's just as pretty as you said she was. I'm glad to meet ya, hon." When Lydia smiled shyly and offered her hand, Mickey knocked it out of the way and pulled her into an embrace. "Shoot, girl, we don't stand on formalities here."

Lydia seemed surprised at first, but she returned the hug. Ryder was pleased by Mickey's reaction. Usually his sister was good at reading people and knew in an instant if she liked someone or not. It was obvious she approved of Lydia. Another good sign.

Mickey led them inside. The second Ryder walked into the living room, his six-year-old twin niece and nephew jumped up from the video game they were playing and raced over to greet him. "Uncle Ryder!" they screamed in unison like a well-rehearsed duet as they hurled themselves at him. Ryder lifted one child in each arm, laughing at their exuberant welcome. “Easy, you little crumb snatchers. Your uncle isn't as young as he used to be, and you two are getting heavier. What's your mom been feeding you?”

Taryn giggled, displaying a smile with two missing front teeth. She was the spitting image of her mother, with a halo of blonde curls framing a cherubic face. “Oh, Uncle Ryder. You're exaggerating again. You're almost as strong as Daddy. So what did you bring us?”

“Yeah! You always bring us something when you go away,” Tate added.

“Kids! You know better than that.” Mickey lightly scolded.

“Don't worry about it, Sis; they're just being kids.” Ryder laughed, putting the two of them down. “I'm hurt; you only want me for my presents, but alas, I didn't get a chance to pick you up anything from the island. But…” He dug into his back pocket and produced his wallet and handed each child a twenty-dollar bill. “Don't spend it all on candy.”

Mickey shook her head. “You spoil them, Ryder.”

“Hey, what are uncles for?”

“Well, it was nice of you. Thank your uncle, kids, and tell him that you appreciate him adding to your savings account.”

“Awww.” The twins groaned.

Taryn placed her hands on her nonexistent hips. “But we always have to put our money in a savings account. Why can't I buy what I want with my money?”

“Because you'll appreciate it later on. Now say thank you and no more back talk. If you haven't noticed, we have company, and I want you to show Miss Lydia the two of you have manners."

Taryn pouted for a moment before releasing a sigh. "Thanks, Uncle Ryder."

"Thank you, Uncle Ryder," Tate echoed.

Ryder ruffled the children's hair. "You're welcome. Hey, you guys, I'd like to introduce someone to you." He tugged Lydia's wrist to pull her closer and wrapped his arm around her waist. "Kids, this is Miss Lydia. Lydia, these two rug rats are Taryn and Tate."

Lydia seemed a bit nervous, but she smiled at both children. "Hi, Taryn and Tate. I like your names."

Taryn cocked her head to the side and gave Lydia a long, assessing look. "Are you Uncle Ryder's girlfriend?"

"Taryn!" Mickey yelled.

Taryn's hand flew to her hip again. "What? I'm just asking a question, Mom. You always said if I want to know something, I should ask."

"I think she's pretty, Uncle Ryder." Tate looked Lydia up and down. If his nephew weren't six, Ryder might have been jealous at the competition. The woman had an effect on men of all ages, it seemed. Ryder hugged her close to his side.

"Yes, she is." Ryder groaned inwardly, noticing the maroon undertone of Lydia's dark skin, indicating a blush.

"Sorry I missed you coming in; I was out in the back with the grill. Steaks should be done in about ten. How's it going, Ryder?" Graham, Mickey's husband, walked in through the patio door and strode over, with his hand extended.

The two men shook hands. “Can't complain. Graham, this is Lydia.”

Graham smiled, offering his hand to Lydia. “Pleased to meet you. Hope these two little monsters haven't said anything too embarrassing.”

Mickey shook her head. “You're too late for that.”

Graham raised an eyebrow at his children. “Should someone's video game privileges be taken away?”

“Oh please don't. They're so funny and cute.” Lydia spoke up, much to Ryder's surprise. He liked that she put herself in the role of their defender.

Graham chuckled. “Don't let the cuteness fool you.”

“They were both fine. Honest.” Lydia winked at the twins and shot them a conspiratorial smile.

“If you're sure.”

“Positive.”

Tate took Lydia's hand. “Miss Lydia, let me show you our new video game. It's really cool.”

She looked at Ryder, as though asking what she should do next. He nodded his encouragement.

“Okay. I'd love to see it.” Lydia allowed the twins to lead her to the television, where she sat on the floor between them. Taryn handed her a controller.

Tate sat so close to Lydia, he was almost on her lap, but she didn't seem to mind. “Miss Lydia, to play this game, you have to hold the controller like this. The *X* makes the little man run, and the circle makes him jump. The square makes him shoot. All you have to do is shoot the red and green monsters. The gold monsters are the good guys. And the blue ones give you health."

Lydia scrunched her nose. "This sounds awful complicated. I don't know if I'll get very far."

Tate patted her shoulder as if he were reassuring a child. Ryder couldn't keep the smile off his face at the sight. "Oh don't worry, Miss Lydia. If Taryn can get to level five, anyone can. It's really easy."

Taryn nodded enthusiastically. "Yep. I can get to level—Hey! That wasn't nice. I can get further than you!" She leaned over until she was in her brother's face.

"Can not. You stink, and you know the only reason why you even got to level five was because Daddy helped you."

"That's not true! You big jerk!"

"Hey, that's enough, kid." Mickey intervened.

Lydia looked over with a smile. "They're just passionate about the game. Okay, you two, no more arguing. How about we take turns, and we try to get through the levels together? Taryn can go first, and then you, Tate, and I'll go last. And we'll win or lose together. What do you think? We could all take turns playing different games to see who gets the furthest, but I think it would be so much more fun playing as a team."

Tate rubbed his chin as though contemplating it. "That sounds like it could work."

Lydia grinned at Taryn. "How about you, hon?"

Taryn offered her a dimpled smile. "I think it would be really fun."

The three commenced playing their game, giggling like three conspirators.

Ryder was impressed with Lydia's ability to relate with the children. He saw the side of her she'd kept hidden, but one he knew was always there: a warm, kind, and caring woman. It made him realize she'd be good with kids of her own one day. It only made his feelings for her deepen.

“Wow, the kids don't usually warm up to strangers this quickly.” Mickey observed. “I like her, so far. She's definitely an improvement over the bimbos you used to date when we were younger.”

“Gee, thanks, Sis.”

“I'm serious. She seems like a nice lady. Polite. She works at your company, so she must be smart, attractive, and she doesn't seem to mind kids. Looks like you picked a winner. But I do have to offer you a word of warning.”

Ryder tensed, not liking the change in his sister's tone. “What?”

“The parental units are coming for a visit at the end of next month. They're staying with us for two weeks, God help us, so you know what that means?”

“Shit. I'll just have to tell them I'm going out of town.”

“Hey, if I have to put up with them for two weeks, I don't see why you can't have one lousy dinner with them. They're your parents too, you know.”

“Too bad we couldn't pick our parents? I guess you're right. If I don't have dinner with them at least one night, I'll never hear the end of it. Damn it. I forgot their annual visit was coming up. Next year I'm definitely scheduling an out-of-town trip."

Mickey punched him on the arm. "You will not. As long as I have to suffer, so will you."

Graham opened the patio door and poked his head inside. "Steaks are ready!"

Later, after lunch was consumed and the children had gone to bed for naps, the adults sat outside at the patio table, having drinks.

"So, Lydia"—Mickey leaned over with a smile on her face. Ryder groaned inwardly because he knew the real questioning was about to begin—"tell us. How did you come to work for Ryder's company? Have marketing and advertising always been your thing?"

Lydia took a sip of her spiked tea. "Actually I really didn't know what I wanted to do with my life when I got out of high school. I've basically supported myself since I was seventeen, and at first I just took jobs where I made enough to pay the rent."

Mickey raised a brow. "Like what?"

"Waitressing, which was about the only thing I could get at my age with no formal work experience, but after a while I really wanted to go back to school to get some direction in my life. So I worked my way through school while holding down some office temp jobs. I temped for an ad agency and realized I liked what they did and I had tons of ideas, so I switched majors and completed my BS with a minor in marketing. I was fortunately hired at the job I had been temping for. After a while I decided I needed a new challenge and moved to Austin. I found Ryder's company through a temp agency."

"And when I saw how sharp her mind was and how much she contributed to the team, I knew I'd be a fool to let her go."

Mickey seemed to relax, sitting back in her chair. "Beauty and brains. Nice combo."

Lydia smiled. "Thank you."

"So how long have you and my brother been dating?"

She opened her mouth but closed it again. Lydia looked over to Ryder.

"It's still kind of new, Sis." Ryder wanted to wring Mickey's neck for putting Lydia on the spot, but he knew the interrogation wouldn't end until his sister's curiosity was satisfied. And it didn't. But Lydia held her own. For every question asked, she had an answer.

Ryder was so proud of Lydia. She kept her composure the entire time, answering Mickey's blunt questions, and when the kids returned, she played with them some more. By the end of their visit it was clear Mickey had placed her full stamp of approval on Lydia, and Graham seemed to like her as well. Everything pointed to the fact that he and Lydia belonged together. That the family members who counted were as taken with her as he was only sealed it. If she thought he was letting her go now, she was crazy.

* * *

By the end of the weekend, Lydia was more exhausted than she had been before it began. She'd actually enjoyed spending time with Mickey and her family. Mickey talked a lot, but she was likable, and while Graham didn't speak nearly as much as his wife, he was quite affable and charming as well. The children were sweethearts. Ryder seemed to spoil them, which was understandable. They'd been a lot of fun to be around.

Lydia felt a twinge in her breast. What would it be like to have Ryder's child? Would he or she be as rambunctious and adorable as the twins? She immediately shook that thought from her mind. Feelings she wasn't quite comfortable with were beginning to creep beneath her defenses, and Lydia wasn't sure she liked it at all. Besides, she'd probably never carry Ryder's child, or anyone else's for that matter, with her condition. It was all fantasy, and she'd do well to remember that.

Now home, ensconced in her condo, curled up with a book by her favorite author, something gnawed at her, like she was missing something. Or someone. Before she could examine her feelings, the phone rang, cutting into her silent musings. Glancing at the phone, she smiled when she saw the number. She picked up the phone.

They hadn't spoken for a bit, mainly due to their busy schedules. "Hi, Sammy Jo. Haven't heard from you in a couple of weeks. How's it going?"

"Things have been a bit hectic at the office lately. My boss has been a dragon. The firm has just landed an account with one of the largest finance corporations in the city, and it's going to bring in some big money. Gina will be working with the head guy himself, and I think he flusters her a bit."

"Gina? Seriously? Nothing seems to get to her."

"I didn't think so either until Cary Hathaway crossed her path." Sammy Jo chuckled.

"Cary Hathaway, as in the Hathaway Group? Are you shitting me? That's not one of the largest finance firms in the state. It's *the* largest in the state and dare I say, possibly in the country."

"I wouldn't go that far."

"Well, I know Ryder has wanted to do business with them for a while. It would be a feather in his cap to land an account like that. So they've contracted the consulting agency you work for. Will you be working with the big man as well?"

"That's all Gina. I think she may be so flustered because she has a bit of a crush on him."

"Isn't she married?"

"Like that's ever stopped her. You have no idea how many times her husband has called the office and she was on one of her *business lunches*. There's more drama in my office than a soap opera."

"Is he interested in her other than in a business sense? He is one of the city's most eligible bachelors. And if I remember correctly, judging from that picture in the newspaper of him, he isn't hard on the eyes."

"I don't think so. He seems a bit intense. I try to stay out of his way as much as possible when he comes to see Gina. Anyway, that isn't why I called. I have some fantastic news!"

"What? Is it about Melody? How is my ray of sunshine, anyway?"

“She's doing great and missing her godmother. I hope you'll stop by for a visit soon.”

“I will. I promise. Tell her I'm thinking of her.”

“Will do. She's excited about going to the second grade next year. Three more weeks and school will be out, which ties into my news. My mother-in-law is taking me and Melody on a one-month cruise to the Mediterranean. Isn't that terrific?”

“Sounds good, and you deserve it. Will you be able to take that much time off?”

“I had a lot of vacation time owed to me, and though Gina wasn't happy about it, she knows I can use the break. I'm really excited. Marvin and I were going to go on a cruise on the Mediterranean, before… Well, now we'll get our chance.”

“We?”

“I'm taking him with me, silly.”

By *him*, Sammy Jo meant Marvin's urn. “Well, I'm happy for you, hon.”

“Thank you, sweetie. And how about you? How are things going with that fine-ass boss of yours?”

“I don't know. I know I'm crazy to have an affair with my boss, but Ryder seems so different from Kevin and Casey. Part of me wants to give him a chance. I mean, really give him a chance. But the other half of me is waiting for him to screw up.”

“Have you thought he might not?”

“I can't afford not to. Letting my guard down is what's gotten me in trouble before. I think this thing will eventually run its course, which is why I don't understand why he took me to meet his sister and her family. They were all lovely, and I enjoyed myself with them, but while I was there, I felt like a big fake."

"How so?"

"I felt that they would see things for what they really are. That Ryder and I are a temporary fling."

"Well, hon, you know best." That was one of the things she loved about Sammy Jo. The other woman listened without judgment. "But I do think you should talk to Ryder about what he thinks of it."

It was sensible advice, but Lydia was terrified. "Maybe."

What she didn't want to admit to her friend was that she took comfort in the not knowing. As long as she didn't know his true intentions, she couldn't get hurt.

Chapter Fourteen

Lydia rubbed the bridge of her nose. Her eyes were practically crossed from looking at the computer screen. Glancing at the clock on her desk, she noticed it was going on eight. Time had gotten away from her. The rest of her team had already gone home, and no one was left in the office except her and Ryder, who was currently on a conference call in his office with one of his foreign clients.

She really wanted to do a good job on the Rawlings account, her first big job at this agency. Actually it was the biggest project of her career, and the last thing she wanted was for her colleagues to think she'd gotten lead on the project because she was sleeping with the boss.

She would be blind if she didn't notice some of the looks she got around the office. It was as if everyone knew something was going on between them. A couple of the women who had been friendly with her before barely spoke to her now. And some of the men gave her knowing looks. If she really gave a damn about what they thought of her, she might have been upset, but it still made things more than a little awkward.

Ryder made no attempt to play down their relationship. Although he kept things professional at work, he never crossed the line when others were around. But the way he'd look at her, touch her arm, or smile at her made it apparent to anyone with eyes, their relationship went beyond that of mere employer and employee. It was like he was advertising their affair to the world. Lydia wasn't exactly sure what to call it. She supposed they were dating, but how they got to this point, she wasn't sure.

It had been three weeks since the weekend he'd practically kidnapped her, and she was surprised to find she really liked Ryder the man. He was as fun to be around outside the bedroom as he was between the sheets. The two of them had started spending a lot of time together. They'd work late, and afterward Ryder would order takeout and either hang out at her place for the night or take her back to his place. All they did was talk, watch movies, and cuddle. Not once did Ryder attempt to have sex with her, which frustrated Lydia a bit. But if she were being honest with herself, she kind of liked their quiet time together.

Having worked so closely with him on the Rawlings account these past few weeks, she'd absorbed a lot about the business she didn't know. It was no wonder his agency had grown to the level it had. He had a drive and a know-how that left most of his competitors in the dust. She'd learned so much from him. She loved watching him in action. Yet there was still the big question mark about what was happening between them. Even though she found herself looking forward to those nights alone with Ryder, it scared her that he had this effect on her. Was she setting herself up for getting hurt? As if her thoughts had conjured him up, he walked into her cubicle.

"Lydia, you look tired; let's get out of here. When was the last time you ate?" Ryder placed his hands on her shoulders and massaged her tense muscles.

"Hmmm, that feels good. I just want to finish this last little bit before we go. I thought your conference call would be longer."

"We were able to come to an agreement sooner than I anticipated. You didn't answer my question."

"I dunno. I had a sandwich for lunch."

"Which you probably picked at and didn't finish. What am I going to do with you, woman? Sign off, and let's go. This stuff will keep until the morning."

"But—"

"No buts." He leaned over and grabbed her mouse, clicked on Save, and closed her documents. "I'll take you home and fix you something to eat."

"I still need to go grocery shopping."

"Then I'll take you back to my place. Stay the night, and I'll take you home in the morning or not. It's Friday, so it's not like we have to come to the office tomorrow. We both could use the break."

She should have protested, and maybe a few weeks ago she would have, but she couldn't think of anything more relaxing than snuggling next to Ryder with a belly full of one of his fabulous culinary concoctions. "Okay. Let me sign off, and I'll be ready."

* * *

She was silent on the ride to his place. Lydia mulled over this thing they had together. She wanted to ask him to clarify what he expected, but she wasn't really sure how to phrase it. Did she just come right out and ask? Would it be too forward to mention that she missed being intimate? Hanging out and getting to know one another was nice, and she wouldn't trade it for the world, but she missed the sex too. Maybe he was trying to show her he really cared for her. He had been attentive and sweet, but she had needs only he could fulfill.

This was probably her fault for fighting him so hard. She was starting to trust him now, a little bit anyway. Maybe she should just tell him she was ready to take that giant leap into a relationship. He had taken her to meet his sister. That meant he was serious, right?

When they arrived at Ryder's house and settled in, he fixed her a glass of wine. They migrated to the kitchen, where she kept him company while he began the food preparation.

“Okay, spill it. What's up with the frown?”

He was way too perceptive sometimes. Biting her lip, Lydia debated how much to tell him. There was no way she was going to come right out and ask him for sex, so that part was out.

“Where do you see this going, Ryder?” That was safe. It didn't demand anything, and it allowed her the opportunity to hide the depth of what she felt for him.

He paused in the midst of chopping vegetables, piercing her with an unwavering stare. “Where do *you* think it's going?”

He wasn't smiling, and there wasn't a trace of humor in his voice. Lydia shivered at the intensity of his stare. She didn't have an answer, because she honestly didn't know. In all her past daydreams of her future, it had never included a man, especially not one like Ryder. "I guess we're seeing each other?" Weak, but it was all she had right now.

"Yeah, we are definitely doing that." His gaze swept down her frame, causing her nipples to tighten and her juices to flow. "But that isn't what I asked."

"I really don't know," she admitted. "Which is why I'm asking you."

"So whatever I decide, you're good with?"

He was testing her, but that didn't mean she had an answer. On the one hand, she didn't like the sound of just going along with whatever he wanted. She was an independent woman who could decide for herself what she wanted. If only she knew what it was.

"Come on, Ryder. You know what I'm asking." She sighed in frustration. "I really don't know where this is heading, and to be honest, I'm not sure where I want it to go. I just want to know what you expect."

"I don't expect anything. I just know I want to be with you. As far as I'm concerned, you're my woman." He said it so simply, as if that were all there was to it. He must have sensed her growing agitation, because he put down the knife and walked over to engulf her in his arms. It was impossible not to melt into his embrace; it just felt too good.

She was overwhelmed with emotion; silent tears slid down her cheeks. Just great. She hadn't planned on making a fool of herself, and now Ryder probably thought she was a big baby.

Alarm etching his eyes, he cupped her face between his hands. "What's the matter, baby?"

"I just... You're being so good to me, and I don't know how to handle it."

"If you don't believe you deserve to be valued and treated like a lady, then you're nuts. Haven't you figured it out yet, Lydia? I'm in love with you." He wiped away her tears and gently kissed the tracks they had left.

A soft gasp escaped her lips. "But you can't. It's too soon. You can't love me."

"I probably fell in love with you the moment I set eyes on you. Yes, we've only been together for a little bit, but I don't need another year, a month, or even another week to know how I feel about you. It's not just lust. What's in my heart is real." He released her face to take her hand and placed it against his chest. "See, darlin', this is what you do to me. I can't eat, sleep, breathe, or move without thinking of you. I want to be the man who makes you laugh and cry with tears of joy. I want to be there in your triumphs and comfort you when you're sad and lift you back up when you fall. I know you may not be ready to say it back to me, but I'll wait for as long as it takes."

She moistened her suddenly dry lips. "You're going to have to be very patient with me. Love is a tough thing for me. I thought I was in love before, but...I ended up getting hurt. Badly."

"Tell me about it. Let me take that pain away for you. Use me as your sounding board."

He seemed so sincere, and she'd already opened up to him about some of her past. “The first boyfriend I had was a user. Oh, he did all the right things and said all the right things, in the beginning. He convinced me to let him move in. I was so in awe of him. I was only nineteen and never been kissed; he was twenty-six and seemed so much more worldly than me. Things were good at first, and then it became apparent he couldn't keep a job. I thought my love for him would get us through the hard times, but he wasn't interested in working when he had me to support him. When I objected, he became physically and emotionally abusive. I would have left him, but I didn't have anywhere else to go, and I was terrified he'd find me and hurt me even worse. It went on for about three years.”

Ryder's green eyes nearly darkened to black in his anger. “Where is that bastard now?”

“Dead. He got into a fight and was killed.”

“Good. Because if he were still alive, I would have done it myself.”

A sad smile touched her lips. “After Kevin, I needed a fresh start. So I moved and landed a position at PRL. It's where I met Casey. He pursued me, and I was flattered because no one like him had ever taken an interest in me. Turns out he only wanted one thing.” It wasn't a lie. Now knowing Casey's motivation for what he'd done, she wasn't sure if it would be fair to tell Ryder, his boss, what he'd done in the past. It could jeopardize his career, and even though he'd hurt her, it wasn't in her to destroy the man's livelihood.

Ryder's lips tightened. “I see. It's why you left PRL, isn't it?”

“Yes. So, you see, I may not have a lot of experience with relationships, but the couple I've had didn't turn out well for me. I don't think I could take the disappointment if you let me down too.” Tears streamed down her cheeks again.

He grasped her chin. “Baby, I would never hurt you. Ever. I love you. Please believe me. I intend to spend however long it takes to convince you of my feelings and to show you that you are worthy of being loved. Look, Lydia. We can take it as slow as you need me to. I'm trying not to rush you into anything; I just can't stand it when you push me away. Until you're ready, don't think about something beyond what we are right now. I will wait.”

“Is that why you haven't tried to…you know?” Her face burned just asking the question. It just slipped out before she could stop herself.

Ryder went completely still, his arms tightening around her. She felt his cock growing against her belly. She could have sworn she heard a low moan, but it was so hushed she couldn't be sure. “No, I don't know. Why don't you tell me?”

Ryder felt like a walking hard-on. It was impossible to be close to Lydia and not want her. She was right; he had held off because he didn't want her to think that was all he wanted from her. She was so damn prickly, and he was scared if he pushed too hard, he would frighten her off again. He was probably pushing now, but she had started it.

“Sex,” she clarified. “Is that why you haven't tried to have sex with me?”

"Maybe I was waiting for you to make the first move."

When she looked up at him with those big brown eyes, he lost all willpower. He took her lips forcefully, using her hair to tilt her head back. Damn, he'd missed this. It had been pure hell to hold out this long. Knowing that she wanted him, that she missed this too, only made it better. Still, it was wise not to rush it.

"I need to finish dinner, or we'll both go hungry," he murmured against her soft lips. He didn't want to stop, but if he didn't, he was going to take her right here on the kitchen table.

"I'm not hungry…for food."

Aw hell, he was a goner. So much for stir-fry. Thank God she wore a dress; he didn't think he had the patience for pants. He lifted her to the counter, pushing up the skirt of her dress as he did. She was wearing garters again, with the nylons that stopped at the top of her thighs. He loved those things. She always wore the sexiest damn underwear.

"Did you miss me, baby?" He breathed the question against her skin, biting down on the crook of her neck.

"Foreplay later. I need you now."

He hid his smile, slowly unzipping the back of her dress. There was no way he was going to hurry this. It was the first time she had admitted to wanting him without coercion. He wanted this moment to last so she would never forget it. He knew he wouldn't. He lifted her dress, leaving her bra and naughty thong and garter set.

Ryder enjoyed the way her body trembled against his. He skimmed the tops of her breasts with his fingers where the lace edged along her skin, and watched in fascination as her nipples became even harder. He couldn't resist scraping his teeth over the diamond-hard points through the flimsy material. Her thighs spread as he pressed his mouth against her breast.

"Damn it, Ryder, don't play with me."

Music to his ears, but it didn't deter him. He intended to drive her as crazy as he had been, making her experience the hell he'd suffered through without her in his arms. Pushing her bra cups underneath her breasts, he repeated his action on each mound until she moaned and ground her silk-covered core against the bulge in his pants. He ignored the tugs on his hair until she panted heavily. Even then it was hard to lift his head.

"But playing is fun." He pressed his thumb against her clit through her underwear. "Don't you want to play with me, Lydia?" Slipping one finger inside the band of her panties, he lightly traced the seam of her pussy. She was wet and ready, but he wouldn't end the sweet torture anytime soon. At least not until he tasted her.

"I don't want to play. I need you." Lydia attempted to move her hips, to force his finger inside her.

Giving in to her demands, Ryder pressed two fingers deep into her pussy, curving upward the way she liked it. "Tell me where you need me, darlin'." He scraped his teeth against the lobe of her ear, never pausing the deep strokes of his fingers. "Tell me how you want me."

"Your dick, your mouth, just fuck me!"

"You're going to get it, baby. All of it."

Without missing a beat, he lowered himself and suckled her clit into his mouth. Ryder loved the way she gyrated her hips, pressing her cunt against his face. She was hungry for it. He wanted to make her hungrier. "Like that, darlin'?" He chuckled lightly. Ryder was full of masculine pride that he could have her begging for him like this.

"Oh, Ryder, that feels so..."

He raised his head to meet her desire-filled gaze. "What, baby? Tell me."

She licked her lips, a motion that made his cock so fucking hard, he didn't know how much longer he'd last. "I feel like I'm flying."

As compliments went, he couldn't have gotten a better one. It made him want to make this even more special for her.

"Then let's soar together." He thrust his fingers faster as he flicked the nubbin with his tongue while sucking ravenously. She wrapped her legs around his shoulders and rode his face. He lapped at her pussy, reveling in the taste of her on his tongue and the scent of her arousal. Lydia's intoxicating flavor and her soft whimpers spurred him on. He sucked harder, plunging his fingers deep inside until she shook and cried out his name.

"Ryder! Oh God, I'm coming." He waited until her tremors lessened before easing his fingers out, but he didn't move. Instead he replaced the digits with his tongue, going in for a second attack. "No more, please. I can't take it."

He pulled back slightly, not because she asked, but simply because his cock was painfully pressing against the zipper of his pants, ready to be set free. Even more than that, he needed to be one with her. Lydia's pussy was so enticing, he couldn't go without one more taste. Returning his attention to her pussy, he thrust his tongue in a pantomime of what his dick would soon be doing, pausing only to swirl it around her clit. She whimpered for him to stop even as her hands gripped his face closer. An animalistic growl was his only answer. He couldn't stop. Not until she screamed his name at the top of her lungs did he even consider it.

Rising slowly, he stared down at the woman he'd grown to love. He loved seeing her like this: her eyes hazy and replete with a dichotomy of bliss and hunger. He expanded his chest with pride, knowing he had done this to her and made her feel this way. He felt more like a man than at any other time in his life.

"You are so beautiful." She was. So fucking perfect. His heart swelled with not just passion but a love so deep, he could barely stand it. Maybe Lydia had a propensity for closing up tighter than a clam, but he saw her for who she was: a woman with a beautiful spirit and the capacity to love with everything in her being, if only she allowed it. His woman.

When she gave him a devious little smile, sliding from the counter down to her knees in front of him, his gut clenched. He didn't move a muscle, didn't dare breathe. His eyes screwed shut; he was half-afraid of the vision of Lydia kneeling before him; her sweet lips less than an inch from his shaft were just his mind playing tricks on him. He had dreamed about this, had wanted it badly, but never dared to ask. It was something she would have to give freely. He never dared hope it would happen so soon.

"Ryder, open your eyes." Her breath wafted across his heated, tight flesh. His eyes snapped open, just in time to watch in utter fascination as her tongue snaked around the mushroom-shaped head of his cock. *Fuck!* He had to lock his knees to keep them from buckling. When that same bulbous head disappeared between her lips, he wanted to howl, beat his chest, and come at the same time.

"Shit, baby, that feels so good." His voice was nothing more than a rasp. He couldn't even clear his throat. She took him in, moving her mouth slowly down the pulsating length of his cock. Ryder grasped the sides of her head. In response, she started to hum, and Ryder felt his eyes cross. The vibrations shot straight up his shaft down to his balls, making the sensitive sac tingle.

But then she did something he never in a million years would've expected. Just when he thought she would surely go down no farther, he felt the tip of his cock hit the back of her throat. Lydia cradled his balls in her hands and fondled and cupped them.

She pulled away from his cock, only to suck his sac in her mouth with fervent tugs. Ryder thought he'd pass out right then and there. Her ministrations were hot as hell, yet they were laced with enough innocence that was uniquely Lydia. She used her tongue and nipped with her teeth.

"Oh God. Baby! I—" He realized if he didn't stop her, he'd come in her mouth, and he wanted to save it for her warm, tight pussy.

Lydia was far from finished, it seemed. Releasing his balls, she took his shaft in her mouth again, one hard inch at a time. The warm, wet suction of her mouth was delightful torture; the feel of his cock working down her throat was enough to drive him out of his mind. With an effort of will he never knew he possessed, he slid his dick out of her mouth, damn near whimpering as he did so.

"I have to have you now!"

Lydia didn't have time to blink before she found herself on the kitchen table, her legs spread wide, her pussy stuffed full. She gasped at his welcome thrust. God, she'd missed this. Missed him. There, she'd finally admitted it. This wasn't just hot sex, but something more.

Ryder gripped her hips, his eyes closed and his breathing shallow. He looked like he was in pain. "Ryder?"

"So fucking tight. So good. My pussy. Say it, Lydia."

"Your pussy. All of me is yours."

His eyes popped open. "'Bout time you realized that." He growled before thrusting so deep in her, it was as if they'd merged into one being. And she loved it. Lydia could feel the veins that lined his shaft against her vaginal walls, could feel each time it jumped inside her. She whimpered from all the emotions swirling within her.

Something was different this time around, and it suddenly clicked for her what it was: she was open. For the first time in a long time, she had allowed someone else in other than her best friend.

Ryder dug his hands deeper into her hips, fingers pressing mercilessly into the cheeks of her ass, pulling her into each power-driven thrust. There was no air to scream or to cry out; she could only pant as he took total possession of her body. Her heart thundered, as she realized with each drive, he was irrevocably breaking through the wall she had built around her heart and taking permanent residence there.

It wasn't sex, it wasn't making love, and it wasn't fucking either. He was claiming her, marking her as his for all time. Each stroke hit her G-spot just right. She fell back on her elbows, placing her feet on the edge of the table as she canted her hips to receive him.

"Mine!"

"Yes." She couldn't deny him anymore. "Oh God, yes, yours!"

It seemed to only fuel the fire. His eyes blazed with green fire as he gazed down at her so possessively, a shiver ran through her body. Ryder lowered his head; his teeth tugged the hard kernels of her nipples just right.

He didn't pause his delicious movements. He plunged deeper and deeper, reaching her womb. Ryder swirled his tongue around each taut peak before raising his head again. "Look at me, Lydia."

Their gazes connected, and something seemed to go off inside of her. Her limbs trembled in forewarning. She was on the verge of something bigger than she had ever felt. The tingles started in her toes, gradually working their way up her body. It was too much.

The detonation started deep in her core, radiating out to every nerve of her body. She shook hard, her muscles seizing. Throwing her head back, Lydia screamed, her body breaking apart and flying at the same time. Her head swam with the sensations battering her from the inside out. She felt his cock spasm inside her, heard his answering roar. Oh God, it was so good.

When she would have fallen back against the cool oak table, he pulled her into his arms, then kissed her face with tender reverence. She hadn't a clue what he murmured as he smoothed his hands down her back; she didn't care. All that mattered was what had just happened, the coming together of two halves to make a whole. No matter what might happen in the future, she couldn't regret this. She had given him everything, and she was glad. And for the first time in her life, she felt something she never thought she'd experience. Love.

Chapter Fifteen

Lydia woke to a delicious soreness. Despite the cool air conditioner's breeze, she felt warm and cozy. Ryder's leg was slung over hers, his arms wrapped around her waist. It felt good and right to wake up like this. Although he had kept her up most of the night, his cock was hard against her thigh. There was no way in hell she could take him again, but it was nice to know how much he still wanted her. It gave her a sense of power that was purely feminine. His fingers trailed up and down her spine. It made her feel like a well-fed cat.

"How do you feel?"

He had to be kidding. She felt like she could scale a mountain if she wanted to.

"Sore but good."

"Good." He planted small kisses across her shoulders, up the column of her throat, across her cheek. "Hungry? I can whip us up something to eat, and then we can crawl back into bed. I want to stay in bed with you all day."

"I can't think of anything else I'd rather do." Surprisingly it was true. Giggling like kids, they went down to the kitchen naked, pinching and caressing along the way. They were lip-locked in a soul-searing kiss by the time they actually made it downstairs. Neither of them heard the door unlock or footsteps heading their way. Lydia didn't hear anything before the screech.

"Ryder Hamilton Garrison!"

Lydia's head whipped around at the sound of feminine outrage. Her brain assessed the situation before her body could move. Standing directly behind them were Mickey and an older couple who needed no introduction. The small blonde woman was a dead ringer for Mickey, and the tall, broad man looked like an older, version of Ryder. His parents gaped at them with horror. Disgust was clearly etched all over his mother's face, while his father looked as if he smelled something particularly foul.

If Lydia could have buried herself ten feet under, she would have. While Mickey looked like she wanted to burst into remorseful tears, Ryder's parents were not happy. Luckily Ryder thought on his feet, shoving her behind his back while cupping his hands over his privates. All she could do was bury her burning face against the smooth skin of his back. "Oh God, please take me now." She groaned under her breath.

"Mom, Dad." Ryder greeted them as if there weren't a thing wrong. "Thanks for the call, Mickey."

"Mikayla tried to call you," his mother announced in the snootiest voice Lydia had ever heard. "You didn't answer your phone. I insisted we come by to make sure you were all right. I must say, Ryder, I'm appalled."

There were plenty of things more horrifying than finding your grown son lip-locked, buck naked with some woman in his home, but it was pretty damn embarrassing for everyone involved.

"Ryder, Lydia, I'm so sorry," Mickey blurted.

Although Lydia couldn't see her—there was no way in hell she would lift her head to witness the distaste on his parents' faces—but she could clearly hear Mickey's remorse. "I swear I did try to call. I thought Ryder would be...out." Meaning she had thought Ryder would be at Lydia's, where they had been spending a great deal of time lately. Lydia just felt more comfortable in her home, and he understood that.

"I think this can wait until we are all dressed." Ryder cut his sister off. "Could you all please turn around?" They must have done as Ryder asked, because a second later he shepherded Lydia back up the stairs. "I am so sorry, darlin'," he told her once they were safely in his bedroom. "That was definitely not how I wanted you to meet my parents."

"I can't go back down there, Ryder." There was just no way in hell she could face his parents again today, if ever.

"I know, baby. I would never ask you to. I'll get rid of them. I promise."

Despite the bravado he had shown Lydia, Ryder was part furious, part terrified to face his parents. He didn't fear them necessarily; he just knew what was important to them. They would never accept Lydia; he had no misconceived notions they ever would. Not that it mattered to him, but he'd hoped to prepare himself for the confrontation he knew was coming. He certainly hadn't wanted to go through this while Lydia was here. It was a relief she didn't want to come downstairs with him. He didn't want her to hear what they had to say. He had a feeling it would only upset her. Ryder pulled on a pair of shorts and a T-shirt before heading back downstairs.

He found his family in the formal dining room. Of course Phillip and Elizabeth Garrison wouldn't stoop so low as to sit in the more-informal den. They looked like the perfect older couple as they sat stiffly in mock outrage. Or maybe the outrage was real; one never could tell. They were plastic people, more concerned with appearances than anything real.

All Ryder's life, what he wore, how well he did on the football field, whom he dated, who his friends were, all that was more important than how he felt, what he wanted, or even who he really was. They looked at him with profound disappointment as he entered. It surprised him how little their displeasure affected him. He simply didn't care what they thought.

"Would you care to explain yourself, Ryder?" Phil Garrison was a towering figure of a man. His dark blond hair was mostly gray now, and the green eyes Ryder had inherited flashed fire. So the emotion wasn't feigned, then. Ryder still wasn't moved. "What could you be thinking to be cavorting with a woman like that?"

Ryder strolled into the room as if nothing at all were amiss, kissed his sister's cheek before standing against the mantel of the fireplace. "A woman like what, Phil?" He had long since stopped referring to his father as "Dad." Right around the same time he started paying his parents' bills.

"Really, Ryder, I think you know." Liz Garrison sniffed. The years and various plastic surgeries had been kind to his mother. She looked like a woman in her forties instead of someone fast approaching sixty. Her bright blonde hair was impeccably styled, and there wasn't a wrinkle in the silk sheath she wore. A single strand of pearls completed the ensemble. The very picture of the perfect Texan housewife.

Very few knew she had flunked out of college, unable to get past her professors with a pout and a stomp of her tiny feet the way she had in high school. She had tried modeling but had been unable to make it to her assignments on time or work well with photographers. She had attempted to become an interior decorator and failed miserably. Apparently clients had expected service rather than a past beauty queen who wanted the world to wait on her.

What a sad, tragic couple they made. Phil stuck in middle management at an oil company, Liz desperate to be the queen bee of her small circle of social-climbing friends. The older Garrisons had expected far more out of life and had been shocked to find that just because they were beautiful didn't mean they could get their own way.

It rankled them to no end that people they had tormented in high school had gone on to flourishing careers, while they had been caught in a rut. They expected their children to accomplish what they had failed so miserably at. For Mickey, that was easy enough. She'd won several beauty pageants before settling down and marrying the "right kind" of man—a lawyer whose future looked promising. Ryder had been both their greatest joy and biggest disappointment.

While he had succeeded in making a lot of money, owning his own company and being a success in life, Ryder tended to cultivate the wrong friendships, being a tad too liberal in his thinking and dating the wrong types of women.

He didn't give a shit about appearances, much to his parents' horror. He didn't try to get in the right clubs or make the right friends.

"Actually I don't know," Ryder finally answered. "You don't know Lydia, so what you could possibly be referring to escapes me." He knew quite well what they meant, but he wanted to hear them say it.

"Mom, Lydia is a really nice person." Mickey tried to ease the tension that was growing in the room by leaps and bounds. "The kids love her."

Liz gasped, staring at her daughter like she had just grown another head. Poor Mickey. The last thing Ryder wanted was to make this any more difficult for her than it already was.

"I find it hard to believe Graham would allow that woman to be around the children." Liz sounded perfectly horrified. "How could you, Mikayla? I raised you better than to let such, such…trash in your home!"

"You refer to Lydia as trash one more time, and I will cut you off." Ryder's ire rose to dangerous heights. All attention swung in his direction as he pushed himself away from the mantel and walked to stand directly in front of his parents. "You have no right to come into my home and disparage my woman. If you can't keep a civil tongue in your mouth, you can leave."

"Don't talk to your mother that way, boy!" Phil bounded to his feet. "You are the one running around naked with that…that woman."

"This is my home, which you came into unannounced, and if I want to cavort around naked in my house, I will, and there's not a damn thing you can do or say about it."

"Good God, boy, don't you have enough sense to at least take her to some motel if you have that kind of an itch? There is no telling what you could have brought into your house. She could be casing the place as we speak!"

Ryder silently prayed for the Lord to give him the strength not to punch his father's lights out. "Oh yeah, I should have taken her to a motel, because there's no telling what kind of black-woman cooties she could have spread just by being here."

"Exactly. You never know what someone like her could be carrying." Phil smiled smugly. Apparently grasping sarcasm wasn't his strong suit.

"I guess if I'm foolish enough to bring her over here again, I'll be sure to lock up any of my valuables. You've made me see the light. What was I thinking to get involved with someone like her? I guess she must have put some voodoo curse on me or something. That's what her people do, isn't it?"

Liz sniffed. "Well, we all make mistakes, Son. While your extracurricular activities turn my stomach, you could have at least been discreet. In a neighborhood like this, you're lucky none of your neighbors called the police when they saw her enter your house."

"Yeah, I shouldn't have risked my valuables. Her being black and all, she'd probably rob me blind. You know, I only hired her because of affirmative action. Had to get the Feds off my back."

Phil nodded his head enthusiastically as if he were at a backwoods Sunday revival. "You have to be real careful of her kind."

Even Ryder didn't think his parents were this damn thick, and it saddened him a bit to be proved wrong. But perversely he wanted to see just how far they'd go, so he wouldn't feel a bit guilty when he had to kick their asses out of his life. "How about we put it down to a weak moment on my part? The little head getting in the way of the big head. Guess I wanted to find out if they were as wild in bed as people say they are. That's what I get for watching too many rap videos, huh? Poor woman thinks I'm actually in love with her. You give her people an inch, and they'll take a mile."

Mickey covered her mouth to hold back the giggles. Ryder was gratified that at least his sister got it.

Phil smirked. "Yes, well. Just let it never happen again, will you, Son? Now that we've got this unpleasantness out of the way, get rid of her, and we can all go out for breakfast."

No doubt they were looking to be treated, but Ryder had had enough. "Are you people slow? Do you not realize how ridiculous you two are to believe that crap? By the way, it's called being facetious. Look it up in the dictionary. You two have probably never had a meaningful relationship with any black person to make these idiotic judgments about them. News flash, I have no intention of getting rid of Lydia."

His father's mouth fell open before he sputtered, "S-so you're choosing to humiliate your mother and me over this little fetish for some ghetto trash?"

"My feelings for her have nothing to do with you. This isn't some kind of fetish," Ryder glared at his parents. "Lydia is not trash. She's a beautiful, intelligent woman. I could've done a hell of a lot worse had I followed any of your advice. How about you worry about paying your own damn bills and keeping your wife out of boutiques you can't afford and let me live my own life? I love her, and I'm going to be with her, and there isn't a damn thing you can do about it. This isn't some temporary fling, so you can get the hell out of my house until you learn to deal with the reality!"

Phil drew himself up to his full height, standing nose to nose with his son. Ryder saw doubt and confusion flicker in the older man's eyes but knew he wouldn't give. Too bad; neither would he. There was no way in hell he was giving Lydia up to make his parents happy.

"Until you come to your senses, you are no longer my son. Mikayla, I will be speaking with Graham about this. If anyone hears about what your brother has done, it could seriously damage his reputation."

"Come on, Dad. Step into the twenty-first century. Graham likes Lydia as much as I do. You're both being ridiculous." Tears flowed down Mickey's face. Ryder knew she hated being in between him and their parents like this. He wished it could be different, but he wasn't going to give in on this one. Not even for his baby sister.

"I hope you didn't leave Graham alone with that woman." Liz picked the wrong time to speak. "You know how those kind of women are."

"Get the fuck out of my house!" Ryder roared.

He was done. His head ached; his gut was sour. His parents were hateful, bitter people. He felt tainted by their very presence. In the past he had looked past their narrow-minded prejudices. It had never really had an effect on his life before. Now he just couldn't stomach it. Especially not with Lydia upstairs waiting. Maybe sometime in the future he would try to reason with them, but he just couldn't do it now.

"You will regret this," Phil whispered as they were leaving.

"I think you will regret it far more than I will."

After closing and locking the door behind his uninvited guests, Ryder ran back up the stairs. He prayed with every step Lydia hadn't heard any of it, but tempers had been running high. She probably couldn't help but hear snatches of the yelled conversation.

"Lydia?" He checked the bedroom, but she wasn't there. "Lydia, honey, we need to talk." She wasn't in the bathroom either. He checked the entire second floor, but she was nowhere to be found. Running back downstairs, he checked the kitchen, then the den, but still there was no sign of her. She was gone.

* * *

Lydia sank back against the leather interior of the cab's backseat, struggling to keep the tears from falling until she was safely locked inside her condo. She held her breath, casting glances behind her. She didn't know why she bothered. From what she had heard, Ryder was just about done with her now that his parents had talked some sense into him.

"*How about we put it down to a weak moment on my part? The little head getting in the way of the big head. Guess I wanted to find out if they were as wild in bed as people say they are. That's what I get for watching too many rap videos, huh*?" She thought he could have been joking, but when he mentioned the part about really not loving her, she couldn't listen to another second of what he had to say. That last bit tore into her like razors.

Despite her best effort, moisture leaked from her eyes as the words replayed in her head. It didn't make any sense; yet she had heard his words loud and clear. How could she have been so stupid? Just when she thought that maybe there was a happily ever after for her, reality smacked her dead in the face. Why had he led her on so cruelly? She had told him things she'd never admitted to anyone. She'd let him in and rejoiced at their final coming together, all while he'd probably laughed behind her back.

Lydia felt like a fool of momentous proportions. How could she have believed his lies? He didn't have to tell her all that bullshit about waiting for her and loving her. She'd never asked him to love her. What kind of sick psychopath just came right out and told a woman he loved her when he was preparing to kick her to the curb? If it were just sex he wanted, she would have given it to him.

It made no sense. Why go through all that they had for a "weak moment"? She had given him the perfect out, and he hadn't taken it. He had pushed and pushed until she fell in love. This was far worse than Casey, or even Kevin. What got to her the most was, deep down, she'd believed Ryder would hurt her all along, yet she'd gone willingly into his arms anyway.

Her stomach roiled as she thought about all the things she had done with him, all the things she had allowed him to do to her. No wonder he thought she was some cheap piece of meat. She had let him have his way with her. Men didn't respect women like that; they used them. The hurt and pain were not worth the momentary pleasure of what he'd offered.

Beads of sweat broke out on her forehead as she struggled to keep her emotions under wraps. No matter how hard she tried, she couldn't still the roller-coaster ride her stomach was taking. Rolling down her window, she pressed her head against the metal frame to allow the fresh breeze to graze her face. She felt physically ill. Although she hadn't eaten that much in the past twenty-four hours, what little she had eaten was threatening to make an appearance at any second now.

"Miss, are you okay?"

Shaking her head, Lydia clutched the side of the door, knowing she needed to purge. "Please pull over for a minute," she croaked out past dry lips. As soon as the car stopped, she pushed the door open and leaned over, just in time to retch violently. She was wrung completely out. Weakly she resumed her seat and closed the door before fishing a tissue out of her purse to wipe her mouth. "Okay, we can leave now."

As soon as she got home, she fell into her bed, then pulled the covers over her head. Hot, bitter tears fell freely.

The harder she tried to forget Ryder, the more she hurt. She'd heard about men like Ryder—emotional pariahs who enjoyed building people up only to shoot them down. He'd done a damn fine job of that.

Lydia cried until she had no more tears left, and then just lay there. It took too much energy to move. The phone rang almost nonstop for a while, before falling silent. There was no one she wanted to talk to. Besides, why would Ryder call now? His "weak moment" had passed.

Lydia drifted off to a restless sleep before being awakened by loud banging on her door.

"Lydia! Lydia, let me in!"

Ryder. What the hell was he doing here? Hadn't he hurt her enough? As much as she would've loved to wrench open the door and tell him off to his face, she had no words. She couldn't bear to face him. Maybe tomorrow, when she figured out what she was going to do. But not right now. She was just too tired.

The pounding and yelling stopped after a while, and she drifted back to sleep, but her dreams were haunted by the man who had trampled all over her heart and her pride: the playful, naughty Ryder on the island; the sincere Ryder at the office; the dark, passionate Ryder at home, had all been a charade. It was hard to reconcile the man with his words to his parents. By the time morning came, she was relieved, but she still couldn't work up the motivation to get out of her bed.

Some women nursed heartbreak with ice cream and chick flicks, but Lydia had never been one of those types. She wondered, as she lay, if they helped. After managing to crawl out of bed, she made her way to the refrigerator to see what type of ice cream she had in stock. There was a tub of unopened Chunky Monkey, but as soon as she opened it, the scent made her feel nauseated, and she raced to the toilet, where she dry heaved until she cried. Heartbreak sucked so bad.

It was a shame Sammy Jo was away. She had no one to discuss this with. Feeling weak, she knew if she continued to feel like this, there was no way she'd be able to make it to the office on Monday. Not that she was sure she wanted to go back at all.

No. She couldn't run away. Not again. She had let Casey do that to her; she wouldn't let Ryder do the same. Besides, as hurt and betrayed as she felt now, she wasn't really sure she wanted to move away. Not yet. How pathetic was that? She still cared. Her phone rang, but she didn't bother to answer, figuring it would be Ryder again. She plopped on the couch and listened to the answering machine pick up the call.

"Lydia, baby, if you're there, please pick up. I don't know why you left so abruptly, but please at least call me back to let me know that you're okay. Whatever is wrong, we can work it out. I love you." *Click.*

Liar.

She saw right through his act, and she wasn't playing along anymore. Lydia must have dozed once more, because she woke up to a voice on the answering machine again. "Lydia, sweetheart. It's Mom. Could you please call me back when you get a chance? It's been a long time, and I've been thinking about you, honey." *Click.*

She released a moan. Her head was throbbing, and her stomach still felt queasy. What did her mother want? She hadn't called in a few weeks. After the room stopped spinning, Lydia sat up, reached for the phone, and dialed her mother's number.

"Hello?" Rhonda Morris-Jackson-Fields-Waters answered on the second ring.

"Mom. It's me, Lydia."

"Oh hello, Lydia. I didn't think you'd call me back so quickly. I was heading out to the store for a minute. But I'm glad to hear your voice, sweetheart."

"Really?"

"I know we don't talk often, but I do think about you, honey. I actually called to ask if you wanted to come visit for a bit. I sure would love to see you."

It had been a few years since she'd last seen her mother face-to-face, and it had been awkward, with neither of them having much to say. "I, uh, I don't know, Mom. I've got a lot going on right now."

"Oh." The disappointment in her mother's voice zinged Lydia straight through the phone. "I understand, sweetheart. But when you get the chance, please visit."

Lydia felt like a jerk for fobbing off her mother, who was obviously trying to make an effort. "When my schedule winds down, I promise to come out."

"That sounds really nice, sweetheart."

They chatted for a few more minutes before hanging up. Not even a minute after Lydia replaced the phone on the receiver, it rang again. She glanced at the caller ID. *Ryder.* She waited for the answering machine to pick up.

"Lydia, me again. I'm really worried, baby. Please call. If I don't hear from you within an hour, I'm calling the police." *Click.*

Shit. She had to get out of here before Ryder made good on his threat, and there was no doubt in her mind he'd carry it out. If she called a cab to come get her, she could pack quickly while she was waiting. She'd have the driver take her back to work to pick up her car; then she'd call her mother to say she was coming.

Lydia couldn't face Ryder yet. She just wasn't strong enough.

Chapter Sixteen

Ryder was beside himself. How could she leave him without even a good-bye? She'd obviously snuck out the kitchen door. How she got home, he wasn't sure, but it worried the hell out of him that something had happened to make her run off the way she did. To compound the matter, she didn't answer his calls or the door when he'd gone over to her place. He'd made good on his promise to call the police, who'd gotten the condo manager to open her door, only to find she wasn't there.

When he'd driven by the office to see if her car was still in the parking lot, he discovered it was gone. It was as if she'd disappeared without a trace. Frantic with worry, he'd staked out the front of her condo, hoping to catch a glimpse of her, but she never showed up. By Monday he was a mess. He'd been unable to sleep a wink as he'd lain in bed wondering what might have happened to her. He didn't want to go in to the office but realized he had a few important meetings he couldn't put off.

Lydia didn't show up to work, and when he received a message from the office manager that she'd called in sick, his disappointment and worry increased. She was avoiding him. She had to be. Had his declaration of love freaked her out?

Or was it the way his parents had treated her? Whatever the reason, he was bewildered and hurt by her sudden disappearance. He'd never opened up to a woman the way he had with Lydia, and it was as if she'd thrown his feelings back in his face.

Somehow he made it through his conference calls and meetings and decided to head out early, a rarity for him. He was nearly out the door when someone called his name.

"Ryder?"

He stiffened. This was one person he could have done without seeing. He turned around to face the owner of the voice. Ever since he'd found out Casey and Lydia had history, he'd tried not to let his personal feelings get in the way of their professional dealings, but knowing just how badly he'd hurt Lydia—to the point where she was scared to share her heart with another man—made Ryder wanted to knock the other man out. Grasping at the calm he needed to deal with his employee, Ryder took a deep breath. "What can I do for you, Casey?"

"I see you're on your way out, but do you have a minute?"

After the day he had, talking to Casey Werth wasn't on the top of his list of priorities, but he had an open-door policy in his company. And he had always made it clear that any of his employees could come to him at any time.

"Sure. Walk with me to my car, if you don't mind."

"Not at all."

Ryder didn't bother to modify his strides for the shorter man, forcing Casey into a near trot. "Ryder, I really don't know how to put this, but is everything all right between us?"

They were in the parking lot now, only a few yards from Ryder's car, but he halted. "What do you mean?"

"Do you have a problem with me?"

Ryder raised a brow. "Should I have a problem with you?"

The other man flushed. "I don't think so, but I get the sense that you don't like me for some reason."

"And what exactly gives you that impression?"

"For one thing, you barely speak when we pass each other in the hall; you seem to look right through me in meetings. And when you do speak to me, it's with short, curt sentences."

What the hell was this? High school? "Listen, Werth. I'm a very busy man, and I have over fifty employees under me, and we're still growing. I don't have time to hand hold every single one of you. I expect you to do the job you're paid to do. And if you think I'm not giving you the attention you feel you need, then perhaps this isn't the agency for you."

Casey turned a bright shade of red to the roots of his auburn head. "That's just it. You haven't allowed me to do the job I believe I was hired for. When I interviewed with you, you told me there would be a few large accounts coming our way and because of my experience you wanted me on the team. You said I'd be working closely with you on the ones you took the lead on. So I was surprised when I wasn't even named a member of the team on the Rawlings account. I've basically been given projects that usually only the junior staff members would be handling. Is it because Lydia told you what I did?"

Ryder saw red. He didn't want this man to even speak Lydia's name, and that he'd so casually bring up what he did pissed Ryder off beyond words. The little prick. Forcing himself to remain calm, he clenched his fists at his sides. "She mentioned it, but what happened in the past is the past. I generally don't let personal issues get in the way of business."

"Then why? If it isn't because I stole Lydia's idea at PRL, then what?"

Ryder stiffened. "What did you say?"

Apparently sensing the imminent danger he was in, Casey took a step back. "Uh, you did say she mentioned it? That I presented an idea of hers as mine? Look, it's something I will never do again, and I've learn my lesson—Ugh!"

Casey wasn't allowed to finish before Ryder slammed his fist against the other man's face. "You weaselly son of a bitch! How could you do that to her? Do you know the damage you caused from what you did?"

Casey held his face. "I thought she told you." The whine of the other man's voice worked Ryder's last nerve.

"Obviously not. Get the fuck out of my sight before I kill you."

At least the other man wasn't dumb, because he scurried away, but not before he muttered a weak "sorry."

That wasn't well done of him, and hitting that bastard could possibly come back to bite him in the ass, but hearing what Casey had actually done to Lydia sent a rage shooting through Ryder the likes of which he'd never experienced. By the time he was behind the wheel of his vehicle, Ryder was seething. When he finally caught up with Lydia, she had a lot of explaining to do.

* * *

Lydia woke up to something damp and cool being pressed against her forehead. She groaned, pushing away another wave of nausea. When she tried to move, a hand gently grasped her shoulder and nudged her back down. "Stay where you are. If you make any sudden moves, you're bound to be dizzy."

Her eyes popped open. She wasn't in her own bed. It came back to her that she'd driven to her mother's the day before. It had surprised the hell out of her when she'd pulled up to the neat house in a middle-class suburb with identical manicured lawns and white picket fences. She had to look at the address her mother had given to verify this was the right place. It wasn't her childhood home. Rhonda had obviously done well for herself, and this was a far cry from the little apartment Lydia remembered.

Her mother had surprised her as well. Though it had been at least four years since they'd seen each other face-to-face, her mother hadn't seem to have age a bit. She was still a very attractive woman who looked to be in her late thirties, even though she was pushing fifty. But what had surprised Lydia most of all was the greeting. Rhonda had hugged and kissed her, telling her how glad she was to see her. She had never been this affectionate in all the years Lydia had lived under her roof. But Lydia had been in no condition to examine these changes in the older woman, because she'd felt like shit. During the entire three-hour ride here, she'd felt like throwing up, even though there was nothing in her belly. Her head was killing her, and she was irritable.

Rhonda had taken one look at her face and marched her daughter to bed, where she had spent the rest of the night taking care of her. If she weren't so sick, she might have thought her mother was snatched by aliens and replaced with a pod person. And now her mother sat at her bedside, rubbing her forehead with a damp cloth.

"How are you feeling, honey?"

Lydia licked her dry lips. "Who are you, and what have you done to my mother?"

Rhonda gave her a small, sad smile, guilt lurking just beneath the surface of eyes that looked so much like her own. What was this? Guilt from her mother? Surely it couldn't be true. Her mother had never once considered anyone other than herself. Lydia had to be seeing things.

"I haven't always been there for you, I know." Rhonda turned her head away, looking for all the world like she was battling tears.

"Try never." Lydia took a deep breath, knowing that hadn't come out right. Regardless of the past, it was obvious her mother felt bad about it. The least Lydia could do was hear her out. Too bad her stomach was in constant upheaval, her head ached, and she couldn't make up her mind whether she was starving or wanted to throw up.

Rhonda sighed, taking the cloth off Lydia's head and placing it in a bowl on the nightstand. Tears streaked down her face. "All I can say is I'm sorry. I have no excuse for ignoring you; none that would be enough, in any event. I willingly traded my daughter's well-being because I was so terrified of being alone. I never realized until it was too late that I was only running from myself, hiding from realities I didn't want to face. I was so busy trying to find someone to take care of me, I forgot to take care of you."

"You're damn right you did." All Lydia's hurt and anger came pouring out. "You have no idea what you've done, do you? I question my choices in men because of you. I'm scared to open up to people, and it's hard for me to trust, because the one person who was supposed to always be there for me was always too caught up in the current man in her life." Tears flowed freely down her face now.

Rhonda lowered her lashes, but not before Lydia caught a glimpse of shame in the other woman's eyes. "And I'm so sorry, Lydia. You mean the world to me. I just never realized it until it was too late. I've done a lot of soul-searching since Mark was sent away to prison. I took a long look at my life, and I didn't like what I saw. It's then I discovered that not only did I no longer know who I was but I also didn't have a relationship with you. I wanted to get myself together, not only for me but for you as well. I've spent the last few years bettering myself, and for the first time in my life, I love me. I've learned to stand on my own two feet, and I love it. Not to say that if the right man comes along, I won't give love a shot. I'll just be more careful."

The declaration left Lydia feeling more uncomfortable than she liked. It kind of took the wind right out of her sails. Everything she had been ready to accuse her mother of, Rhonda had just admitted on her own. Lydia didn't want to let go of her anger, though. She needed it to get through the pain Ryder had inflicted. At least that was what she told herself.

When had her life turned to shit? She had worked so hard not to become her mother after the fiasco with Kevin. And what had she gotten for it? A boatload of heartache and not much else.

"I'm sorry for being so surly, Mom." She sighed, closing her eyes. "I just… I don't feel very well. But I'm glad to hear things are going well for you."

Rhonda gave a low laugh that wasn't really mirthful. "I deserve your anger. I will be the first to admit that. I placed my marriages above my baby. You have every right to be resentful. Ironically I thought I was providing you with a stable home. What I didn't realize was that you needed me more than anything."

"I see." The steady parade of stepfathers had been anything but stabilizing, but at least she could understand her mother's point of view a little better.

"I can't blame you if you don't believe this, but I do love you. Look, Lydia. I got pregnant at sixteen. My parents were very disappointed, especially when shortly after you were born, your father took off. My mother kept saying it was my fault. She said that if I hadn't been so loose to begin with, maybe my first husband would have respected me."

Lydia raised a brow. "You never talked about my father like this before. You were always so vague about him, I just assumed you didn't know who he was."

Rhonda grimaced. "I should have been up front with you, I know, but I was so ashamed. In my mind, I believed I was saving you from the heartache of knowing your father didn't want to be a part of your life. But deep down, I knew it was me he didn't want."

Lydia's heart went out to the scared sixteen-year-old her mother had probably been. Strangely she didn't feel this sudden need to go find her father. That time had passed, but out of curiosity she had to ask. "Do you know where he is now?"

"I'm sorry, sweetheart, but he passed away ten years ago in a car accident. I should have told you about him."

The pain in her mother's voice was so pronounced, so real, Lydia found herself drawn into the world in which the older woman must have lived. Things she had never understood started to click into place. "It's okay." Lydia couldn't bring herself to be mad.

"I never wanted my life for you, which is why I tried to push you to meet life on your own terms, not someone else's." Rhonda kept going, only this time she met Lydia's gaze head-on, the earnestness of her words shining through. "I probably managed to mess even that up. I knew on an intellectual level what I was doing wasn't healthy. I knew I would never really be happy marrying anyone who would have me without taking the time to see if we were in the least bit compatible, but every time a marriage failed, my mother's words came back to haunt me."

Suddenly not ever seeing her grandparents made a whole lot of sense. Lydia trembled; man, was she grateful her mother had the foresight to keep her away from such simpleminded people. "I didn't realize."

"My parents were from a different era, when family meant a mother and a father. My mother never understood times had marched on and sometimes it was better to be alone for the right reasons than be with someone for all the wrong ones. They basically disowned me when I didn't marry your father. Not that he was marriage minded anyway." The older woman smiled down at Lydia tenderly. She felt the love for her pouring off her mother. A love she had never felt when she was a child. It was impossible to reject it, not after she had hungered for it for so long. "You will be a better mother than me. We'll work on it together."

Lydia had to laugh out loud at that one. For one thing, her polycystic ovary syndrome made pregnancy unlikely to begin with. Though her symptoms weren't as bad as some women with her condition, her periods were few and far between. One year, she hadn't menstruated at all. When she'd asked her doctor about it, she'd been informed that her chances of conceiving were slim to none.

Then there was the fact Lydia sincerely doubted she would ever trust a man enough to even try. "I'm sorry to tell you, Mom, but you're probably never going to have grandchildren." Funny, she had never felt sad about it until now. Although in the last couple of weeks she had secretly allowed herself to visualize little green-eyed, golden-skinned babies with Ryder's devious smile. Yet another indication of how foolish she had been.

"Oh, so you've decided not to keep it?" Rhonda's eyes got round and troubled. "Oh, Lydia, I really wish you'd reconsider. I've managed to work myself through nursing school; I'm a certified RN now. I can help you. I would love to do that. There is plenty of room here. Together, we can give this baby a much better life than either you or I had. I know we can. Oh, honey, please think about this carefully."

Lydia stared at her mother as if she were speaking Japanese. What the hell did she mean by that? Keep what? "No! I'm sick; I'm not pregnant. I can't be." A full-blown panic settled deep into her bones. It just wasn't possible. Life couldn't be this cruel. She had the flu. Plus, she was heartsick. The combination was knocking her off her ass, not anything else.

"Lydia, have you actually taken a pregnancy test?" Rhonda prodded gently. Just to stop her mother's nagging, she jackknifed off the bed and swung her legs over the side. A wave of dizziness promptly knocked her right back on her ass.

It didn't prove anything. "I'm not pregnant." This just could not get any worse.

"I'll tell you what"—Rhonda sounded as if she were talking to a recalcitrant three-year-old—"if you aren't feeling any better in a couple of days, we'll get you a test, just to make sure, okay?"

"Fine, but I'm not pregnant."

Two days later while driving back to Austin, Lydia found she had to face facts. Her mother was right. She was carrying Ryder's child. There was absolutely no question she was keeping it. She loved the tiny person inside her with a passion that almost scared her. The question was how to handle this.

At least one good thing had come out of all this mess. She had gotten the mother she never had...maybe. They would have to take it slow and get to know one another, but

Lydia felt a glimmer of hope. The bigger question was whether she should tell Ryder. Even if he had just been experimenting—according to his words to his parents—he still had a right to know.

She wasn't the kind of coldhearted bitch who would hold his child hostage, if by some miracle he actually wanted a relationship with her or him. For all she knew, he might complain and even accuse her of trying to get his money. But she wouldn't ask him for a dime.

Lydia would tell him, but everything was still so new to her. She needed to get used to the idea herself. She just had to be careful and keep it hidden until the Rawlings account wrapped up. With the bonus as a lead on this account, she could move closer to her mother. No point in tempting fate by living together. Lydia had been on her own for far too long.

She would work hard to find another job as quickly as possible, to support herself and her child. And if Ryder ever wanted to visit, that was his choice.

The first inkling of doubt filtered through the fog of her pain. Not for the first time, she wondered why he would say the cruel things he'd said about her behind her back after confessing his love. Maybe she had misread the situation. No, there was nothing wrong with her hearing. She'd heard what she'd heard. Simple as that.

Chapter Seventeen

Ryder watched and waited for a chance to corner Lydia, but she was becoming way too adept at avoiding him. She'd returned to the office on Wednesday morning, apparently, but he'd been out of town for an overnight trip to meet with a distributor.

When he'd returned on Thursday, he found himself right back where he'd started with her before they'd gone away to the resort. Square one. Part of him wanted to demand she talk to him, but he couldn't bring himself to use strong-arm tactics. He wanted her to want to come to him, without his badgering her. Yet the more she ignored him, the more he hurt. The pain of losing her and not knowing why was killing him. She acted as if they hadn't shared something special, and it hurt unlike anything he'd ever experienced.

Of course with the Rawlings account, she had to speak to him, but she kept conversation at a bare minimum and didn't stray beyond work-related issues. Soon the project would be moving to the production team, and he wouldn't be working that closely with her anymore until the next big project he decided to put her on.

He'd called her several times, had even gone by her condo, but to no avail. It was as if he was persona non grata. By Friday he couldn't take it anymore. He had to know why. Ryder had tried to give her space, but the sleepless nights were getting to him and affecting his business like nothing else ever had. He snapped at and was short with anyone who crossed his path. He couldn't deal with clients without zoning out, and he'd been in such a foul mood this morning, Donna had walked away from her desk in tears.

He felt like shit and realized he couldn't go another day without confronting Lydia. His resolve to have her come to him had vanished. As he walked out of his office, Donna called out to him. "Ryder."

He paused. "Yes?"

"Thank you for the flowers. It means a lot, and yes, I accept your apology."

He smiled. After he'd seen how he'd upset the woman who'd been his right hand almost from the time he'd started the company, he knew he had to fix things. So he'd called a local florist to have a large arrangement sent to her immediately. He'd had a card added that simply said, *Sorry for being a jackass. Ryder.*

"You're welcome. I'm glad you like them. And again, I didn't mean to talk to you the way I did this morning. It's been a challenging week."

The redhead nodded. "I know how you feel. My husband can be like a bear with a sore head if things don't go his way at work, so I'm used to it. Normally I would have taken your lousy mood in stride, but I guess it's been an all-around miserable time in my life right now." She sighed.

Ryder hadn't had a chance to talk to his assistant on a personal level for a while, and he felt bad for not giving her the attention he once had. He valued her as more than just his assistant, but as a friend. “Is everything okay, Donna?”

“It's just that they're having layoffs at Jeff's company, and he's worried that he'll be next. My oldest was accepted into an expensive private college, my middle child wants to study abroad, and my youngest needs braces.” She gave a humorless laugh. “Life sometimes has a way of kicking you when you're down.”

“I'm sure things will work out for you. Jeff works in accounting, right? If he's laid off, I could hook him up with a few of my contacts in that industry.”

Donna grinned. “Bless your heart. Hopefully it won't come to that, but I certainly appreciate the offer. Oh, and by the way, the Sanderson Group wants to reschedule your meeting from Tuesday next week to Monday, same time. I told them I'd call to confirm once I spoke to you.”

“That should be fine. Thanks again, Donna. I'll be away from my desk for the next hour or so.”

“No problem, boss.”

As he walked away, he made a note to give her a significant increase in salary. The agency was doing well and was projected to do even better in the coming months. Besides, Donna deserved it.

Ryder found Lydia in conversation with one of the team members on the Rawlings account. She was so into what she was saying that she didn't notice his approach. He took a second to observe her. Something was different about her today. Her hair, which was usually piled or twisted into a bun, was pulled back with a red ribbon to match her short-sleeved knee-length dress. She was absolutely gorgeous. But it wasn't her hairstyle. There was something about her he couldn't quite put his finger on.

Amelia noticed he was standing there first, and stopped talking. “Hi, Ryder.” She beamed.

Ryder saw Lydia's body stiffen. She kept her back to him, however. He nodded. “Amelia. How's the project coming along?”

Amelia sidled next to him, a bit closer than he was comfortable with. She was the office flirt, and he'd never minded before, because she got the job done. But with Lydia standing only a few feet away, he didn't like the way her scarlet-tipped nails curled around his arm. “Everything is going great. We've been in contact with Jasper Rawlings, who's very pleased with our progress, and if all goes well, we should be sending this to the production team next week.”

“Good. That's what I want to hear. Amelia, could you please excuse us? I'd like to have a private word with Lydia.”

The blonde poked her bottom lip out in a pout that made her look childish rather than the sexy she was probably going for. “Okay. See you later.” She walked off, but Ryder didn't spare her another glance.

Lydia kept her back to him. “Did you want to talk about the Rawlings account?”

“Would you at least look at me?”

She huffed before turning around. There were bags under her eyes, he noticed for the first time. Was she not sleeping either, from thinking of him? "What can I do for you?"

"I think you should take a walk with me on the path by the pond everyone seems so fond of using."

"I hardly think that's necessary to talk business."

"But I wasn't interested in talking business, and unless you'd like the entire office to know some very personal details about us, I suggest you take that walk with me."

She folded her arms across her chest and pursed her lips. "Blackmail, Ryder? Is it really that serious?"

"Obviously it is. I think you owe me an explanation for your little disappearing act on Saturday. Now let's go."

Her nostrils flared. "Fine." She walked past him, forcing him to lengthen his strides to catch up with her.

Lydia knew she'd have to speak with him sooner or later. She might as well do it now, even though she'd die before she admitted to him what she'd overheard. The hurt was still raw, and she could barely bring herself to look him in the face after he'd completely duped her into believing they had something real. He wasn't the man she believed he was. Once they were on the walking path, they went a few yards before Ryder broke the uneasy silence between the two of them. "So are you going to tell me what the problem is, or do I have to read your mind?"

"You're the one who wanted this talk, not me."

"Don't give me that shit. I fucking pour my heart out to you, and you basically throw it all back in my face by leaving without an explanation. Do you know how I felt when I realized you'd left?"

Was he kidding? After what he'd said, why the hell would he care whether she stuck around, unless he was just the type of guy who couldn't stand losing? It dawned on her that Ryder wasn't upset that she'd left, but that he wasn't the one to tell her to leave. It sickened her to think she'd given herself to such a whack job. Thank God she hadn't told him she loved him—that would have made things worse. "Look, Ryder. I was hoping you wouldn't make such a big deal about it, but I think this little thing we had…well, it's run its course. At least for me it has."

All color drained from his face, leaving him pale beneath his sun-kissed skin. "What?"

"Oh come on, Ryder. Let's be adult about this. You've wanted to get into my pants since I started working here. And I was wary at first because I wasn't looking for any romantic entanglement. But you were persistent. I was horny, and you were a good lay. I figured if I wanted to get laid, I'd play along with your little game. But on Saturday I had an epiphany."

His chest visibly rose and fell; his lips thinned to an angry white line. "And what was that?"

"That beyond sex, there's really nothing I want from you. And I could probably get good sex from any number of places without having to deal with the mushy stuff."

"The hell you will!" He looked like he'd explode like Mount Vesuvius. Taking her by the forearm, Ryder hauled her against him. "What the hell has gotten into you? You aren't the loving, sensitive woman I fell in love with."

She laughed harshly. "I don't know who you think I am, but it sounds to me like you've built a fantasy in your head. There's nothing between us beyond sex, and the sooner you realize that, the sooner you can move on as I have. I'm not ready for any heavy involvement. My main focus is on my career, and I hope you don't make things difficult for me because of this."

His eyes narrowed, and his fingers dug into her arms, making Lydia gasp. "Do you think I have so little integrity that I'd allow our relationship to get in the way of business?"

"You tell me, Ryder. I noticed Casey has a black eye. I wonder how that happened? What's the matter? Are you upset because he had me first? Or maybe you're upset because he actually might be a better lover than you?"

"If you think..." Just as quickly as it had appeared, the fire went out in his eyes, and he released her arms and took a step back with narrowed eyes. "What game are you playing, Lydia?"

She moistened her lips with the tip of her tongue. "I don't know what you're talking about."

"You almost had me fooled, but you laid it on pretty thick. A little too thick. Why are you trying to make me hate you? There's something going on here. Call me conceited if you'd like, but there's no way you could respond to me the way you did without feeling a little something for me. What are you so scared of?"

Why was he pushing her to admit feelings for him after what he'd said? Was this some twisted game of his to get her to spill her soul to him and, when she did, he'd laugh in her face? She couldn't be around him for another second. "Look, you're making this harder for me than it should be. We never should have gotten involved. Once the Rawlings project is sent to the production team, it's best I leave Garrison's."

"What are you saying, Lydia?"

"I'm saying consider this my two weeks' notice. And I'd appreciate if you didn't speak to me again unless its business related." She turned on her heel, feeling absolutely sick to her stomach, but most of all to her heart. With tears blinding her, she took off as fast as her legs could carry her. She need not have run, because Ryder didn't follow.

Chapter Eighteen

Ryder gulped the entire contents of his whiskey glass, wincing at the burn of the fiery liquid sliding down his throat. Lydia was leaving the agency and walking out of his life. He could have run after her, could have held her in his arms, could have kissed her until she melted, but it didn't change the fact that she wanted to leave the agency. Leave him. How had something so beautiful gone so terribly wrong?

Everything had been going great until his parents showed up. He wondered if meeting them had scared her off. It was a possibility, but then he dismissed it. He'd made it clear to her what his parents thought didn't matter to him. It had to be something, though, but what? Hell, he was too damn drunk to figure it out. He grabbed the whiskey bottle and took a swig, bypassing the glass altogether this time.

"Ryder!"

Mickey.

He should have known his sister would put in an appearance when he didn't return any of her calls. "Don't you ever knock? I think I'm going to ask for my house key back if you keep showing up unannounced."

She placed her hands on her hips and glared at him. "Well, if you would have answered the door when I rang the bell, maybe I wouldn't have needed to use my key."

"Didn't want any company." He slurred his words.

"What the hell is the matter with you? You're a mess, and you're drunk."

"There's no law against a man having a few drinks in his own home."

Mickey crinkled her nose in her disgust. "Looks to me as if you've had way more than a few. I see you're not bothering to use a glass. Does Lydia know you have these drunken binges?"

"I don't have binges. And I doubt Lydia would give a damn if I drank myself to death. She'd probably cheer me along."

"What are you talking about? Don't tell me there's trouble in paradise already."

"Paradise was just an illusion, it seems. Lydia has decided she wants nothing more to do with me, and to underline her point, she's given me two weeks' notice."

"What? You're kidding, right? You two were so cute together. I've never seen you so happy before. What happened?" She took a seat on the couch next to him, pried the bottle from his hand, and placed it out of his reach.

"Hell if I know. Everything seemed to be going great, and then boom. She was gone."

"Whoa, slow down. Tell me exactly what happened."

Ryder ran his fingers through his hair in frustration. "That's the thing. I don't know what the hell happened.

Admittedly it took some convincing for Lydia and me to get to the point where she would admit she was interested in me beyond sex."

"Uh, do I want to hear the rest of this?"

"Hey, do you want me to tell you what happened or what?"

"Sorry. Go on."

"Everything seemed to be going fine. And then last weekend when you brought Freddy Krueger and Cruella de Vil by, I sent her upstairs to wait for me. But when the three of you left, she was gone—sneaked out the back door. And she didn't show up for work for a couple of days, which isn't like her. She hasn't called out once since she'd started. When she came back, it was like talking to a cold stranger.

"Lydia said some pretty hurtful things, and the next thing I know, she's throwing her resignation at me. I was floored. I don't know what happened in between the time I told her to wait for me until the time she left without a word. I mean, the way she spoke to me made me think she's hiding something and she doesn't want to tell me what. I'm not crazy to think she had feelings for me too, but why the about-face, I don't know."

"If you think she's still in love with you, then why aren't you over at her place trying to get to the bottom of it?"

"Don't you think I've tried to? She won't tell me, and I'm not going to use sex as a weapon. I want her to tell me instead of me having to force it out of her."

"That's understandable, but maybe she's been hurt before and she's cautious."

"She has, and she is. Too damn cautious. I don't see why I have to pay for what a couple of dickheads did to her. It's bad enough I employed one of them, and he serves as a constant reminder of the wall Lydia keeps putting between us."

"You hired one of her ex-boyfriends?"

"Didn't know it at the time. Can't stand seeing the son of a bitch around the office knowing what he did to her. But it's not like I can fire him without possibly facing a huge lawsuit. I'm lucky he didn't press charges when I punched him in the face."

"Oh, Ryder, you didn't."

"He had it coming. Although I should have kept my hands to myself. He's been avoiding me like the plague lately, and that's just fine with me."

"Hmm, just be careful. You never know what the future holds. He could still very well hold this against you."

He shrugged. "Guess we'll see. Not that it matters. Lydia won't be with the company for much longer anyway."

"And you're just going to let her quit like that?"

"What choice do I have? I can't force her to work for me if she doesn't want to."

"There has to be more to it. Lydia doesn't seem like the type to inflict pain needlessly. I definitely didn't get that vibe from her. Do you think Phil and Liz scared her off?"

Ryder raised a brow. "Since when did you start referring to the parental units by their first names?"

"Since I realized what a couple of backward bigots they are. I especially didn't appreciate their lecturing me the entire way home, but to bring it up in front of the twins..." She shuddered. "Those aren't the values I'd like to teach them. Graham wasn't particularly happy about being told who he should and shouldn't allow in his home. I felt as if I'd taken a step back into the fifties. I told them they had to leave. They weren't too happy about it, but I'm tired of it."

"Wow. And you were the good one." Ryder chuckled.

"I'm serious, Ryder. All my life I did the right things, said the right things, according to them. I even participated in those stupid pageants because Mom wanted me to, even though I hated them. As I sat there listening to them spew that nonsense, I realized I didn't really give a shit what they thought about me anymore."

"Well, hallelujah, Little Sis, join the club. So do they no longer have a daughter either?"

"Not sure. They didn't say, but Phil and Liz wouldn't look me in the eyes when they left. Oh well. The sad thing is, they really do seem to love the kids, and they treated them well. The twins will miss their grandparents, but at least they still have Graham's parents, who are really sweet people." She sighed. "I got an idea. If Lydia won't tell you what the matter is, maybe she'll tell me."

Ryder groaned, then pushed himself from the couch and stood up. "No, thanks. I don't need my kid sister to fix my problems."

"Stop being so damn stubborn. I'm not trying to fix your problems, just trying to help. Besides, where you failed, I may succeed in getting the information from her; at the very least I can see if I can read between the lines. What do you say? Let me talk to Lydia."

He was tempted, but what would Lydia think if he sent his sister over? She'd probably cuss him out. But then again, this not knowing was killing him. “I might regret this, but okay. I'll give you the address. But try not to be pushy, okay?”

Mickey gave him a lopsided grin. “You have nothing to worry about. I'll take care of it.”

Her assurance did him absolutely no good.

* * *

“I don't know what to do.” Lydia forced back the tears that threatened to fall as she cradled the phone to her ear. “Mom, he sounded like he was mad at *me*. Like I did something wrong.”

Rhonda was quiet for so long, Lydia began to think maybe the connection had been cut off. “Lydia, honey, are you sure you heard what you think you heard?” It was said with gentle admonishment.

“I was right there. I heard him loud and clear. Maybe I shouldn't have been eavesdropping, but I'm glad I did. At least now I know what he really thinks about me. I just don't get why he keeps bothering me.”

There was another stretch of silence before Rhonda sighed. Lydia really didn't like the sound of that sigh. It made her feel like a child who had just declared she didn't care whether people believed that Santa Claus wasn't real. Taking a deep breath, she forced herself to relax her tone, even if she was still in turmoil. “Maybe he thinks I'm an easy mark.”

"He doesn't sound like a man who would say something so vicious," Rhonda argued. "Not if he is still trying to get you to talk to him."

"Or maybe he's one of those types who can't stand not being the center of everyone's attention. It doesn't matter anyway; I'll be out of here soon enough. I'll be down this weekend to start looking at places for rent until I can find something more permanent."

"You know I have plenty of room. I don't know why you have to get a place of your own."

She really didn't think that was a good idea. Her relationship with her mother might be on the mend, but Lydia didn't want to push her luck. "I've been on my own too long to move in with my mother."

"With a baby on the way, you need to think about saving money. Trust me. Kids are expensive."

"I'll think about it." It was all she could give her mother at the moment. There were so many things she needed to sort out, but she was just too tired to get into it right now. After promising her mother she'd call again soon, Lydia sank down into her plush couch, trying to block out the world. She felt drained; maybe a quick nap would help.

She groaned as someone continuously pounded on her door. It seemed like Ryder had gotten his second wind and was back to torment her a little more. She honestly couldn't understand him. If all he wanted was to cross cultural lines, there were plenty of other women who'd be all too happy to do that for him.

Why he was fixated on her was a mystery. She really didn't need any more of his lies. She had enough on her plate. With resolve she didn't have earlier when he had cornered her, she stomped over to the door, determined to give him a true piece of her mind now that they were away from the office. How dare he think he could talk about her like she was less than he was and expect to crawl back into her bed? She might still love him, heaven help her, but she wouldn't be his fool.

"Why don't you just leave me alone?" she barked before her face turned hot as she saw who had been pounding. This was the last person she had expected. Ryder had sent his little sister after her? What was with this family anyway?

"Wow, and here I thought we got along pretty well." Mickey offered her a sunny smile that was impossible to resist. "May I come in, or am I banished like my brother?"

Lydia didn't want to have a conversation with Mickey. She was part of this whole thing, and Lydia's pride was in the dirt. Lydia didn't think she would ever be able to honestly say she was over Ryder, but she couldn't take any more of the push and pull. Plus, she felt like stir-fried shit right now. The term "morning sickness" was grossly mislabeled. It was more like morning, noon, and night sickness, as far as she could tell. The last thing she wanted or needed was Ryder's sister pleading his case.

"This won't take long." Mickey pushed her way into Lydia's condo. "Plus, I brought margarita mix and some to-die-for steak nachos. We can have some girl talk and stuff our faces."

As Mickey walked past her, the aroma of fresh Mexican food wafted up, hitting Lydia square in the face. Her stomach rebelled almost instantly. She tried choking down the sickness threatening to overwhelm her. Lydia moved quickly to the side, waving a hand in front of her face. It didn't work. She felt the upheaval and knew there wasn't a thing she could do to keep it down.

"Excuse me, I—" She couldn't finish. Lydia made a beeline for the bathroom, where she promptly lost her lunch.

"Lydia, are you okay?" Mickey was right there behind her; thankfully she'd put the food down somewhere. "Are you sick? Can I do anything?"

"I'm fine." Lydia waved the woman away, rinsing out her mouth and splashing some cool water on her face. She knew from experience, now that she'd given up the contents of her stomach, she would feel downright chipper for a little while. And hungry. Just not for Mexican food, and the margaritas were a definite no-no. "Just give me a second and I'll be right out."

"Oh. Okay, sure."

Lydia didn't need to look at Mickey to see the other woman was confused and more than a little suspicious. She probably thought Lydia was on drugs. Given the way Ryder and her parents had sounded, it was something they would all expect. Squaring her shoulders, she marched back into her small living room. Mickey had made herself right at home. Two heaping plates full of nachos were waiting on the coffee table, alongside two tall margaritas. She'd never cared for the mixed kind, preferring the frozen ones more, but she couldn't drink it anyway.

"Uh, thanks, but I can't—don't drink." Lydia frantically searched for a plausible reason. "I'm, uh, trying to lose weight."

Mickey looked at her oddly but seemed to accept the excuse. Patting the sofa, the vivacious blonde grinned broadly. “We don't need alcohol to have a little girl talk. Come on. I promise I won't bite. So what's been going on with you lately?”

Lydia's head began to pound. She so didn't need this right now. All she wanted to do was take a little nap. Eyeing the nachos, she was mildly surprised they no longer made her feel sick. In fact, they looked kind of delicious, and she was suddenly starving. Shrugging, she sat, allowing Mickey to put the plate in her lap. The thick, juicy strips of steak looked so good. Lydia starting downing the food before she realized what she was doing.

“Guess I was hungrier than I thought,” she offered upon seeing Mickey's bemused stare.

“So do you want to talk about it?” Mickey didn't beat around the bush, but didn't come right out and say it either.

A fresh wave of anger washed over Lydia. What was wrong with Ryder? Why send his sister? Hadn't he done enough? Lydia put the plate down and faced Mickey head-on. The quicker this was over, the quicker she could get some sleep. Games were one thing she didn't have time for.

“What is it with your family?” Lydia demanded. “I really don't get it. What more could Ryder possibly want? I would have thought he'd be glad I walked away on my own and didn't take anything from his house or cause a scene when he was done playing around.”

“Oh man, you heard Phil and Liz, didn't you?”

Lydia blinked at the other woman. *Phil and Liz? Not Mom and Dad?*

"Yeah, I heard them, all right," Lydia muttered, looking away. Tears she had been forcing back all day burned in her eyes. She couldn't afford to let them fall now. She leaned back against the cushions and closed her eyes, working on getting a hold on her emotions. It was hell having to do this all the time. All it took was a freaking commercial, and she was bawling like a baby these days. "Look, it doesn't matter. Ryder and I are over. They should be happy. And not once did I manage to bring my homies over to rip him off."

She knew she sounded bitter, but damn it, Ryder's sister had invaded her home. Mickey should have left well enough alone. It was true she hadn't heard Mickey speak derogatorily about her, but she had heard that damning giggle from Mickey during her brother's rant.

"Ryder and I aren't like that at all." Mickey's words had Lydia seeing red.

"Not like that? Really? So when he said I was a 'weak moment' on his part, or when he said he just wanted to find out what it was like to be with someone like me, was that supposed to be a compliment? Being compared to a rap video was some sort of declaration of love?" Getting to her feet, Lydia pointed toward her door. "I don't know what you people are playing at, but I want no part of it. Just leave me the hell alone."

Mickey didn't get up to leave. She didn't even move. She just stared, her mouth hanging open. Dread started to creep up Lydia's spine. Mickey was looking at her like she'd lost her mind.

"Lydia, Ryder was being sarcastic when he said that. He defended you. He kicked Phil and Liz out right after that."

The blonde looked absolutely incredulous. "He loves you, and he told them so. How could you even think he would ever mean something so-so"—she shook her head—"I don't even know what. I thought you were deeper than that. I thought you actually cared for my brother enough to at least give him a chance to explain himself. How could you have spent any time with him at all and not known he would never seriously say something like that?" Mickey rose to her feet.

Lydia's righteous indignation dissolved into horrified contrition. Her head spun as she watched Mickey move toward the door. What had she done? She tried to remember how he'd sounded that morning, but all she could remember were the words. Those words had cut into her and twisted, bringing on pain like she'd never known. Instead of demanding an explanation, she'd run, placing Ryder in the same box she'd put Casey and Kevin.

And why? The answer was more uncomfortable than the truth. In her mind, all men were the same. She had been as intolerant as his parents. Because she had been badly hurt in the past, she expected it. Even though she loved Ryder, Lydia had believed the worst of him at the first sign of trouble.

Ryder would never have done that to her. He would have asked her what the matter was. In fact, when she had tried to push him away, he hadn't believed she was capable of the callousness she had placed on him. Racist was something Ryder was not, yet she had readily believed it. Not only believed it but held on to it. She had planned on leaving without telling him why because she was a blind fool.

"By the way." Mickey sounded bitter and disgusted, and Lydia couldn't really blame her if what she had said was true. It's true; you know it is. You've always known, her heart spoke back to her. "Were you ever going to tell my brother you're pregnant?"

Lydia's mouth fell open. "I'm not..." Her first instinct was to deny it but she realized how foolish that would be.

Mickey's eyes shot blue fire. "So you weren't going to tell him? Well, you'd better, because if you don't, I will. Just because you've decided to use what you overheard as an excuse to dump him doesn't give you license to keep his child away from him."

"I was going to tell him, but I was just getting used to the idea myself and—"

"Save it. I've got your number, Lydia. You would have found an excuse to dump my brother eventually, wouldn't you? Because you're a coward. An emotional coward who is so scared and caught up in your own insecurities, you're willing to hurt someone who would give you the world if he could."

Lydia moved her mouth to speak, but nothing came out. Mickey's words were like bullets hitting their target square on the bull's-eye.

Mickey, however, wasn't finished. "Guess what, Lydia? My brother can't walk on water. He's not perfect, nor will he ever be, but he's someone who will love you with all he has, and if you can't see that, then not only are you not the woman I thought you were when we met, you don't deserve him."

Lydia could no longer meet the blonde's gaze, shaking from head to toe in her shame.

“You have a week. Seven days and I'm telling him. Maybe if you stopped looking for reasons not to be with him, you could see my brother loves you. Don't be a fucking idiot and throw it away.” She didn't slam the door, but the gentle *click* was indictment enough.

Chapter Nineteen

Ryder quickened his pace as he saw Lydia running out of the office behind him. She had been trying to talk to him all day. There was a time when he would have welcomed her attention—hell, he had worked his ass off for it—but that was before Mickey had come over last night. He had been prepared to engage in yet another pity party, getting stinking drunk so he could pass out without dreams of the woman he loved haunting him. However, when Mickey had told him why Lydia had run from him, he saw red. That Lydia could believe he was some asshole who believed that garbage made his blood boil. She'd just assumed he was no better than Phil and Liz, when she should've known better.

They had spent more than enough time together for Lydia to know who he was. There was nothing he held back from her. It had always been Lydia who kept a part of herself from him. He felt like she had been biding her time, waiting for him to screw up. Who the hell could survive a test like that? The woman had ripped out his heart and walked all over it, and he was supposed to, what? Take it? He was tired of tiptoeing around her issues.

He had jumped through hoops for that woman, bent over backward to show her he was for real, and she had believed the worst at the first drop of a hat. If it had been any other woman, he would be able to move on without looking back, but it wasn't any other woman. It was Lydia. As mad as he was with her right now, he still loved her. He had every intention of working this thing out, but just not now. He was still too raw, too hurt. Let her do the running for a while. Lord knew she had put him through his paces.

He understood more about Lydia than perhaps she even did. She had been hurt badly, so she expected to be hurt again. The thing was, he had worked hard to prove to her he wasn't like that. The woman was a head case, but damn if he could stop thinking about her.

"Ryder! Wait!"

Halting at his vehicle door, he coolly watched her approach. There were circles under her eyes, her mouth drawn down into a straight line. His pain seemed to be echoed in her eyes. His heart lurched as she got closer. It looked like she hadn't been sleeping at all, and she was losing weight.

Ryder wanted to reach out and pull her to him, bury his hands in her locs and hold her close, but he couldn't do that. Although he wanted nothing more than to comfort her, Lydia needed to learn an important lesson. Not every man was out to mess her over. He wasn't that jackass Casey or the nightmare Kevin. He refused to be treated like he was.

"What is it, Lydia? I'm late for…something." There, let her think whatever she wanted. It was after six; he rarely made appointments at night. He was throwing out a test to see if once again she would readily believe the worst. They couldn't have a relationship if she weren't willing to trust him. This wouldn't work otherwise.

"Oh, um, I just needed to talk to you—"

"Is this business related?" He cut her off. He wasn't ready for a heart-to-heart.

"No, it's about us."

"I'm afraid I don't have time. Besides, you said there was no us, right? I would think you'd be glad I've finally given up."

Not waiting for her reply, he quickly climbed into his car. He couldn't look back. If he saw that wounded look he knew was on her face, he wouldn't have the strength to drive away. He hated hurting her, and he knew he had, but damn it, he hurt too. She had taken his words of love and devotion and thrown them back at him without stopping to think of what it was doing to him. Why was he always the one giving? This was one time Lydia was going to have to do the chasing.

It dawned on him that she might not. She had absolutely no experience going after a man. She was just as likely to give up. As much as it scared him, he knew what he was doing was right. He was setting her free, so that if she chose to be with him, he would be the happiest man on earth. But it had to be her choice, and he couldn't make it easy.

* * *

Lydia watched Ryder's car fade into the distance. For two straight days he had avoided her. He had stayed away from his office, except when dealing directly with clients.

Ryder tended to stay in a group of senior account reps. He even went to lunch with a crowd. There was no way to talk to him unless she wanted the world to know how stupid she'd been. Maybe that's what he wanted. A public mea culpa. She would do that and more, if only he'd let her talk to him.

Lydia had no doubt Mickey had told him what she thought he'd said. Her reaction played back in her mind and seemed so overwrought in hindsight. She'd been ready to bail on him because she was overly sensitive and mistrustful. She deserved his scorn. She loved him so much, it hurt, and she had ruined it, allowing pride and ghosts of her past to stomp out the hope of having a future with a great guy.

Mickey had been right; she was an emotional coward. She couldn't allow this to end, at least not without telling Ryder how she felt.

Yes, she'd made a mistake, but there had to be a way to make it right. She had worked her ass off to get a degree, to buy her own home; surely this couldn't be as hard? And if it were, it was worth it. She turned and strode to her car, back straight with determination. She would win him back, no matter what she had to do.

* * *

She pulled up to Ryder's driveway, her heart racing a mile a minute. She was taking a chance that he'd gone home straight from the office. Lydia breathed a sigh of relief when she saw his Escalade parked in the driveway. When she made her way to the door, she raised her hand to ring the doorbell, only to have the door opened abruptly.

He was dressed casually in a pair of jeans that molded his muscular thighs so well, her mouth went dry. His buttoned-up shirt was rolled up to the elbow, and the first two buttons were undone revealing his tanned throat and a light dusting of dark blond hair over his chest. He looked good enough to eat. She didn't realize she'd been staring until he cleared his throat noisily.

"What are you doing here, Lydia?"

She bit her bottom lip. He sounded so hostile. Her nerve slowly ebbed away, and Lydia realized if she didn't tell him soon what she'd come for, she'd lose her courage completely. "Ryder, we need to talk."

"Oh? Kind of like how we needed to talk when I came to you to find out what was wrong and you threw my love back in my face? Well, guess what? I'm no longer in the mood for talking. As you can see, I'm heading out and won't be returning until next Tuesday. I trust you'll be able to wrap up everything with the Rawlings account. And don't worry, you'll get your bonus before you go."

For the first time, she noticed the overnight bag in his hand. "Where are you going?"

His nostrils flared, but instead of answering, he stepped outside, forcing her to back up as he pulled out his keys and locked his front door. With that task completed, he sidestepped her and walked to the car as if she weren't even there.

Lydia hadn't been sure what to expect when she'd planned this confrontation, but his coldness chilled her to the core. Part of her wanted to let him walk away and that be it, but then Mickey's words came back to haunt her. No, letting Ryder walk away was the act of a coward. She didn't want to be that person anymore, so caught up in her fear of loving that she would allow something wonderful to slip out of her grasp. Besides, she needed him like she needed no other. Not to mention, their child needed him. Would he be happy about the baby? There was only one way to find out.

"Ryder, wait, I'm sorry, I, uh—" Her heel must have caught on a rock as she went chasing after him, because the next thing she knew, she went hurtling to the ground face-first. She threw her arms out in front of her to brace her fall and landed on her hands and knees. But coupled with the speed she'd been running and how hard she had fallen, her hands slid from under her, scraping against the pavement and sending her flat on her belly. She couldn't cry out, because the air whooshed from her lungs.

"Lydia!"

That Ryder had called out to her didn't register at first. Stunned by the impact of her fall, she lay there until a pair of strong arms wrapped around her waist and pulled her up.

"Oh my God! Lydia, are you okay?"

Still unable to talk, she merely nodded. And then the pain registered. She looked down at her palms to see the heels of her hands were badly scraped, her shirt and stockings were torn as if they'd gone through a shredder, and her knees were bleeding.

"You poor baby. Look at you. You're bleeding." Before she could respond, Ryder scooped her up in his arms and carried her back to his house. After fumbling with the keys and unlocking the door, he carried her to the bathroom and sat her next to the sink. "Don't move." The command, though softly spoken, had underlying steel that Lydia would have been a fool to ignore. Not that she would have. She clutched her stomach, waiting to see if something adverse would happen. It was a good thing she wasn't so far along that the baby would have been affected by her fall; otherwise she would be in panic mode. What was going through Ryder's head? He was probably even more annoyed now that his trip would be interrupted.

He walked back in with a first-aid kit in hand, which he placed on top of the toilet. "Here, let me get that shirt off of you. You're going to bleed all over it." Once her shirt was off, Ryder gingerly worked off her shoes and stockings. He then eased her out of her skirt. She wordlessly let him strip her down to her bra and panties.

With her clothing discarded, he dug through his first-aid kit and pulled out some medicated wipes. Gently he took her hand. "This is going to sting a little bit, baby, but I need to clean the wounds so they won't get infected."

She bit her bottom lip at the sting of the medicine touching her damaged flesh, but she managed not to cry out. By the time he had finished cleaning her hands and scraped knees, the tears freely coursed down her cheeks, but not because of any physical pain. That was all transitory. No, she hurt because Ryder was taking care of her so tenderly, even after she'd treated him like crap, and she didn't deserve it. Not one bit of it.

He looked up at her, his intense gaze full of concern. "It's okay, baby. The worst part is over. It doesn't look like the scrapes are bad enough that you'll need stitches, but if the pain persists, we can see the doctor. Just let me get you bandaged up so we can stop the bleeding."

Once he had patched her up, Ryder stood up with a smile and kissed her on her forehead. His tenderness was her undoing. She burst into loud, body-shaking sobs.

"Baby, it's okay. I know you took a nasty fall, but don't worry. I'll take care of you. We'll get you some ibuprofen, and you'll feel better."

His words made her cry even harder.

Ryder took her in his arms and stroked the back of her head. "Shhh. I know it hurts, baby; I'm here. Don't worry."

"I-it's n-not t-t-that. I do-don't d-deserve your k-kindness. You have every r-ri-right to hate me. I am slime." She sobbed against his chest.

"Don't you dare talk about the woman I love that way. You are not slime. Let's just forget about these past couple weeks, okay?"

"No. I can't forget, because I treated you so… You didn't deserve me walking away without hearing you out. I'm so sorry, Ryder. I should have known you wouldn't say those awful things about me and mean them. You were so perfect, and I was looking for reasons why it wouldn't work. I was so scared of my feelings for you. I started to panic because I believed you'd hurt me first, but I don't care anymore. I love you so much, and I can't go another day without letting you know. And if you still want me in your life, I will be whatever you want me to be. Your employee, your friend, your booty call—whatever, I just—Oh…"

Ryder cupped the sides of her face. “What did you just say?”

She sniffed. “I said I'll be whatever you want me to be, in whatever capacity.”

“No, that part about loving me.”

Lydia took a deep breath. “I love you very much, Ryder. So much it hurts. I never thought I was capable of feeling this way about anyone after what I've been through, but now I realize it's because I hadn't met you yet.”

Chapter Twenty

Ryder couldn't count the many times he'd dreamed of this moment—when he'd hear those three little words from her lips. Of course, he hadn't pictured his woman battered and bruised, but as far as heartfelt confessions went, this was one for the ages. Unable to go another second without tasting the sweetness of her lips, he grazed the sides of her face with his thumbs. "Oh, darlin', I love you too. So much." His lips collided with hers. Damn, he'd missed this.

How the hell had he survived without it? Pulling back slightly, he outlined the fullness of her lips with his tongue, savoring the warmth of her breath against his mouth.

Lydia moaned, opening her lips at the persistence of his tongue. Ryder captured her moan, sucking it into his mouth and loving every second of it. He'd never needed anyone as much as he needed Lydia. His dick was so painfully hard, he was ready to bust a seam. She tasted so good, felt so good. This was his woman. And the fact that she'd finally acknowledged it made it even sweeter. Needing more, he gently lifted her into his arms, careful not to break the contact of their lips.

Lydia returned his kisses wholeheartedly, her tongue meeting his and exploring his mouth. Her enthusiasm for him made his cock even harder, if that was possible. He took her to his bedroom and laid her gently in the middle of the bed.

"Stay still. I want to look at you." Slowly he undressed as he drank in the sight of her, refamiliarizing himself with the curves of her body. He loved the way her tiny waist flared to voluptuous hips. "God, you're beautiful." There was something different about her, though. Her breasts seemed fuller, but the added dimension suited her. He shook in anticipation of running his hands over every inch of her curves.

She giggled. "Even all bruised and bandaged?"

"Yes. You'd be beautiful if you were wrapped up like a mummy."

She raised a brow with a laugh. "Now you're pushing it."

Ryder kicked his boxers off, his last article of clothing, and joined her on the bed. "It's true. I don't think there's anything that would make you unattractive to me."

"I'll hold you to that."

He grinned. "Oh, you can just hold me, all right." Straddling her, he undid the front clasp of her bra to reveal her full brown globes capped with Hershey-kiss-colored nipples. They were way too tempting for him to resist. Bending over, he took one in his mouth. Lydia arched her back, offering herself to him.

"Oh, Ryder, that feels so good." When she would have wrapped her arms around him, he gently pushed her hands away, remembering her injuries.

As he suckled, licked, and laved the hardened tip, he squeezed her other breast, shaping it in his palm.

She squirmed beneath him. "Ryder, please let me touch you."

"No, baby, not until you feel better."

"But I do. Honestly, I'll be careful."

When she lightly grazed her fingers down his back, he inhaled sharply. Ryder could deny her nothing when she looked up at him with those soulful brown eyes. Besides, he'd missed her touch. God, he loved this woman more than life itself.

Ryder pushed her breasts together and took turns licking each nipple before sucking them both into his mouth. He was like a kid in a candy store full of chocolate. Lydia was so sweet, tasted so good. And her soft pants and moans were driving him insane. The scent of her arousal was a heady aphrodisiac that made him dizzy with desire. He began a descent over her body, letting his tongue make a wet path down the center of her torso to her navel. Ryder dipped his tongue into the indentation in her stomach.

Lord, she was perfection. He marveled at her softness and the way she jerked beneath his mouth.

"Hmm, Ryder. I need you. Please make love to me."

"Not yet, baby. I need to taste you first. I've gone nearly two weeks without this. You're not going to deny me, are you?"

She chuckled. "When put like that—Oh!" She gasped as he nuzzled her pussy through her panties. He ran his tongue over her clothed cunt, licking the already-soaked material.

She slipped her fingers through his hair and bucked her hips, pushing her pussy against his face. “Please, Ryder. I need you.”

He caught the edge of her panties with his teeth and dragged them down her thighs. When they were to her knees, he gripped them with his hands and yanked them all the way off. Settling between her thighs, he took a moment to inhale deeply. The musky, tangy, sweet scent of her was like nothing else. He doubted he'd ever get tired of staring at the pretty pinkness of her pussy.

Pressing a deep kiss against Lydia's cunt, he pushed her legs farther apart, damn near pushing her into a split. He wanted her as open to him as possible. “Mmm, delicious.” He took several swipes at her pussy with his tongue before capturing her little jewel between his teeth. This seemed to send Lydia over the edge, because she started to thrust against his face.

“That's it, baby,” he muttered against her pussy before returning his full attention to her clit. He sucked it as hard as he could.

“Oh God, Ryder, I don't think I can take it!”

Ignoring her cries, he slipped his middle finger inside of her and fucked her with it with fervent strokes as he continued to suck the shit out of her clit. The way she writhed and screamed, he knew she was close to her climax. He slipped another finger inside of her and slammed into her harder and faster, sending her over the edge. The sweet warmth of her honey bathed his face as he lapped at her cream like a very satisfied cat. He was addicted to Lydia, yet it was an addiction he wanted no cure for.

He licked and sucked on her pussy for several more minutes before sliding up the length of her body and lowering his mouth to hers. Their tongues dueled back and forth as if fighting for supremacy. As their mouths merged, he slid his hand between their bodies and grasped his cock. He couldn't go another second without being inside of her. She was so wet and ready for his cock, he was able to slide so deep into her cunt, he wasn't sure where he ended and she began. Pulling his mouth away, he released a howl of pure satisfaction.

Lydia let out a soft sigh of contentment. She wrapped her arms around his neck as he slowly began to move inside of her. “I love you,” she whispered.

“I love you too, baby. So much.” He kissed her as their bodies moved together. He braced his arms on either side of her head so he could watch her expression as he made love to her. The reserve that had once lingered in the dark pools was no longer there, and for the first time, she was completely open to him, and he saw something that he hadn't seen before. Love.

Their joining was more intense than anything he'd ever experienced before. With his heart engaged, nothing could compare. As he drew closer to his climax, he pushed deeper and harder, and Lydia met him thrust for thrust, giving as good as she got.

“Ryder, I'm coming!” she cried out.

“Don't hold back, baby. Let go.”

Her pussy clenched his cock, squeezing him so tightly, it sent him spiraling to his orgasm, which was so intense, it ran up his entire body. "I love you!" he shouted before collapsing on top of her.

Tears coursed down her cheeks. Ryder must have felt the wetness, because he lifted his head, alarm etching his face. "Baby, are you okay? Was I too rough? Are your injuries bothering you?"

She nodded. "More than okay. These are happy tears. I love you so much; I don't know how to handle it."

Ryder smiled and kissed the tip of her nose. "How about we take it one day at a time? I've never felt this way about anyone either, but I bet between the two of us, we'll figure this love thing out. Deal?"

Lydia returned his smile. "Deal."

"Of course you know I'm never letting you go. I'm sorry for acting like a jackass these past couple days. I was just hurt when I found out the reason you ran. We could have cleared that little misunderstanding up in five seconds, but you chose to think the worst of me; instead of trying to work it out, you took off."

"No. I should be the one apologizing. You're right; I should have come to you. But when I overheard you say that you were with me due to a 'weak moment,' all my old insecurities came flying back. Acknowledging what I feel about you now and how much pain I was in when I thought you didn't love me anymore is not something I ever intend to go through again."

"As if I'd let you go. And by the way, I expect that you forget this resignation of yours. I can't afford to lose one of my best employees. But on the other hand, if you'd prefer to be a stay-at-home wife, I won't object."

Her smile widened, and her heart fluttered in her chest. "Are you asking me to marry you?"

"Hell no! You're going to marry me, and that's not up for debate. As soon as possible. The only choice you have in the matter is whether we'll have a big to-do or a small civil ceremony."

"Well, neither one of us is from a large family, and I can think of nothing I'd like better than to be your wife. I don't care if we go to the justice of the peace or whatever."

"Good. We'll get married as soon as possible, and then we can work on kids."

She was pleased that he seemed so interested in having children, and it made telling him easier. "Oh? So you're that anxious to have kids?"

"Only if they're yours and mine. Besides, ever since I realized I loved you, I can't get the image out of my head of you pregnant with my child. I know some couples want to spend time together before starting a family, but we have the rest of our lives together, and the way I feel for you, I would love to share this love with our children."

Her eyes welled with tears. "I'd love that too."

"Good. So you'll stop taking the pill?"

"Actually…I was never on it. You see, I never thought I could get pregnant, because I have a condition called PCOS, which causes irregular menstrual cycles and cysts on my ovaries. My doctor said I'd have an extremely hard time conceiving, but that goes to show what he knows."

Ryder grasped her shoulders, his eyes widening. “What are you trying to say?”

“I'm pregnant. I must have conceived on the island. I wanted to tell you sooner, but things were kind of weird between us.”

Ryder's instant joy was apparent in every line of his face. “Oh, baby! Your fall! Oh my God, I made love to you a little rougher than I should have. What if I hurt the baby?”

She giggled. “My, you have a large ego. You're large, but not so big that you'd hurt the baby. Pregnant women have sex all the time. That won't hurt the baby. As for my fall, the baby is too small for it to have made a difference. I'm sure he or she is fine.” The next thing she knew, Ryder's mouth swooped down on hers, taking her breath away.

“I love you so much.” He ran his hand lightly over her belly. “And I already love the life growing inside of you. I can't believe my son or daughter is inside of here.”

“You won't mind if I go back to work, do you?”

“I don't see why not, but I'd like for us to take a visit to your doctor first. Of course, if you still want to work when the baby comes, it's your decision, although I'm not crazy about the idea of putting our child in day care when I make more than enough to support us.”

“Oh, you don't have to worry about that. The baby will be my first priority. Work will always be there, but I don't want to miss the most important years in our child's life. And I don't see why I can't work from home.”

Ryder lowered his head and kissed her belly. “That sounds like a plan.”

"So are you going to start being nicer to Casey now that you know he and I will never be anything other than colleagues?"

He scowled. "Why did you have to kill a beautiful moment by bringing up that jackass?"

"Be nice, Ryder; the poor guy is a nervous wreck, and we've made our peace. If I can forgive him, you should too."

He rolled his eyes. "Fine. I'll give the guy a break if he decides to stick around. I'll even put him on the next big project. But I don't have to like him. Ever."

She leaned over and gave him a kiss. "That's all I ask. I have to give your sister a call and thank her for talking some sense into me. I think she's more than a little annoyed with me right now."

Ryder laughed. "She can be a little firecracker when she wants to be, but don't worry about it. She's not one to hold grudges, and I'm sure she'll be excited about the baby."

Lydia grinned and nodded, deciding not to tell him that Mickey already knew. "I'm sure your parents won't be thrilled."

"I've said it time and time again that I stopped caring what they think of me a long time ago. I doubt we'll be hearing from them anyway. They're too set in their ways to change."

Lydia snuggled closer to her man, enjoying the feel of him. Perhaps he'd never see eye to eye with his parents, but after her reconciliation with her mother, maybe Ryder would have one with his parents. Stranger things had happened.

The heavy haze of sleep was starting to take over. Ryder wrapped his arms around her and stroked her back as her lids grew heavier.

"Ryder?"

"Yes, darlin'?"

"Love you."

Epilogue

"Tristan is an angel. He gets more handsome by the day. He's got the Garrison chin, and he has green eyes. He barely looks mixed," Liz announced as she bounced her three-month-old grandson on her knee.

There would have been a time when his mother's comment would have bothered him, but at least she was trying. He wouldn't have thought in a million years that his parents would swallow their pride and come see him. But he and Mickey suspected losing both their children had been the wake-up call they needed to do a little introspection. Things were still a bit stilted with his father, but Phil too seemed to be trying, and it didn't hurt that they both adored Tristan. The baby sucked on his fist and grinned at his grandmother.

"Hate to disappoint you, Mom, but he may still get darker yet."

"I'm not an idiot, Ryder. And I won't love him less because of it." She gave the baby a kiss on the cheek.

Tristan Ryder Garrison, who had been born a bit prematurely, much to his parents' surprise and delight, was the spitting image of his father with his honey-tinted skin, dark blond curls, and green eyes. Lydia had bemoaned the fact that she'd been nothing more than a glorified incubator. He was a good baby, who had slept through the night almost from the beginning, and he'd somehow worked the miracle of bringing their families together. The twins loved their new baby cousin. Mickey was forever threatening to kidnap him, and Tristan even had Graham talking about having more kids, though the twins were already a handful.

Lydia's mother had moved closer to help Lydia out with the baby. Liz and Phil sent presents weekly.

Today was Tristan's christening, and the family had come back to their house afterward for a buffet lunch. Rhonda scowled at Liz from the corner. Those two didn't get along; Ryder believed it was because they were more alike than either one of them would admit. Rhonda walked over, hands on her hips. "I think you've monopolized Tristan long enough. Besides, he wants to spend time with his favorite grandmother." Rhonda reached for the baby, but Liz held on to him so tight, Tristan cried out in protest.

Liz smirked. "He's already sitting with her, dear."

Ryder knew then he had to intervene before those two came to blows, and he refused to have his son in the middle when that happened. Lydia, who had been across the room in deep conversation with Mickey and Sammy Jo, must have noticed and beat him to the punch. "Um, I think it's time for Tristan's feeding." She scooped their son up before either grandmother could protest and was out of the room with the quickness of a ninja.

Ryder couldn't keep the grin off his face as he followed his wife and son to the nursery. His wife and son. He liked the sound of it and loved both hearing and saying it. He found Lydia in the rocking chair, her nursing bra unclasped. Tristan suckled her with gusto. He was a greedy little devil.

He'd never get tired of watching her nurse their child. She was so beautiful. His heart swelled with love for her and their child. After nearly a year of marriage, every day seemed like Christmas. He counted his blessings for his good fortune.

Lydia noticed him standing in the doorway and smiled. She waved him inside. Ryder watched over them until Tristan seemed to have his fill. Lydia gently pulled him away from her breast and placed him over her shoulder. After a few moments the baby let out a loud belch, followed by a long yawn.

"He's been pretty good today, considering it's way past his nap time. I was going to let him stay up a little longer since he wasn't fussing, but from the looks of your mother and mine, I didn't want our son to be ripped apart in a battle of tug-of-war. I just don't get why those two don't get along."

"Faded beauty queens vying for attention, I suppose." Ryder knelt beside the rocking chair and dropped a kiss on his son's fair curls. "I can't believe he's already three months."

"I know, it seems like just yesterday he was born."

"Makes me want to have another one."

Lydia raised a brow. "So soon?"

"You gotta admit, we make beautiful babies together."

"We certainly do."

"But I'd like to put in a request this time around."

"And what would that be, Mr. Garrison?"

"A beautiful, brown-eyed baby girl who looks just like her mother."

"Hmmm, I'll see what I can do." She laughed before leaning over to accept his kiss.

THE END

Eve Vaughn & Shara Azod

Eve Vaughn enjoys writing above all else. She began writing short stories to amuse herself when she could form letters. Mischievous as a child, she lost her television privileges quite often and found writing to be her outlet. Besides writing, Eve likes reading, baking, volunteering, traveling, and spending time with her family. She currently resides in the Philadelphia area with her husband and turtle.

Shara Azod was born in Florida, grew up in Southern California, and has lived all over the world. A Marine brat, Navy vet, and the wife of a Navy lifer, she has visited four of the world's seven continents. Her favorite destinations are Paris, Hong Kong, Bahrain, the United Arab Emirates and Catania.

Shara married a real life cowboy and has two beautiful children. Currently residing in the South, she enjoys the slow easy pace of life since her husband retired and hopes to keep busy writing plenty of juicy romances.

CPSIA information can be obtained at www.ICGtesting.com
Printed in the USA
BVOW041427190911

271617BV00001B/111/P

9 781607 375319